The Send-Away Girl

The Send-Away Girl

Stories by

BARBARA SUTTON

THE UNIVERSITY OF GEORGIA PRESS   ATHENS AND LONDON

Published by the University of Georgia Press
Athens, Georgia 30602
© 2004 by Barbara Sutton
All rights reserved
Designed by Sandra Strother Hudson
Set in 10/13 Berkeley Old Style
Printed and bound by Edwards Brothers

The paper in this book meets the guidelines for permanence
and durability of the Committee on Production Guidelines
for Book Longevity of the Council on Library Resources.
Printed in the United States of America
04   05   06   07   08   C   5   4   3   2   1

Library of Congress Cataloging-in-Publication Data
Sutton, Barbara, 1960–
The send-away girl : stories / by Barbara Sutton.
p.   cm. — (Flannery O'Connor Award for Short Fiction)
ISBN 0-8203-2655-0 (alk. paper)
1. United States—Social life and customs—Fiction
2. Psychological fiction, American.
3. Friendship—Fiction.   I. Title   II. Series.
PS3619.U89S46 2004
813'.6—dc22   2004007421

British Library Cataloging-in-Publication Data available

To John Keats (1921–2000)

Contents

The Send-Away Girl

Tra il devoto et profano

Marta's grandmother liked to wear a pink housecoat around her large home while completing self-assigned housekeeping chores. Two of Marta's uncles liked to tell their friends that this housecoat made their mother look like a counter girl at Schraft's. Marta's mother liked to sober up at the counter of a coffee shop that some people likened to Schraft's. And the Portuguese lady who was dropped off three times a week to help Marta's grandmother with her housekeeping chores liked when it came time to be picked back up again.

During the era of Nan's pink housecoat, Marta's uncles and mother were away in places purposely devoid of Chippendale and chintz, places where life had the shadeless panache of Manhattan real estate before it became Manhattan Real Estate. Marta considered it odd that her mother even chose to have a baby, given her absorption into the bigger picture of vodka, barbiturates, and boyfriends. And it was the boyfriends, according to Marta's uncles, who were her worst addiction, for they were too old to be masquerading as hippies and took out their anger at this situation on Marta's mother, who, even after all kinds of stomach pumpings, always looked new and supple, like the sixties as *Life* magazine sold it. Marta's grandmother had just become a widow when her daughter announced that she was pregnant and intent on producing a line-item love child. Being utterly disgusted with life, Marta's grandmother vowed never to set eyes on the love

1

child, to make of her first grandchild a symbol for everything that went awry with the morality of her children.

Marta's mother drank and popped pills through her pregnancy, so much so that Marta's uncles predicted a worthless harvest, that whatever their sister expelled would have "that Injun disease." Marta was born during a freak snowstorm in November, was pulled out of her mother by a doctor who was killed in an automobile accident later that same day—slid off a bridge in his Camaro. The doctor did the pulling with forceps, and if there was a struggle or cranial indentations that were later thumbed out by the nurses, no one informed Marta of this matter, especially not her mother, who liked to be out for most events rather than up close and personal.

Marta was born too early, too small, and clumsily angled, and she was so gauche as to arrive with clumps of black hair and feet that, in proportion to her premature size, were simply and inexcusably big—ample reason for people not to love her. Once she made the scene, however, her recalcitrant grandmother—the woman whom Marta and soon everyone else began calling Nan—reluctantly broke her vow. As Nan told it, she could do nothing about Marta being a baby who laughed instead of cried. She said she could not help but to return Marta's coos and embraces, that when she'd put her hand around the child's ankle to keep her from crawling off the dining room table she could feel the pulse of something big, something already grown.

It was common knowledge that Marta's mother, along with Marta's uncles Jim and Bob, made Nan's life extremely difficult, but it was Nan's youngest child, Henry, who actually made her weep. Henry was twelve when his father died and Marta was born. According to her uncles, Henry did not mind his father dying, but he was livid about Marta and her clumps of black hair, big feet, and attendant nurse coming to his house as some sort of replacement, even though he himself never much lived in his house, what with getting into trouble and being sent off to every variety of military academy that promised to build character within the shells of morally gutted WASPs. For years Henry made Marta's life a squeamish affair, despite the soothing presence of Nan in her housecoats, and it wasn't until he enlisted in the army at a bad time to be enlisting in the army that Marta actually thought of Nan's eighteen-room affair as "home."

Marta's father was Italian. Which sort of Italian he was—he is, perhaps—was an issue that her uncles considered perennially open to speculation. According to her mother, this was nobody's business. Marta's Uncle Bob—who still manages to do something moneymaking for NATO—says he was a textile heir who was chummy with Alberto Moravia and a lot of people at Cinecità, the big movie studio, that he was a spoiled brat who traipsed back to his family fortune and now speeds around the Riviera in the boats of subpoenaed politicos too busy for suicide. Henry's version was that Marta came from the sperm of a low-grade Mafia don, a guy with a nickname—"some black, hairy piece of Sicilian shit." He said this to Marta while he was visiting for Easter, after he'd finished basic training. Marta's Uncle Jim—who still makes big money as a vice-something of a Philadelphia bank—had laughed a great deal, slinking down in a leather wing chair. "Now, how the hell would Carol meet a hairy Mafia don at Henri Bendel?" he asked. Henry stubbed out his cigarette on a tray of deviled eggs that were arranged like a halo; he retained the smoke for an unpleasant few seconds before snorting it out of his nose. "They're always buying underwear for their whores" was his rationale. "Ain't that so, sister-chick?"

The Reverend—Ryder Hobbes III, pastor emeritus of Nan's church, world-renowned art historian, and close family friend—was the rare person whom Henry could amuse rather than anger or terrify, and because of this the Reverend had early on become Marta's favorite unrelated-to-her person in the world. Even though he was in a staggering way, the Reverend took Marta by the hand that Easter of the "hairy piece of Sicilian shit" and led her out to the side porch, saying something like, "Freshen your martini there, sunshine?" or "Isn't it just about time for the

Fabergé egg roll?" or "Is that a Boucher demoiselle I see swinging out there?" On the porch the Reverend slipped and fell, and as Marta unsuccessfully attempted to help him up he murmured something about "sister-chick." The porch furniture was new and arranged differently from the previous setup, which was the Reverend's excuse for falling. "I hope Henry gets killed in the war," Marta told the Reverend as she sat down on the floor beside him. "I hope you're wrong, my love," he told her, his legs spread out in front of him. He leaned back on his arms and stared straight ahead, his glassy eyes fixed on something invisible in the near distance—who knows, Marta thought, perhaps he could really see a swinging demoiselle. "I hope Henry gets cured," he said, almost as a mutter. "Then he can help to cure me. Wouldn't that be nice for a change, my love? 'The Curé Gets Cured'—story at eleven."

Military service had taken Henry not into the thick of the world's most photographed mess but to North Africa, where the messes seemed to interest only shutterbugs for *Le Monde*. "Tough break," Marta's Uncle Bob had said on hearing of the posting. "He must have been dying to get over there and wipe out a village, carpet bomb a few orphanages." After that Easter Henry had become a ghostly figure way off in Africa—never writing, never calling. Marta's life had become more pleasant with him gone, and the house came to feel like church on a weekday afternoon. Roaming the beeswax-scented rooms, she'd think that this must be what "the farm" was like when all the boys went off to the thrills of war, because the Reverend was always singing in a hucksterish way, "How ya gonna keep 'em down on the farm, after they've seen Par-ree?"

The Reverend spent the afternoons, the early evenings, and sometimes the late evenings with Marta and Nan, but never the mornings, because that's when he was said to do his writing. In the summertime, when school was out, the morning agenda without the Reverend seemed to consist of Nan in her pink housecoat polishing or waxing expensive objects and touching at the back of her hair at regular intervals. This was also the time of day that Nan seemed to thoroughly enjoy inhaling her Winstons. When she smoked in this manner, Marta would often study her face, trying to memorize the expression of rapture. "There are eyes upon me," Nan would say, not bothering to look her granddaughter's way, "and I'm nowhere near Texas." When the leftover rectory ladies were visiting for a game of bridge or canasta, Nan smoked and touched the back of her hair in a studied, elegant way. But with Marta alone at the long dining table, the touching and smoking were different, and the only break in the drama was the postman's arrival.

Getting the mail provided something of a lilt, for Marta's mother was always sending clothes from the boutique sections of New York department stores, where she was said to live—in the stores, that is, as a joke, as hyperbole. From a heavily tissued box Marta would extract and display to Nan a zippered, pucker-knit sweater or daisy-covered bell-bottoms. "Oh, hooray!" Nan would say limply. "Another outfit for your collection! Go on, then, go put it away." Marta and Nan sometimes got bored with the routine, and as a diversion Marta would feign insolence. "I don't like it," she'd say. "She sent me this same jersey last week."

"I don't believe it was the same."

"Yes it was. It was ugly then and it's ugly now. I won't wear it."

"If my memory serves me, the jersey from last week had that glorious white piping."

"It was purple."

"Purple, yes, the color of passion."

"I hate purple. I hate passion."

"You won't hate it when you get older, when it becomes convenient."

For most of the year, after school was when Marta kept the Reverend company as he drank. Usually she'd bring the record player into the drawing room and spread her forty-fives out all over the Persian carpets and prayer rugs. The Reverend could crack her to pieces by singing along to parts of "Stranded in the Jungle," especially the way he said, "They was a'cookin' me!" Marta can remember one weekend trip she took down to the National Gallery with Nan and the Reverend: he pointed to a Bosch with its customary macabre mayhem—skeletons hanging up their own skins like they were wet suits—and said, "Meanwhile, back in the States." The Reverend seemed to like whatever records Marta liked, but he was especially fond of the Dave Clark Five song "Glad All Over." They'd sing it together, Marta going first: "You say that you love me" / "say you love me" / "All of the time" / "all of the time" / "You say that you need me" / "say you need me" / "You'll always be mine" / "always be mine." One time when Marta and the Reverend were listening to her records with Nan, the Reverend asked, "What is meant by the 'all over'? What's the context? Is he glad all over his body, or is he glad all over again?" Nan did not even look up from the *Times* bridge column to reply: "I should imagine he means both, dear." And the Reverend seemed pleased. "Yes, of course. And what a clever Dave Clark is they!"

Marta was unpopular at school because she thought herself both magnificent and unfortunate. As a consequence, the time spent with her record player and the Reverend was particularly cathartic. When she played her records she'd jump all around the drawing room, and if Nan wasn't there she'd jump on and off the furniture. When she jumped on the furniture the Reverend never bothered to intervene; he'd contentedly observe the floor show, nodding and occasionally offering commentary: "What would Bernini do with you, my love? *Marta in Ecstasy . . . Marta in Ecstasy with Diamonds*. Or perhaps *My Little Marta*." Shortly after any mention of Bernini, however, the Reverend would begin to ramble to the point of inaudibility. His eyes would get glassy, and soon he'd be asleep and would have to be taken home by a man from the Ace Taxi Company, usually Leonard with the scar on his face. If you called Leonard "scarface" he would kill you. Marta knew this because he once said to her, "Call me scarface and I'll kill ya." When Marta told the Reverend about Leonard's warning, the Reverend said, "What if we just called him Paul Muni?" But Marta never called Leonard Paul Muni; in fact, she tried not to say anything to Leonard, especially since he was a friend of Henry's.

Henry was on Nan's mind one memorable Saturday in 1970 because the Tuesday before he had called from some army place an hour away to say he had married an Ethiopian woman named Alda and that he was bringing her and the several suites of furniture she had just purchased out of a highway showroom to live at Nan's house. "Henry, you cannot do this," Nan had repeated, shaking her head. She pretended to cave in at everything, to have a fragile constitution, but to know her, to be there as Marta had to witness her touch at the back of her hair and suck in her Winstons in that odd way, was to know that it was all for show, fakery like the bas-relief swans and tiger lilies on the drawing-room cornices. First she called Marta next to her as she sat on a Windsor chair near the telephone table in the hallway; then she stood, still gripping Marta's wrist. "You're not to come here," she shouted. Marta could hear Henry's voice blaring out of the earpiece, and after a while Nan had had enough and handed the receiver to her granddaughter. Marta held it in silence, away from her ear. "Alda, honey. Alda! Shit! Alda, get your black ass in here!" It was the romantic part of June, and Henry and Alda were apparently in a motel with a balcony, and Alda apparently had to be on this balcony. "Ma, Ma—ya there?" Marta tried to approximate Nan's pained whimpers, but Henry didn't seem to care who was on the other end. "I'm married to a 'colored,' Ma—that's a whole class they got back there, what they call the Lena Hornes. Tell your drunken priest that—we got us a big-tits Negro chick in the family."

It went on—Henry's loud joking—and Marta could tell that this mysterious Alda was pretending to be outraged at his "black ass" and "big tits" and "Negro chick" and was slapping him and grabbing to get at the phone in that playful way certain couples establish as the gist of their relationship. Finally she got hold of the phone and started talking without pause, as if reading a prepared statement. "Hello there, Mother. Henry is a bad boy. Mother, I am not black. My father is Italian. My father has blacks for servants, no good servants. My father is a rich man. My father lives in a villa. My father makes his own wine. The blacks—they drank their beers. But my father makes his own wine. Mother, I am telling you now that my father is Italian."

That Saturday morning the store on the highway phoned Nan to say that someone would be by in an hour to deliver Alda's furniture. By the tone of Nan's voice, Marta could tell that her grandmother was conversing with a type of man she was not used to dealing with. He seemed to be telling her that he had a lot of furniture that had to go somewhere, that he was a busy man with a delivery slip, and that he didn't have time for people's problems. Half-past eight was too early for the Reverend, but Nan phoned him in a panic, and the first thing he did when he arrived at quarter-past nine was to pour himself a drink and then offer one to Marta. "Em, Em, Em," he said with a velvety voice, even though his appearance this early in the day rendered him roughshod and salty, grizzled and gray. "Just relax, dear. I'll talk to the man. As far as I know, one cannot in this country force furniture into the home of another. It's all in the Bill of Rights, within the purview of the inalienables—or does it fall under quartering of troops?" He looked at his watch, which seemed to be missing from his wrist. "What time is? Is that war of ours still going on? What do you think, my little cabbage?" he said to Marta. "Quartering of troops is it?"

It was funny to Marta how Nan's immediate neighbor, the eighty-two-year-old optometrist forever pruning his shrubs, seemed the priestly one, decrying debauchery such as the Reverend's, having sympathetic chats with Nan when she was angry at the Reverend and happened to be dallying by the hedge in her Mardi Gras gardening hat. Nan, the Reverend, and Marta still went every Sunday to the Reverend's Episcopal church with the red doors, even though he complained that church cut into his routine. It was said that the Reverend did his writing in the morning, and that Sundays proved, for reasons people attributed to the existence of a benevolent Redeemer, particularly conducive to "ideas." But on weekdays and Saturday, when he got to Nan's house just after one, or on Sunday, when Marta and Nan picked him up at 9:52 for the ten o'clock service, he always looked like he just got up, like he hadn't had an idea since the days before women started wearing pants.

The Reverend was one of the few people in the world who could look at a Caravaggio canvas and give the whys and where-fores of its composition—or look at a bogus Caravaggio, it was said, and begin with a look that could freeze the spigots in hell. He could do this, and then he could turn around and amuse and enlighten with a marvelously witty discourse on why Corot, as brilliant at landscapes as he was at figurative painting, was the most important artist of the nineteenth century. Marta remem-bers him many times being called off to Europe to inspect a paint-ing, and she remembers many times spying on him and Nan in her grandfather's library, with Nan sitting at the desk, drafting a check from her dead husband's leather-bound ledger book.

The three of them—the Reverend, Nan, Marta's grandfa-ther—were famously close since their youth, since Marta's grandfather and the Reverend were Yale men and Nan was the fifteen-year-old sister of the girl they were both said to be crazy about. According to Nan, everyone was crazy about Evelyn right around the time she married a financier and moved to Argentina, where she died a few years later of some mysterious viral infec-tion. With Evelyn gone, Nan became the center of things. She was called Emma, or Em, by the Reverend, and he was called Ryder by her. Marta's grandfather's name was James; people who didn't know him well called him Jim; people like Nan and the Reverend called him James. People remember Marta's grandfather as a fair-play capitalist, a man who listened rather than shot his mouth off, a WASP who hadn't forgotten the "P," who didn't blush at the naïveté of Christian charity. He had a heart attack at sixty-eight, dying in a cab somewhere in Midtown. The driver apparently did not know Marta's grandfather was dead in the back, and because the lunch-hour traffic was particularly heavy that day, he took a circuitous, illegal-turn-intensive route to get Marta's grandfather to his lunch date at one. Marta's Uncle Jim always made a joke out of this—a joke that would bring his mother to tears. According to Marta's uncle, arriving somewhere exactly on time was "making it DOA."

When the Reverend took Marta with him on his trips to the city, she would speculate aloud as to which street it was that her grandfather died on. "Do you think it was here?" she'd say to the Reverend. "I'll bet he died right at this stoplight." The first time she made such a conjecture the Reverend acted uncharacteristically stern, advising her that she should be more interested in where her grandfather was born. But when she replied, "Why? He wasn't *born* in a cab, because they didn't even have cabs back then," the Reverend laughed and patted her on the head, like she was a good dog behaving well in the city. The Reverend's trips consisted of visits to the Met and the Frick, sometimes to Trinity, and then always to a dark town house where he drank with three other men dressed as priests and where a lady who looked like Miss Hathaway from *The Beverly Hillbillies* would first bring Marta meringue cookies that made her lips chalky and then later an incongruous glass of ginger ale to wash away the chalk. The trips always began at the Met, and the Reverend would be irritated at the gobs of people milling about until he and Marta made it to *Concert of Youths*. At the Frick they usually met a woman in a blue angora coat that looked brand new but was from the fifties, which at that time was the worst possible period, fashionwise, to be from. The coat had one of those collars that served as a scarf, and the woman would loop the scarf-collar in a chic way and clip to it an oval pin covered with blue gems. She'd look at the pictures with the Reverend and Marta, and Marta would always check to see if the stocking-muted blue veins on her feet still matched her coat. Marta was not aware then that this woman had been one of the world's most sought-after art restorers, that she had retired herself sometime back because her eyesight was just about shot, and the chronic pain pulsing though her neck and shoulders was almost unbearable. All Marta knew was that the blue veins on this woman's feet matched her coat, not just well, but exactly.

Marta could never remember the names of whatever people were coming into or going out of the Reverend's life—an ambivalence that flowed smoothly into the way that he, on different days, seemed to alter his appearance and even his smell. Sometimes he looked much younger than Nan, as if he had blackened the hair that was combed back at his temples, and he sometimes smelled not so bad, almost good in fact, like pine. On those rare occasions that he looked young and smelled almost good, Marta was startled by the thought that he had once been an extremely handsome man, and she would feel nervous taking hold of his hand, touching his moist palm. He was always so tall above her, and in Manhattan his paleness rendered him invisible up there among the buildings that seemed to grow into each other at the top. He'd curse at bad drivers, wave away street hustlers, and then a few minutes later he'd laugh through his nose and say, "And you a man of the cloth!" On the first of these trips Marta showed off to the Miss Hathaway woman, to the woman in the blue angora coat, and to the men dressed as priests by asking, "What have you done with your cloth, Reverend?" But later she realized that when adults laughed so merrily at her comments they looked at her as if she were that well-behaved dog—something only the Reverend was allowed to do. As such, she made it her policy to listen rather than speak, just like the Portuguese lady who helped Nan with the housework.

Nan's house was only a block from the church and a block minus a house from the vine-covered, Tudor-style rectory in which the Reverend lived. It was a good thing for the vines, Nan always said, because the building was sprawling and ugly. The Reverend had what today would be called a studio apartment in the back. The new young pastor and his unattractive wife and two equally unattractive boys inhabited that part of the rectory which, like a day lily, opened up in all directions from an inauthentically opulent foyer. The Reverend was a symbol of the way arrangements could be made, of how small, under-the-table worlds could be crafted out of big, administrative ones. Marta's grandfather could have bought a big house anywhere around New York, but he chose the Reverend's parish, where turn-of-the-century Tudors stood next to neo-Colonials next to Victorians next to English cottages next to Mediterranean stuccos next to stick-and-shingle piles. Marta's grandfather chose none of these: his was a modest federal-style mansion built much earlier by a man named Tarsis—a man who, according to local legend, went mad one June day and shot everyone's horses, some right out from under their riders. When Marta and the Reverend would look at *The Polish Rider* at the Frick, the Reverend could always make her laugh by saying, "And then, alas, whom did he meet up with but Mr. Tarsis."

Alda's furniture arrived at ten o'clock in a tractor-trailer with pilgrims painted on the side. To see such a monstrous vehicle not on an interstate or a turnpike but on Nan's quiet, sleepy road made Marta feel like worlds were colliding, like one of those prickly National Guard situations that the nightly news was always hyping had finally erupted in her front yard. She had wanted to go out with the Reverend, to stand a bit behind him as he talked to the two men who came with the trailer, but Nan grabbed her arm and pulled the girl in front of her, clamping her hands onto Marta's shoulders. Nan and Marta watched from the bay window in the drawing room as the Reverend gestured with his arms, turned to face the house, and pointed up and down the road as the men went about their unloading preparations. Nan's front lawn was lush that spring, and the Reverend and the movers seemed like some kind of litter blown from far away.

"Shouldn't you call Uncle Jim?" Marta asked Nan, knowing full well that there was little for him to do from Philadelphia, or that he wouldn't even care to do anything if he had been there in Nan's drawing room and not in Philadelphia. There was Marta's mother on West 57th, but she was never home. Marta's Uncle Bob was in Vienna at a conference on mutual and balanced force reductions; this she knew by heart because she had recited it so often to the older boys idling with their bikes on the church green. The Reverend walked back toward the house with his head down and a small piece of paper in the hand that wasn't holding his drink. In the hallway Marta could see that he was laughing and that the piece of paper was a tattered business card. "Sorry, Em, dear," he said. "I told them to put the furniture on the lawn. It was either this or get into a fistfight with the two of them or call the police right now, which I know you don't want to do." Nan gasped at hearing "furniture on the lawn," and having loosened herself from Marta, she was now pacing with her arms folded. "They were kind enough to give me this number of EZ Liquidation"—he was reading off the card—"a similar group of men who will come over and take the furniture away in an hour or two if we pay them a hundred dollars, which sounds to me as good a deal as any."

Marta had already run back to the window, looping herself up under the silk curtains, which she always liked doing because it gave her a bridal veil. Waiting for Alda's furniture to come down the ramp, she thought vaguely, in a way that seemed behind her, of how to other people it looked like Nan and the Reverend were married, the way he said "if *we* pay them a hundred dollars." Marta so remembers this scene because when the first piece of furniture came down the ramp, the bright morning sky had been dimmed at the center with a cluster of ashen clouds, like God had suddenly decided to pull a tarpaulin over the day. But this kind of sky only made the greenery more luminous and vivid, and when the wind blew the trees the undersides of the leaves flickered strange colors. This was how the world looked when

Alda's furry red and blue Mediterranean-style sofa was placed squarely in the center of Nan's lawn.

There was to follow more from this suite—a loveseat and two chairs with ottomans, all upholstered with fabric that was exactly like the fur on the stuffed animals that hung over doorways and pushcarts on 42nd Street. The upholstery was the red of a sweater Marta once wanted to have from Bloomingdale's, but Nan said it was too nauseating; the Moorish inlay color was a too-light navy blue. There were some tags and plastic, but not on everything. There was a vinyl yellow hassock that was as wide as Nan's pantry. There was black Naugahyde office-type furniture like the kind advertised on fliers that came with the Sunday paper. There was a chaise with fur, or long black hair. Marta had seen pillows like this in a display that involved slouching mannequins in glittery Halston clothing, also at Bloomingdale's. When she had reached to stroke the fur Nan said, "You don't need to touch that kind of thing." The bedroom furniture was white and a baby's blue; the monstrous upholstered headboard was tufted and puckered with dozens of gold buttons. "What kind of French is that, Nan?" Marta yelled, not turning around. "Is that Louis furniture?" She soon realized that Nan and the Reverend were back in the library—that, for Nan, the arrival of so many strange fibers and materials was not such a fascinating diversion. What struck Marta about the movers' labor was not how quick and agile they were, being just the two of them, but how they took the initiative to arrange the furniture by room, as if filling an invisible ranch house that only they could see.

After the tractor-trailer had lumbered off down the road, when the invisible ranch house was vacant, Marta ran out to inspect, to see how this kind of furniture felt to sit on. It was two weeks into summer vacation, and already she seemed to have done nothing and was tired of everything. If this had been any other neighborhood in the country, the optometrist dallying out in his front yard would have been right over to ask, "What's up with all this furniture?" But in Nan's neighborhood, bouncy or jovial neighborliness was considered poor taste and an unenlightened way to snoop into the affairs of those who lived around you. The optometrist wore an oyster-colored fishing hat, and the lenses of his thick, tiny glasses glimmered like lighthouse reflectors. The Reverend and the optometrist did not speak, and each, like two dogs not wanting to fight, pretended the other did not exist, although when talking to Marta the Reverend called the optometrist "the human laxative." The human laxative had a name — Dr. McCurdy — but Marta rarely used it, because it wasn't difficult to see that his priestly routine was exclusively for adults. Dr. McCurdy hated children in a way that only children could decipher. He once yelled at Marta, "Why don't you go to a playground! Go away and don't be ruining your poor grandmother's beautiful lawn. You tramping around here — it's a sin, girl!"

Marta sat first on the furry, long-haired chaise and decided she didn't like the level of incline, the way the part where her legs rested arched up unnaturally. She tried to pretend she didn't know that the optometrist was scrutinizing her with his lighthouse glasses, but his presence was impossible to ignore. He had walked right through his shrub hedge, into Nan's yard, and stood there staring at her, as if she were an extension of the furniture, as if she had been bought out of a showroom on a highway. Being stared at by the optometrist suddenly brought to Marta's mind a disturbing image — that terrible black eye she saw staring at her from a rhubarb patch on the farm of some distant relatives in Pennsylvania. It was an opossum that presently emerged in full form to reveal his onerous dirty-water hide, his onerous dirty-rope tail. Marta felt something equally hideous about the optometrist — plus, being alone with the furniture in the invisible house and with the sky so dark and the wind whipping up made her think of the ghosts that probably went with the house, the ghosts that Alda bought out of that showroom. What the Reverend would call "the tableau" spooked her, and she ran back to the house so fast, with such traction, that she could almost see the grass staining the white rubber soles of the sneakers that came out of a box from her mother she had just opened that morning.

In the library lived a stillness thick with memory and un-changeability. Marta had seen old photographs of people—her grandfather, Nan, the Reverend, comely women in cloche hats and crocheted handbags, men in ecclesiastical garb or the pin-stripe suits of a certain era—taken in other parts of the house, and everything looked so different, more floral and alive with peony fabric and white wicker, rosy draperies and fringed dav-enports, lamp shades with indentations like the cuttings of a diamond. She was sure that her grandfather's library, though never photographed, was always the same. Nan was sitting in the monstrously shaped leather wing chair Marta had never liked. Her nylon-smoothed old lady's legs were crossed at the ankles, and one elbow was on the armrest, holding up her head like it weighed a ton. The Reverend was at the bar (small in comparison to the one in the drawing room and the one in the dining room), pouring something straight from the bottle. Without looking at the Reverend, Nan held up one arm and wiggled her fingers. Marta had never seen Nan accept a drink before the cocktail hour, and right then she decided that, because this appeared to be a crisis that did not involve her mother and because she was almost ten, she'd finally have that drink the Reverend was always offering her.

The Reverend delivered the drink to Nan's awaiting hand and then sat on the chair's other arm, leaning into her space, strok-ing the waves of her snowy hair with his rough knuckles. The two of them seemed to Marta like a pair of melancholy pigeons, cooing and roosting on a distant ledge. They must have thought she was pouring soda water for herself at the bar, because she used a tall and innocent water glass rather than a short and crafty liquor glass. Marta remembers pouring both vodka and gin, and then both tonic and soda. She remembers the implements—the crystal and the much-polished silver whose engraving was muted to a mere suggestion of birthright. There was always a set of tongs, but the ice bucket was usually empty. There used to be a full-time Belinda who might respond to your call for ice, but Marta had never met this Belinda, who was replaced by the occasional Portuguese lady who liked to keep her mouth shut. The Portuguese lady would bring the cubes in a colander and dump them into the bucket like she was a kitchen boy at a fast-food place replenishing ice at the salad bar.

After just a sip or two of her invented cocktail Marta felt so soft, like a third roosting pigeon. "Let's inspect the damage, dear," she heard the Reverend propose to Nan, petting and shaking her shoulder, "and then I'll ring the men." Like pigeons with legs they made their way out of the house, out to the lawn, and it surprised Marta that, in unison, they plopped themselves down on the red sofa and had the presence of mind to put their glasses on the laminated-top Mediterranean coffee table. Marta was there behind them, in front of them, to the side of them, like a small dog at the arrival of company, and she put her drink on the laminated-top Mediterranean coffee table as well.

"Look at all this," Nan said, limply slapping the cushion to her side. "I have no dignity left. I can't even take care of my own house. There'll be holes in the yard. Like a golfing course arranged by a drunk. All my beautiful grass. God forbid Henry shows up."

"I'm afraid, my love," the Reverend began, "that even God cannot forbid Henry from being Henry."

"You can always make him sound like some colorful figure," she said, "someone out of Molière, someone out of Wilde. But he's a monster, Ryder. Henry is a monster."

"Rembrandt clouds," the Reverend muttered, letting his head fall back. "Haarlem clouds."

"Do you suppose they'll come in the rain, the men?"

"There's a Caravaggio I'd like to see before I die," the Reverend went on, paying no heed to Nan but doing so in a courteous way. "Gone missing. Judas betraying Christ. The Kiss of Death, like in the Mafia movies." He spoke of this lost Caravaggio so often that people close to him didn't even hear it; to Marta it was as regular as the clearing of his throat before a nice big spit into his handkerchief.

Lying on the furry chaise lounge, staring at Rembrandt's churning clouds, Marta felt superb. She said aloud, "My uncle is in Vienna at the conference on mutual and balanced force reductions," only she didn't say it all arrogant like she did to the older boys idling with their bikes on the church green, because when she did they whipped pieces of tar at her. Somewhere way off was her drink, and she could feel how she and Nan and the Reverend looked, the three of them in this invisible house.

"I didn't want Henry," Nan said with a terrible lowness to her voice, "and I have been punished for not wanting Henry. I have been punished by not liking what the rest of them have become. Selfish and hollow. How could anyone like what they've become? They treat me like a concierge — someone to clean up their messes, pay their tickets, fetch them a taxi to the airport. Worthless they are. No integrity. Integrity would have been too much to hope for."

"We know that, dear."

"Who are they after all? Where did they come from?"

"Mustard seeds, dear."

"I gave those mustard seeds everything, Ryder."

"Everything, my dear, and yet they betray you. The Caravaggio, for instance — the Caravaggio I mention presents the decisive moment; Jesus is captured in Gethsemane, betrayed by the mustard seed with that beautiful surname. Iscariot is almost as sweet as Caravaggio, wouldn't you say? Caravaggio even put himself in the thick of it, on the right side of the group, naturally, holding the lantern."

"How vain of him!" Nan nearly shouted. "How vain to see himself as holding the lantern!"

"Artistic liberty, Em, delusions of grandeur — what does it matter? Every permutation of life is there on the canvas, *tra il devoto et profano*."

"*Profano,* Ryder," Nan insisted. "*Profano et profano et profano.*"

When the storm hit it was like someone had plunged a bowie knife through God's tarpaulin, allowing all the detritus of heaven to crash to the earth. The rain poured through God's tarpaulin at full throttle, pinning Marta to Alda's furry chaise. Marta let the rain clear the hair off of her forehead, let it fill up her ears; she could not move, but she still felt quite good. She remembers this feeling lasting a very long time, and then she remembers the Reverend's voice close to her face, his bony arms beneath her; she remembers Nan kissing her cheek, the old woman's breath smelling as acrid as turpentine.

It stormed and rained for hours on Alda's furniture, but Marta slept right through it. She woke up Sunday morning and tasted something that was awful in a new and foreign way. Alda's furniture was ruined, but on that blurry, humid Sunday the furniture proved to be a most inconsequential matter. Marta wore her nightgown around the house the better part of the afternoon, even with so many people coming in and out. Around dinnertime a white Ferrari rumbled up the drive, and because of all the other cars the Ferrari had to park where it stopped, which was normally never done. Marta's mother got out of one side, and a short man in clogs got out of the other. Marta watched them from the bay window, in her nightgown and bridal veil, just as, half an hour before, she'd watched four men from EZ Liquidation turn Alda's new furniture into junk, hurling it onto the open beds of two muddy trucks. She was told on that Sunday the child's version of what had happened—that both Henry and Alda were dead, that they had died on Saturday morning. When she finally got dressed, she was taken by taxi over to the mothball-smelling house of one of the leftover rectory ladies, the one the Reverend called Nappy Thaline. Because the driver from the Ace Taxi Company happened to be Leonard with the scar on his face, Marta learned, during the five-minute ride, the adult version of what had happened: that Henry had shot Alda eight times in the head and then himself once, also in the head, in their room at the Wiltshire Arms Motel, their room with the balcony. Leonard told Marta that they were both naked except for the fact that Henry was wearing white socks. It was a real mess, according to Leonard, whose parting words — "Tell them I told ya and I'll kill ya" — provided her with yet another option for being killed.

People long ago forgot about the person known as Henry, but even many years later everyone seemed able to recall the detail of the white socks. Five or so summers ago, when Marta was visiting her uncle and his family on Block Island, they were sitting on the beach late one day, and as her Uncle Bob found his bored gaze stuck on his stretched-out middle-aged legs, he shouted, "Christ!" and pointed down at his feet, because he was wearing white socks. Then, out of the blue, he said, "Did you know that Henry was the Reverend's son?" It was certainly a good secret, but Marta had no way of knowing if it was true. Her uncles — the bank president and the NATO lackey, one with prostate problems and the other having just undergone a triple bypass — still hadn't grown up, even though they had both acquired young wives and small children. Marta's uncles still liked to be tattlers of tales, and their easiest mark in this regard was Marta's born-again mother, who years ago became so religiously dried out that she all but negated the lesson of Augustine and continued to put her complete faith into words told to her by anyone at any time.

The Reverend died three years before Nan, when Marta was sixteen; he had a stroke while sitting in his and Marta's least favorite furnishing — the leather wing chair in her grandfather's library, the room with the smallest bar — and he never regained consciousness. He never got to see the lost Caravaggio, *The Taking of Christ,* which turned up in the dining room of a Dublin rectory some years ago. It had been there for decades, in the same place, as the Jesuits broke their biscuits, poured their tea, inhaled their liquor, completely ignorant of the company they kept. Marta can remember the woman at the Frick, the woman in the blue angora coat, once asking the Reverend, "Why would you choose to paint a figure about whom practically nothing is known?" They had stopped before a large oil canvas of the apostle Simon, and the Reverend was scratching the bristly hair that grew down the back of his neck. "Everyone cannot have lived a celebrity life," he said. "Judas proved a difficult act to follow."

The Reverend always said that his best liquor was what the old ladies and the not-so-old widows brought back from abroad—stuff spontaneously sprung for at airports the world over. When it was announced that those aboard the plane would have yet another opportunity to purchase duty-free gifts, these women would pass on the cartons of Dunhills in favor of a second bottle of Cutty Sark for the Reverend. Some would be compelled to festoon the boxed or unboxed bottles with scissor-curled ribbon or adhesive-back bows. "Just a little something, Reverend. Your suggestions proved so felicitous. We quite enjoyed hiking the Dolomites. Florence—truly a Godsend! The Uffizi was indeed stunning, most exquisite. We went to the monastery, St. Mark's, to see the Fra Angelicos. And, my, my, wasn't Sienna lovely this time of year!" On those rare occasions Marta went to the Reverend's too-small apartment—mostly to snoop among the papers strewn across his desk at the window—there would be these duty-free gifts, these little somethings, and when she'd read the cards aloud to the Reverend he'd say, "Direct from the Magi, the dears."

When Henry died, Nan's many longtime friends could think of nothing better to do than send expensive bottles of liquor, as anyone temporarily holed up at the house was assumed to be perpetually in need of a drink. There were multitudes of cards and flowers, but the postman always had a parcel in need of a signature, and it turned out that even a child could sign for scotch. Marta remembers lining up these gifts on the perfectly polished Steinway that nobody ever played and waiting for the Reverend to arrive sometime around one. In the weeks after Henry died, before school started, she and the Reverend would have long conversations, stretched out further by the number of times the Reverend remade his drink. She had asked the Reverend, "Was

Henry a murderer? Should somebody be praying for him?" And he said, "Henry was a sick soul, and prayer can do no good for sick souls." She said, "Everyone's happy that Henry is dead, and that Alda is dead, too." And he said, "That is our wretched condition." She told him, "We are the only people Nan likes. She would only cry if we died." And he said, "How can I say you are absolutely right, my love? But you are." This memory is so sharp—lining up the expensive bottles of liquor on the perfectly polished Steinway that nobody ever played and waiting for the Reverend to arrive and eventually say, "You are absolutely right, my love." She would greet him with, "Look! More from the Magi, the dears!" And he would smile at her with glassy eyes and stroke his rough knuckles across her hair, like a benediction.

The Art of Getting Real

I don't think my dad was ever any age, any particular age. He never seemed old, didn't do stupid things that made him seem old. I can't see him licking a finger to separate the new twenties in his wallet after saying he'd spring for what everyone in the van has just ordered at the Burger King drive-through. Or getting into his Eddie Bauer pants and cruising the Home Depot all day Saturday. He never seemed young either—young like it was an act, like Andy's divorced father putting on his brand-new Gap cargo pants so he can dry hump the girls who come home with Andy's sister over Christmas break. My dad always seemed the age of some guy in the back of a car that you meet for five minutes at night—a guy crammed in with all these other people, a guy wearing some kind of special jacket, only you can't tell what kind of special jacket. My dad wasn't just no age: he was no canoe trips and no camcorders, no curfews and no catcher's mitts. The man was just gone—gone daddy gone, and fuck if I ever cared.

But then my dad is dead, and he is already sort of famous in the clan for being dead, for being only forty-three and dying of a heart attack. Because he died at forty-three in the way most guys die at seventy-three, he will always be thought of as "too young." I'm so sick of those words, and my mother's hiked the amp on the whole thing because "Forever Young" is a song on the Chris Isaak album she's been playing over and over these three days since he died. He hasn't lived with us in years, and in the three days of him being dead my mother hasn't pissed a tear—at least none

23

that I've seen. But then I guess he was there, doing something or other at some present tense in her life, and I guess Chris Isaak's wailing is what cools her jets.

The only thing that made my dad interesting to me was why my mother married him. Everyone says this to their parents: "Why'd you guys get married? You hate each other." I know my mom wasn't pregnant when she got married, but I also know that her getting married is a subject I'm never supposed to talk about. "I'll tell you anything you want to know about the day you were born," she once told me, "anything about the greasy-spoon second you shot out of me, but don't ask me about the blackout during which I got married."

I don't hate the guy; you can't hate a guy like that. He was my dad; I look just like him, and I can't hate him for that either. What I hate is the idea that this has to be a big thing for me; what I hate is all these people hanging around, acting like they were authorized by the DMV to get under my hood. My grandparents are a wreck; they're the ones who need the cards that say "with deepest sympathy" and "in this time of sorrow." My dad was the loser of his family, but he was a miracle baby, born late to my grandmother after she'd had some miscarriages and was warned by the doctors that it was too dangerous to keep trying. His real dad also died too young, in his late forties, when my dad was still a baby, and then his stepdad was about the best father any kid ever had. But, there ya go, right? A wasted six-lane is a wasted six-lane.

Even though my dad was an only child, beyond him the clan is huge, with tons of his cousins and tons of their kids and everyone loving to hover. Me and my mom are holed up and don't know what to do. I don't want to do anything but go around like the seventh kid in a pack of eight or nine, just a walk-on, just like I was a few days ago. That forever-young dad of mine, he's done it again—fucked up the works by not being around.

People want to talk to me about this "congenital" thing, this "heredity" thing, this thing with my heart. Odds are I'll keel over at forty-three, just like my dad, or else have to suck up to rich teaching hospitals so that they'll let me buy one of the hearts they get from their organ pimps in Peru. People think I'm traumatized because I'll have to die or else suck up and then probably die anyway, but this is because all of them are way past forty-three, and the thought of dying freaks the shit out of them. To me, forty-three doesn't seem that young or that old, and dying doesn't freak the shit out of me. Even though there's a Pavement song that goes "simply put I want to grow old, dying does not meet my expectations," I'm not scared to die; I expect to die. All I want to know is who my relatives are forever comparing me to. They seem to think that the right way to act is a numerical constant—say, pi—which would mean that there are all these pi guys roaming around out there consistently doing the right thing. I'd like to know what the correct version of me looks like and sounds like and smells like. That's my big question, the one that pissed off my mother's brother, Phil the Drill, in regard to the "attitude situation" of yours truly: "Who's fucking pi, Phil?"

My mother was always sending my dad away, and he was always coming back from where he was sent—not right away, but he always came back. I picture it like having to cross a desert on a tank of gas: you could just drive straight through and pray you hit a Texaco oasis by the time you're on empty, or you could drive to some stupid half-tank spot and then turn around and come back, to get more gas. This is what my dad always chose. He never did anything bad to us, but that just went along with doing nothing at all to us. My grandparents paid his way, supported my mother and me, bought us this house. Now they say, "He loved you *in his own way*," and I wonder how they can say "love" when he never let me and my mother get in the way of anything he wanted to do, even though he didn't do one friggin' thing with his life. Most of my dad's older cousins have been playing *60 Minutes*, spilling their guts for the camera, saying that "down deep" the guy was "responsible" because when he was a teenager he taught their kids how to ride a bike. "Great," I said.

"That's just great. He doesn't even know if I ever had a bike, but he teaches your brats to ride some merchandise, so he's suddenly Ward Fucking Cleaver. Did he teach them to chew gum and fart at the same time?"

The last time I saw my dad was at Christmas, and the cousins and their kids kept yapping about how I'd shot up, was already a head taller than him. Here I was getting pats on the back for being a successful sperm, and my dad just smiles, all mellow and faraway, like I had nothing to do with him, like I was just some Wonder Years graduate loading sacks of topsoil into his trunk. Maybe my being a head taller than him is what made him shake hands with me like I was someone he just met at a sports bar.

What my dad and I had in common the last time I saw him was Television, not the thing but the band. It used to be just the Band we had in common, but now it's these two things, even though with him dead, I don't suppose we have that much in common anymore. It was this past Christmas, and we were getting all scruffed up to shovel my grandparents' driveway. It's such a guy thing—hardly any talking—and it's always somehow fun in a way you'd never want anyone else to know about. We were in the garage picking out tools from my grandfather's stockpile, considering instruments like a dental hygienist thinks about which silver hook will best get the crud out from between the teeth you lie about ever flossing.

"What are kids listening to these days?" my dad asked as I decided on the shovel he should use. How do you answer that sort of ass-minded question? "I don't know what *kids* are listening to," I finally said. Then he said, "OK, so what are *you* listening to?" I said, "I don't know. Stuff by Television." He banged the shovel on the concrete floor of the garage and said, "Man, I used to do that. That's what I listened to. I used to do that kind of . . . that way, I mean," and then his words trailed off, like he was all of a sudden remembering where he could go to get more gas for the desert.

My friend Andy listens to practically everything you can

download—no discrimination whatsoever—just like any other watered-down shit who couldn't go twenty-four hours without taking four showers. My girlfriend, Alicia, likes good music, plus all that vagina stuff, but like she says, "Ya gotta take the shake with the fries." She's also always saying, "Call me your Pop Queen or bite my ass." The last time she said "Call me your Pop Queen" I said, "OK, honey," grabbing an empty pretzel bag. "I'll call you my Pop Queen if you wear this here cellophane over your head, if you be my Bachman Lady." Alicia's my girlfriend because she laughs when I say things like this; she laughs and says, "Fuck yourself like you're really into it." I feel lucky about Alicia, because sometimes music feels like that's all there is, like it was the closest to you that anything could get. Sometimes when I'm in my room I smell the paper they print the liner notes on—I don't know if it's the ink or the paper or both—but this particular smell makes me feel safe, makes me feel good when I'm alone. Sometimes this is the only thing I like about any particular day.

I have no "role models"—that's what the guidance counselor tells me—but I wouldn't mind turning out like the guys at the used-record store near where my mother works, the used-record store that doesn't sell any used records, just CDs—promo CDs and all the crap people buy and leave for dead. Buy and leave for dead. I can't stand it, being around the store's idiot customers, but I like being around the record-store guys—Michael, Milt, and Heinley. Michael put me on to the Band, to MC5 and Television, that sort of stuff. Michael talks to me like he means it, like I'm not wasting his time.

They're all old, the record-store guys. I don't say this because their being old ever struck me from shooting the shit with them, but because they say it to each other and to people who come into the store, mainly Michael's on-and-off girlfriend, Gretchen, who retaliates by estimating the size of their dicks (Milt's and Heinley's, I mean) in millimeters. Once when Milt was complaining about how lately all his rubbers were busting on him, Gretchen said, "Go for the armor, Milt. Use a thimble." When it's just Michael, Milt, Heinley, and a couple dweebs roaming the bins, the conversation never goes in any specific direction, but it's always entertaining, like eight bucks for a movie without spending the eight bucks. Sometimes I think I'd like to write it all down, what they say, for no particular reason, just because I think I understand, even though I haven't been there and done that.

Michael is not one of those guys who hates practically everything that's happened to music in the past twenty years, but he really can't stand the trend to use tracks that are just some moaning white chick, what he calls "buttercream orgasm in a frosting can." "It's cheap," he told me, "it's such a fucking cheap thing." He said it reminds him of being in junior high, when one of his twit friends (all of his friends were twits, according to him) was excited because his dad had just bought this organ with all the synthesizer features a jerky family that loved throwing money away would want. Michael said that this twit friend pointed out the fact that the organ had come with color-coded, one-finger "sheet music" to the *Abbey Road* album, which back then had kicked its shelf life to death. This twit friend played for Michael "Maxwell's Silver Hammer" using one finger and a calypso beat, and Michael just about lost it, lost it with everything. "I thought, you know, 'I gotta get outta here!'" he told me. "And I meant, like, outta my skin." What I like about Michael is that when he's talking to me he'll use what he, Milt, and Heinley call Punk Latin. Michael speaks in Punk Latin to me even though when he's talking to Milt or Heinley he sounds like he's got shitloads of degrees, degrees in everything.

They all love to rag on me, rag on me for being my age, but it's never anything that makes me mad. Just last week Milt asked Heinley, "So, did ya get that K2 snowboard you wanted for Christmas?" And Heinley said, "No, man, but what I wanted was, like, that chick I saw riding one in a magazine — that chick with the Hello Kitty tattoo and the bra with the two orange smiley faces on her tits. That girl was mad awesome." Even though they'll rag on you, Michael, Milt, and Heinley are about the only older guys I respect. They know what they are, and they never try to make you believe they don't.

My mom keeps pissing off my grandparents by saying "the festivities"—this is what she calls all the funeral-home stuff we have to go through before they put my father in the ground. "What's next with the festivities?" she'll say, and everyone will look at her like they want her to go home, even though she's already in her home.

The worst part of my father's festivities doesn't have to do with funeral homes. It happened just this morning, when Alicia finally came over. Like, here she is my girlfriend, and it's been three days, and tomorrow's the wake, and the day after that the grand finale, the giant slalom into the hole, and today she finally finds the time in her busy schedule to drop by. She was at the back door with her brother's big plaid jacket and her hair looping down from the way her hair is usually brushed up. She wasn't wearing makeup, which meant things were bad, because usually she's got the mascara all smeared on purpose—that's how she looks when she says "Fuck yourself like you're really into it." "You sure look like money," I said to her, and she tucked her arms into her chest and sort of fell into me, crying. I mean, she was really crying, like it was someone that died on her. I asked her why she was crying—I said, "You saw my dad ten minutes, tops"—and she said she was crying because I wasn't crying, because I *wouldn't* cry. For me, that right there was bottoming out to China—my own girlfriend wanting me to be some way that wasn't real. At least she could've been crying at the thought that I'll probably be dead by forty-three.

Alicia's father is a real asshole; that's what she calls him all the time, to his face: "You are such a Papa Asshole, asshole!" And yet this morning she told me that she'd die if he ever died. She said "if he ever died" as if dying was something that only might happen to people, as if dying was as random as Ed McMahon stopping you in your driveway and sticking a giant sweepstakes check up one of your nostrils. Alicia's father is an orthodontist and has so far saved ninety-two thousand dollars for her college education. When she's eighteen he'll stop saving, and she can draw from the account to pay for her college or whatever she wants to do with her life. She says she can't wait till she's eighteen, to get the cash and get away. I know that this is a cool thing for a father to do, but still the man's an asshole.

What everyone says to their parents when their parents say some half-assed thing—like when they make some big fucking proclamation about what you're never allowed to drive again or what you've got exactly fifteen minutes to clean up—is "Get real." It doesn't really mean anything; it's just what you say. It's like filler for when there's nothing going on inside your head. If I think about what I myself would have to do to get real I get a wicked headache. It probably amounts to a religion if you can do it—a religion or some kind of art. Which is probably why everyone throws it at their parents, because if their parents could hack art then they'd be somewhere else, somewhere doing the big time, and would not have any kids to scream at. My dad never asked me to do anything, never gave me an order, but at Christmas when we were out shoveling my grandparents' driveway he said from the blackness a ways off, "Do this one thing for me, will you?" I remember I stood up straight and looked at him even though I couldn't really see his face, and he couldn't really see mine. I remember this was so weird, me waiting to hear the one thing he wanted me to do for him, because for a minute the world was so frozen and silent that it was almost not there. It was as if all the relatives crammed into my grandparents' house were in some Apollo or another and we were out dangling by strings, with no air, just us two out in the black galaxy, with nothing but a stupid job to do. "Don't ever give your mother a hard time" is what he told me. That was it, just not giving her a hard time. I remember feeling really bad and really alone then, and all I could think to do was bend back down to the shoveling and say "Get real," digging into my shitty filler as I dug into the shitty snow.

"What did you say to me?" he asked.

I sort of laughed. "I told you to get real," I said, and then the world seemed even more silent than before, because suddenly I felt like a milked-down bowl of oatmeal, being sad and mad and a prick-on-purpose all at once. "Chris," my dad said in a low voice, "that's the worst thing you could say to a person." I shrugged and said, "I didn't mean nothing by it"—said it all stupid, like some plank-brained linebacker caught pissing into a nice lady's shrubs. My dad was quiet again, and I could see him standing with both hands on the handle of the shovel, like those old pictures of farmers thinking deep thoughts about how to harvest a bowl of dust. "You're not even seventeen," he said. "You don't know shit. What's real to you is something I wish I could go back into, like a tree house. Like a tree house to hide out in. That's what's real to you. You can tell me to fuck off, you can tell me to stick the world up my ass, but don't tell me to get real. And don't tell your mother that either."

The last time I was in the record store a funny thing happened. I mean, it was a situation that started out funny but then went to someplace I wasn't sure of. I was talking to Michael—actually Michael was talking to me—when Heinley warned, "Prick up your ears, dudes. Fast approacheth Ye Olde Wretchin." "Wretchin" is what Milt and Heinley call Gretchen. It's a joke I half wish I could get a drag of, but I know by the sucking-lemon look on Michael's face that a low shit like me could not afford to laugh at "Ye Olde Wretchin." And besides that, Gretchen always looked to me relatively beautiful. They used to call her—all of them, before they got old—"Fetchin' Gretchen." This, according to Milt and Heinley, was before she'd even consider going out with Michael, when she thought that going out with Michael would be a joke, what you'd do if you were on Noah's Ark and needed a date for the Christmas party.

Like always, Michael and Gretchen moved a ways off down the

counter, to talk that girlfriend whispery talk, with the girlfriend looking around suspiciously at the other guys making like they're busy. It's never that these other guys are trying to hear what she's saying—it's only other girls who want to hear what she's saying. The guys just like the sexy sound of this whispery girlfriend talk, and only if it's not their own girlfriend who's doing the talking.

"For Christ sake, Michael!" Gretchen shouted. "You're thirty-nine. Why can't you even think about doing something real for a living?" This sort of blew the whispery moment.

"This is a job that matches my life," Michael said looking down to the mess of empty jewel boxes in front of him.

"Well, yeah, that's exactly what I already knew," she said, soft for a change. "You know, Michael, you've finally completed the mission. You got me into this from the real world. You pulled me in from the outside. It's like I went out of my sane way to get a disease, and now I'm stuck with this disease. I spent too many years loving you for no reason, and now you've really done it—you went and broke a diseased heart."

Once Gretchen was out the door, Milt said, in a lame version of his usually perfect vice-principal voice, "Now that was completely uncalled for." All three of them stared after her through the store's mud-streaked window, stared after her as she walked off under the snow-blinding sunlight, stared after her like she was the last female on the desert island and was leaving them for another desert island. I felt my throat tighten, what I remember feeling as a kid, what I remember feeling those times that the whole fucking world seemed to be leaving me for dead. On our side of the store's mud-streaked window it felt like a sad old movie, mainly sad because I wasn't around in the old days of Michael, Milt, and Heinley, wasn't around then to see and understand how this could be happening. I guess I felt like crying because my sadness was for them, not for me. I felt like crying for Michael, because he was so decent, and for absolutely no reason I can tell he just fell through some big crack in the world, and for Gretchen, because she was relatively beautiful and had a life going on someplace else, and yet she still came into this shitty used-record store that didn't even sell used records anymore.

If I cried over my dad I'd be crying for someone who didn't even exist, because I'd have to cry for the dad I didn't have, the dad of that kid loading the sacks of topsoil into people's trunks. They say it's my age that makes me "heartless"—that's what all of my father's cousins have been mumbling, "heartless," all these dicks who didn't shoot out of their mothers with one diseased heart preinstalled. They say it's my shit-for-morals generation, that's what they say. But I know that Michael would act the same way I'm acting, even though he's almost as old as my dad was just three days ago. I think of that day that Michael didn't cry, standing there over the empty jewel boxes, a bunch of plastic with no music inside. If I was Michael right now I'd have about four years left, and if I was Michael with four years left, I wouldn't know how to find a real thing to do with my life either.

This is what I plan to think about during the wake tomorrow and the funeral the day after. This is what I'll think about when I'm supposed to be sobbing like a simp or else looking like I'm holding it all in for the sake of my mother, who's supposed to be throwing herself and her coat and her shoulder bag over the top of her husband's coffin, like they do in Mafia movies.

It doesn't bother my mom that I am the way I am, and no one has to tell me never to give her a hard time. When I tell my mom to get real she throws a dish towel at me—a dish towel or a sneaker or one of the two Little League trophies I got for merely showing up—and I like this. Sometimes she rolls her eyes and yells "Jesus-fucking-Christ-Almighty!" before she throws a trophy at me.

I think people cry because they're afraid of getting real, because that might mean thinking about how much they don't love their loved ones. And I think maybe that's the reason Michael didn't cry that day at the record store. He would never put on an act. But then I also wonder about crying, because if people can cry when they're happy, then they can also not cry when they're sad. And the more I think of all this, the more I just don't know—don't know if I'd just stand there being real when a relatively beautiful girl was walking away from me, or if, with just four years left, I'd close up my jewel boxes and do something else, anything else, to get her not to leave, to get her to stay with me till it was over, till the end.

Maybe, Maybe Not

I just married the boy next door from thirty-one years ago. He was my neighbor for a year, maybe less, in a town half a state away from where I live now. His family had moved up from Pennsylvania, and then as soon as the neighborhood got used to their license plates they disappeared to Ohio. The father was a claims adjuster, the mother barely seen on account of the venetian blinds that came with their house. Two boys on bikes was the relevant story. Both were a few grades ahead of me, went to a different school, and displayed what I took to be a big-city sharpness. My parents never bothered to speak to the Glenshaws because the Glenshaws never bothered to remove the labels from their new aluminum trashcans. There was definitely something imperma- nent about them, which must have been the reason for their acute appeal to me.

Who winds up to be your immediate neighbor is one of the chanciest things in life — as much of a crapshoot as picking up the paper and never knowing what you're going to read. On a recent Sunday I happened to read the *Times* obituaries because an article from the front page jumped close to that section. One of the obits was for a guy named Gary Glenshaw, who'd devel- oped some kind of robotics technology and was a famous person within the scientific community — three school-age children, sad ending from a brain tumor at age forty-four. When I got to the "is survived by" wrap-up, I remembered this guy and his brother as having lived next door for a speck of time when I was young.

Why on earth did I remember that the father was a claims adjuster? I must've liked the way the words sounded together—I must've invented a complex of meaning. I scrolled through the names and faces randomly packed in my memory to calculate the distance between then and now as thirty-one years.

I paid a lot of attention to my neighbors thirty-one years ago because I was an only child—a condition I came to consider a personal failing. As if to hammer home this character flaw, my parents bought me a swing set with one swing. "Why spend the extra cash?" was my father's rationale. Kids didn't want to play in our yard because you had to take turns on the swing, and the swing set wasn't long enough to allow more than one kid to hang by her knees from the axle bar. We didn't own a barbecue grill; no game with balls, birdies, or wickets was ever played on the grass. Ours was the lonely backyard of old people, mainly because my parents, like vampires or Austrians with rare skin diseases, never went outside during the day. Inside was their domain, where they were forever chiding me for idleness and mopery—the eighth and ninth deadly sins in their book. They were always on my tail, driving me out of the house, and the single swing was the most effortless place to wind up. The swing set wasn't taken down in the winter; the snow liked to drift around it as the cunning rusting process continued underneath. Under the single swing was a deep rut, the distinct parabolic shape of which was molded by my feet. Sitting on the swing with my heels dug into the earth was like saying, "This is the outside, and this is mine."

The Glenshaw family's importance to me stemmed from an incident involving Mr. Glenshaw and our neighboring backyards. The incident occurred in the late fall, and I can even remember what I was wearing that day: cutoffs rolled up to mid-thigh, red wool kneesocks that came over my knees, penny loafers that were water warped out of shape, a purple parka with a strip of red elephants around the chest. I had put on this parka in the kitchen, just as my mother was stuffing a lot of cabbage into a Crock-Pot to stink up the house for days. "Dinner won't be until nine-thirty.

Do something useful until then." She didn't say anything about the fact that I was wearing shorts with a parka; this I distinctly remember.

I liked to sit on the swing doing nothing, waiting for smaller ordeals (for instance, slow-cooking cabbage) and larger ones (say, childhood) to be over and done with. I'd twirl around to twist the swing's chains as tight as I could get them; then I'd release myself so that I could spin—slowly at first and then fast, faster, and finally zip! the end of the show with a jerk to hurt your neck, as if you were practicing for a public hanging at a later date. That day must have been typical of so many others—probably not a pink sunset, but let's remember one anyway—a sunset making the hues of everything in the yard deeper, richer, like every object had a grand and noble purpose. Rusted things looked especially good under the sepia glow of those kinds of sunsets, and there were a lot of rusted things in our yard. That wheelbarrow tilted against the house seemed to be rusted into place. What the heck was that doing there? It had nothing to do with my father, who'd have needed an illustrated manual to work the handles. It must've come with the property, like the Glenshaws' venetian blinds and maybe even myself, because whenever my father caught me just standing around he'd ask, "What—you came with the property?"

That evening of the sunset that might or might not have been present, I saw Mr. Glenshaw come out the back door of his house holding something in his hand. I remember first hearing the screen door slam shut and then looking up for a story to go with it. Each neighbor's screen door slamming shut made a different sound, and I could determine what kinds of domestic situations were occurring by the kinds of slams I heard. Mr. Glenshaw stood in the yard after this particular slam, and I could tell that what he was holding was a pie, because a pie is about the only thing you'd hold that way with one hand. Before I had time to consider what was going on, he hurled the pie at the birdfeeder in our yard. It did not seem like a real pie; it made a cracking sound upon impact, and it scared me. The feeder fell over, and then everything was still and seemed to get darker by the second. I took personal offense at this violent act because I had made that birdfeeder in Girl Scouts; it accounted for one whole badge. It was supposed to have had a mansard roof, though in my rendering you couldn't tell this architectural feature. It took forever to get my father to put it on a pole and put the pole in the ground. He complained that it ruined the yard, that it would attract squirrels, that no one in our family had ever liked birds anyway.

"Mr. Glenshaw just threw a pie at our birdfeeder!" I exclaimed, breathless from having raced into the kitchen. My parents didn't seem alarmed, but both changed out of their reading glasses at the same time — open one case, close the other, the two of them in stereo, ad infinitum until I was of voting age. "Why did he do that?" I kept asking them. I felt that there had to be an explanation, that perhaps throwing pies was something an adult did when he lost his job or bought worthless stock.

By the time my parents got to the kitchen window, you could see the darkened figures of the two boys picking up the debris in our yard and putting it into a trash bag held by the smaller of the two; we watched them as they stood up the feeder on its pole and secured it in the ground. My father said, "I should pay them to rake the leaves."

"But why did he do that?" I continued to ask.

"Do we know what their names are?" my mother inquired of no one in particular, but they both looked at me. I shrugged. "Maybe and Maybe Not."

"Don't be a wise-aleck," my father said. "And what the heck are you wearing on your legs?"

"Not much," my mother replied.

The funeral for Gary Glenshaw was to be held at a Methodist church near Mount Kisco the next day. I wondered if someone at the funeral would be able to tell me why the father of the deceased had thrown that pie at our birdfeeder — maybe the father himself, or else the mother or the brother. From this nuclear group, only the brother was mentioned in the *Times* as being a survivor. I tried to remember what the survivor was like as one of the boys next door. I'd had some brief conversations with him, if what kids say to each other can be construed as conversation. When you asked him a yes-or-no question, he'd say, "Maybe, maybe not." That was his schtick the entire time he lived next door to me — "Maybe, maybe not" — and I had thought it an especially clever one, like something said by kids in more advanced parts of the country.

I really don't know why I decided to drive to Mount Kisco the next day, except that this is the sort of behavior that junk psychologists are always urging on recently divorced women ("embrace spontaneity!"). At the funeral I sat in the back of the church like police detectives do in movies. It turned out to be a packed service with a lot of crying children. There must've been an entire middle school in attendance, presumably the classmates of Gary Glenshaw's children. Surrounded by an entire middle school of weeping kids, I regretted this impulsive action.

You don't really need a program to figure out the principals at a funeral. Even in dysfunctional families the heaviest criers sit in the front row, and this family was no exception, although the Glenshaw brother, the survivor whom I recognized right off because he's the spitting image of his father, wasn't crying and sat a few rows back. He looked like the actor Joel McCrea because his father looked like the actor Joel McCrea. That's all I can remember my father saying about Mr. Glenshaw after it was determined that the labels would not be removed from his family's trashcans — "That guy next door looks like the actor in those Preston Sturges pictures." At least I think he was referring to Joel McCrea; with my father you always had to connect the dots, do the math. His motto, if he had one, was "A word to the wise should be sufficient."

I left the church within a stream of penitent children — they were heading for school buses, and I was intending to take my losses (one day of work and a dollar-something in tolls) and head home. But something made me proceed along with the funeral entourage to a cemetery that was much more effortlessly upper middle class than the one that housed my parents. The scene was as bucolic as a movie set because, luckily for us all, movies constitute most people's experience with burial sites. I'm always conflating my only two burial-site experiences with things I've seen in movies—like there being a steady downpour, men holding black umbrellas above their bowler hats, a priest saying things in Latin, someone suddenly taking off on a horse. My parents died within a month of each other, so in my memory it felt like just the one burial. I purchased the same casket twice—Mr. Oloff gave me a big discount on the second one. Initially I thought this was standard undertaker kindness. Later I learned that Mr. Oloff had been sent two of the kind of casket that I ordered for my mother, and the second one, which had been damaged in transit, had been a bone of contention between wholesaler and retailer, so Mr. Oloff already had the second one kicking around in the garage when I called him again.

"Do I know you?" the survivor asked me as the mourners were leaving the gravesite. I had lost track of him during the "ashes to ashes" part, right about when I lost myself in daydreams about my own funeral and its almost certain lack of drama (I'd have to hire a stranger if I wanted someone to take off on a horse). "Or do you know me?" he persisted.

Because I was caught unprepared, the truth was my only option. "You and your brother lived next door to me in 1971," I told him. "I read the obituary in the paper yesterday. I came here because I wanted to find out something. I don't usually do this kind of thing."

"Did the paper say that?"

"Say what?"

"That we lived next to you in 1971."

"No."

"So what did you want to find out?"

"I saw your father throw a pie at our birdfeeder one night, and I've always wanted to know why he did this."

"Sure," he said, as if nothing about my presence or professed motive was out of the ordinary. "I remember that. I can tell you about the pie." He looked around at the departing mourners, ignoring numerous overtures, people beckoning him toward them. "Do you want to go somewhere for lunch?" he asked. "My sister-in-law hates me. If I go back to her house, I might throw a pie. Look—she's staring at us. Look sad for my sister-in-law. Let's wave at her at the same time."

Though I can't say I had come up with any picture of what the boy next door would turn out to be like, this seemed a plausible result—a little flip, a little renegade. I followed his inexpensive rental car to an expensive restaurant that had once been a stable; I was feeling impressed with myself for not being nervous, for having gotten this far without embarrassing myself. I was planning to pay for the meal with a spare credit card that I'd never used; I practiced sentences that made me sound like Diane Sawyer. Although my original intention was to resolve the pie-throwing mystery for my own satisfaction, I was beginning to feel altruistic, thinking that perhaps the odd encounter would make the flip and renegade survivor feel good about people in the weird way a Preston Sturges picture makes you feel good about people, would confirm for him that we are not all so separate and isolated, although I had no idea why I thought myself capable of this.

Inside the restaurant, however, my confidence began to sag because the brother of the late Gary Glenshaw seemed completely different from the way he had been not twenty minutes before. He was much less secure, maybe even unhappy in a more underlying way than bereavement would call for. He was nervous; he kept lifting the saltshaker and tapping it against the olive oil plate. He cut his lamb into smaller and smaller pieces as he went into more and more detail about some topic that wasn't even audible to me. He would ask me a question but not wait for a reply. "Do you read the *Economist* I read the *Economist*." "Have you been to Japan I've been to Japan." "Are you allergic to shellfish I'm allergic to shellfish." His nervousness was distracting and disorienting, although I suppose it didn't matter given that he never let me get a word in edgewise. Did he really care whether I read the *Economist,* visited Japan, or was allergic to shellfish? Both of his parents were dead; that's one thing I learned. One of his former girlfriends was in an AT&T commercial. Five years ago he borrowed from his brother a lot of money that he never repaid. While his brother was dying, his sister-in-law sent him an invoice for this loan with a 15 percent interest rate compounded over the five-year period.

Toward the end of the meal, I was finally able to ask my own question: "Are you going to tell me the pie story now?"

"I don't think I can today," he said with a pained expression, suggesting that I understood the story as an emotionally complicated one—which in some sense was true. After tapping his coffee spoon against the saltshaker he said, "But I'd like to tell you about it tomorrow."

On the drive home I regretted my impulsive actions. I was hoping he'd forget about tomorrow, was wishing I'd given him a false name and a false number. He was certainly an appealing man if a man was what you were after, but romantic prospecting seemed an unwholesome motive under the circumstances. And besides that, many things about him were sketchy. He seemed to have been through hundreds of jobs but had no discernible career—lots of higher education and then a big gaping black hole. He talked about houses he'd owned in Pennsylvania and yet was living out of a suitcase in someone's apartment on the Upper East Side. He had a name, Kyle, but I felt uncomfortable using it.

The next day he drove up the Taconic Parkway to have dinner at a restaurant I like. He looked much better when illuminated by the lights of this restaurant. In fact, he now seemed different in a new way—not flip, not nervous, but quite comfortable with me, like we'd remained Christmas card friends all these years, like yesterday when he seemed so aggrieved was a tiny blip in a larger narrative, like we had a history of these sorts of ups and downs.

"You start," he said.

"Tell me about the pie."

"OK, but first tell me about you, what you do. I was rude last night, blabbering on and on about myself. I can be like that—rude. Rude when you least expect it, or maybe when you most expect it. Anyway, I'm sorry."

I started to say something, and he interrupted. "I remember you . . . so well. I just wanted you to know that."

This was a difficult comment to gloss over because it was such an outright lie. Maybe he thought I was going to buy him meals indefinitely. Maybe he was even more of a cad than my suspicious mind could anticipate, marshaling all of his charms in a campaign to sustain the pie mystery. I don't know why things happened the way they did aside from the fact that these charms of his were quite potent. He spoke with an intimacy that suggested we were coconspirators in some kind of liberation effort. We spent the entire dinner talking about everything but the reason we were having dinner. "Life in the contemporary world" seemed the gist of it. He acted very interested in what happened to my hometown after his family left, which I found hard to believe given all the places they had lived when he was growing up.

"Let's go there now," he proposed in lieu of coffee. He meant our houses in that little city. "Let's drive there. It's just a couple hours. We'll re-create the pie-throwing incident, like we're detectives, and then you'll know why my father did what he did. Let's see if we can find our houses."

I hesitated before saying, "I lived there until I was twenty-one."

"Great!" he replied, not at all chagrined to have overlooked this obvious—perhaps essential—aspect about me. "You're the expert; you be the guide."

Against my better judgment I consented to be the guide. Curiosity had given way to a mild obsession—I now needed to know what the survivor was looking for, and why I had become part of the search.

It was decided that we'd take my car, which did not surprise me—me driving and him talking. It was somewhat amusing to think that the common denominator between this man and me was a place I hadn't seen in ten years. My parents had selected their cemetery in a larger city where none of us had ever lived. Whenever I visit their graves, I do something a tourist would do; I get a map from the Chamber of Commerce.

"Gary and I used to play all kinds of driving games with my father," he told me soon after we set out. "When we were driving back from Arizona once and he was tired, he played a game to see how many exits he could go before pulling off the interstate and checking us into a motel. We kept ticking off the numbered exits because it was like The Highway versus Dad, a contest. He ended up driving all night and half the next day until we were home. No one said anything for six hours at a stretch. Now it sounds crazy."

"Is that why he threw the pie at our birdfeeder?"

"Dad? I don't know. My mother was the one. She was institutionalized when I was fifteen."

"I don't think I ever saw your mother."

"You were lucky."

I was hoping he'd stop there with his mother because I sensed thickly settled issues, but we had just gotten on the Thruway. Proceeding along on the Diane Sawyer path seemed the decent thing to do, however, so I drove headlong into his issues. "You weren't close to her?" I asked.

"I never thought of her as being close to anyone. She was an only child come to think of it, like you. She was close to my grandparents, I guess. From Lake Placid, though I don't know what that means. That she should have been placid maybe? She was never placid. She was afraid of everything. Always jittery, like an electric toothbrush."

"What was wrong with her?"

"I don't know . . . some kind of depression. She'd drink, she'd stay in bed, she'd fall and hurt herself, we'd drive her to the emergency room at four in the morning. This seemed like the only way it went with us. They gave her drugs, I suppose, but not Prozac-type drugs. Hard stuff, in between the shock therapy."

"That must've been hard."

When he said, "You know something funny?" I could tell that what came next would not make me laugh. "She was the one who got me and Gary saying 'Maybe, maybe not.' This was the sign that she was coming out of it, getting in a better mood. Sometimes she'd shock you by showing up in the living room dressed in street clothes. That was my Dad's word for it—'street clothes,' versus the 'bed clothes' she usually wore, that he was always trying to get her to change out of. When you asked, 'Mom, are you OK?' and she'd say, 'Maybe, maybe not,' it was a big relief, like she was giving you the high-five."

"So did she get better?"

"Killed herself. OD'd."

I was hoping he wasn't waiting for an apology—we're always apologizing about death, and it's the people who don't give a shit who seem the sorriest of all.

"She did it when she was let out with my father for a weekend," he continued, looking out the passenger window. People do that in cars at night—look out the passenger window like it's a video screen showing their own personal past. "He could've saved her," he said, "at least that's what we think. It was his choice. He was a smart guy really. He was in insurance. 'They'll nickel-and-dime ya into the ground'—that was his motto."

"Everyone should have a motto," I said with synthetic cheer. For the remainder of the drive we talked about celebrity dogs, rich people in jail, and mobile telephony—this in addition to music, politics, and the decline of Western civilization.

Our old houses looked small to us, which meant that we'd both grown perfectly typical. I estimated that old people lived in my old house, because even though it looked small to me, it looked the same in most respects; his house had been converted into apartments. We got out of the car and stood on the sidewalk. Both yards were fenced, so we decided not to try to sneak onto anyone's property to re-create the pie-throwing incident.

"We're too old for that kind of thing anyway," I said.

"Is that what we are?" he said with a laugh. Then he looked around, as if we had alternative locations to consider. "Do you think they still have that dump around here?"

"They turned it into a playground a long time ago."

"The way of the world," he said sadly, "ruin a perfectly good dump."

Without much fanfare, we got back in the car and sat there.

"Are you cold?" he asked. "Do we need some heat?" I turned on the car and the heater, and he started talking again. He told me that his mother never cooked dinner; the boys made things from cans, jars, and packages—macaroni and cheese, franks and beans, spaghetti and Ragu. Their father would bring home buckets of Kentucky Fried Chicken. Fast food turned out to be the prelude to his story about the pie.

"One day I got home from school early," he began, "cut class I think. I was always truant, always in trouble at that school. Anyway, I came home, and there was this noise in the kitchen. I go out there, and it's my mother dressed in street clothes; she's making something. Cooking or baking, whatever. The oven was on; she was baking something. She told me to 'go play' because she was making dinner. What was I—eleven? Eleven, and she says, 'Go play.' Anyway, you have to picture how this was for me, for Gary when he got home, what kind of big event this was. I hadn't seen my mother cook, ever. It was shocking. She had once been a good cook—that was the lowdown. Good at just about everything was the lowdown on my mother. I suppose I idealized this time when my mother was good at everything—whatever was just out of my frame of memory—one or two years it was, but it might as well have been a million years before.

"By the time Gary got home, she had switched her plan to dessert. She said something like, 'I'm just making dessert. Just dessert. Call your father and tell him to pick something up, what you like to eat. Tell him I'm just making dessert.' She was using an electric mixer; it was too much. What she was making was a lemon meringue pie. That kitchen had small windows, didn't get much light. She didn't have any of the counter lights on; I remember thinking it was amazing she could do this in the dark. We didn't watch, didn't want to make her nervous. It smelled good though. And my dad was so cool about the whole thing—Mr. Nonchalant. She sat down at the table with us; we had the Kentucky Fried Chicken on real plates.

"When it came time, she got the pie from the counter and put it on the table. This pie looked great. No, not just great—'great' would be an understatement. This looked to me like the most beautiful pie in the world. We could hardly believe it. We just stared at it, and then my mother slid it toward my father. 'You're the man,' she said, 'you carve.' My father smiled; 'I'm the man,' he said. 'I'll *cut*.' But when he put a knife to the pie, the knife wouldn't go in. He tapped on the pie, and the most beautiful pie in the world sounded like plaster of Paris. He looked at my mother; she looked confused and then irritated. 'I couldn't find any cornstarch in *your* kitchen,' she said, 'so I used Sta-Prest.' 'Sta-Prest?' my Dad repeated, sounding equally confused. It was Gary, the great mediator, who translated: 'It's that stuff you iron with, Dad. Starch.' My dad just nodded, staring at the pie. None of us knew what to say. And then my Mom said, 'Well, gentlemen, you know what I hope? I hope we all perish in a fire is what I hope. I hope we're dead before Christmas—charred to bits, each and every one.' Then she got up and went to her room.

"After a bit, my dad took the pie and went out the back door. I think it was too much for him—not the dying in a fire part but hearing her say 'in your kitchen.' I mean, it hit me at that moment that she wasn't our mother anymore—she was this totally separate person. All this pretending that we were a functioning family.

She was like a boarder, an inmate in our house. And I think Dad was feeling that, too. Gary and I just sat there at the table. A few minutes later my dad came back in and said, 'I knocked down something in the yard next door. Go over and see what happened. Fix things up.' I remember him saying, 'Fix things up.'"

His version of the story prompted me to recall this important fact from my own: after Mr. Glenshaw threw the pie at the birdfeeder, he started sobbing, crying with both hands over his face. Now I can remember the part of the story where I remained seated on the swing and watched him, or maybe watched over him, because I was afraid that someone would catch him out—someone brutal and cruel, like either of my parents or any of my neighbors slamming their screen doors. I felt intense pity for Mr. Glenshaw, although as children we were taught not to pity adults. We were supposed to be shielded from feeling pity for anyone but ourselves. Don't hog the toys, don't have tantrums—that was about it.

"I don't remember you at all," the survivor confessed after what felt like a long period of silence. "I wish I did though. I wish I paid more attention."

I now felt intense pity for this man who, through no fault of his own, grew up to look exactly like his father. I kept hearing the word echo inside my head—*pity, pity, pity*. And what did pity do? Pity only exacerbated the world's excessive sadness. I had to do better than that. But what, exactly, did I think I could do? "Make people laugh" is the way I had always understood altruism—make like a Preston Sturges picture and illuminate the perimeters of this loopy, madcap world. There should've been a joke to crack about the birdfeeder, something like "Your dad sure was a home-wrecker!" But now the survivor himself was crying, crying inside my own car, and all I could think to do was reach over to turn off the heat. I had been a willing accomplice—no, an agitator, an initiator—in this historical reenactment of grief. I had found out the answer, but the answer for me was a painful point of inquiry for him. It suddenly seemed to me that there was no such thing as "personal history," that his life, his father's life, my life, and maybe the lives of a lot of strangers were a continuum, all of it just one long story with an endless number of weekly installments. He kept crying despite his muscular efforts to hold it in, so that soon his face got all knotted up like a walnut shell.

He finally put both hands over his face, just like his father did that day in the yard. This I could not bear. "Don't do that," I said, prying his hands away from his face—first one hand and then the other. I pulled hard like I was husking corn, although I didn't mean for this gesture to be hard. And when I saw his Joel McCrea face in such a state, this thought struck me as a revelation: I could take him home to live with me. It wasn't that I particularly liked him or wanted him or needed him, but I could so vividly picture him standing in my yard wearing swim trunks when it was hot. I told myself that we did have things in common—for instance, both of our fathers had had mottoes. I told myself that there had to be a basis for a lifelong union with this man and his big gaping black hole of a life. Long story short: we were married in a civil ceremony attended by four people (not including us).

So far my wifely project has been getting in the habit of calling him Kyle. I've also been trying to reconcile him with his sister-in-law—though with little success. My initial effort in this regard was writing her a check for two thousand dollars as the first installment of the delinquent loan, but she tore up the check in front of me. "Come off it," she said. I did come off it, and I did have second thoughts about being the wife of Kyle Glenshaw, but only for a minute. I can say with confidence that there was never any question of turning back, that I had no choice in the matter once we'd agreed to go looking for our homes.

On the drive home that night after learning about the pie, I felt a huge relief, like I'd finally come clean on a lifelong lie. The survivor fell asleep in the passenger seat, but I was awake enough for the both of us. I remember being perplexed at how his father could make an entertainment-worthy children's game out of counting highway exits that were already numbered—my father would've been asking, "Where's the game in that? Where's the game?"—but I didn't dwell on this because I didn't want to think about my father. Instead I thought quite intensely about that night of the pie throwing, and in doing so I realized that it presented me with the saddest, most vivid, most beautiful moment of my childhood. The most beautiful moment—and I wanted this moment back, to have and to hold from this day forward. I wanted it, with or without the sepia sunset, like it was some terrifying intoxicant. I wanted it and would pay vast sums for the luxury of having it. I wanted it to stay with me forever, or at least until I was dead—until the "ashes to ashes" part, until they put me in the ground, shoveled in the dirt, and signaled for the guy I hired to take off on his horse.

The Brotherhood of Healing

What they do is take a vein from your leg," Mrs. Rodgers had been told by the fat contractor always hanging around the counter of her sister's bakery. "They go in there and get the vein from your leg, stick it in your neck—the old switcheroo. Zip, zip, zip." With each "zip" the fat contractor used his index finger to make a zig, a zag, and then another zig motion, as if slashing his throat—as if slashing his throat would dispel any doubt as to his expertise on surgical repair of the carotid artery. "I seen it on that cable station," he told Mrs. Rodgers, "the whole thing—no commercials."

"Better check your own plumbing" is what Mrs. Rodgers thought at the time, but this was before her second minor stroke. "Three strokes and you're out," she figured after Stroke No. 2, sitting in the Catholic hospital's emergency room, subtracting numbers from one hundred so that the young guy pretending to be a doctor would believe she still had a brain. Intern, resident—what did it matter? The kid had acne; he needed a dermatologist or at least things in tubes from the drugstore. "You're a walking time bomb," he told her confidently when the nurse was out of earshot.

It was the primary care physician of Mrs. Rodgers's sister who'd diagnosed the initial stroke of bad luck, prescribed another blood pressure medication, made a referral. Mrs. Rodgers let a month go by before acting on the referral. Her own doctor was dead, like most everyone she knew, so she had to rely on her sister. It wasn't just that Mrs. Rodgers did not like this man whom her sister had recently chosen as primary care physician from a long list of unpronounceable names the HMO sent out (the guy's first name was Lambert, followed by something else that read like a ransom note). It wasn't just that Mrs. Rodgers didn't like this Lambert character. It was much more philosophical. Some time ago she had decided that she wasn't afraid to die, and the disposition not only grew on her but began to feel like an accomplishment. Not being afraid to die, it seemed, was just about the only thing that Mrs. Rodgers had up on most people. Plus, there was something almost gluttonous about old people being afraid to die — a tenacity that seemed to tip the order of things, as if the more that old people clung so desperately to life the more that small children would run out in front of cars. Mrs. Rodgers didn't want to go back to the Lambert character. She didn't want to go back to the Catholic hospital named after some nun from Montreal. She especially didn't want to talk to residents with acne. But then not being afraid to die was not the same thing as wanting to die, so after the second stroke Mrs. Rodgers began to think seriously about a vein from her leg going into her neck — "zip, zip, zip," no commercials.

The vascular surgeon to whom Mrs. Rodgers was referred was called Dr. Jay. "He's the best," the Lambert character had said. "The best at what?" Mrs. Rodgers thought — "gin rummy, lawn darts?" His office was in a big to-do clinic attached to a hospital, and she dreaded taking the senior shuttle down there because the place had its own exit on the highway. That seemed to Mrs. Rodgers a bad sign. That seemed to indicate that this was "a place where they take you," which is how the oldsters were always phrasing it — to show, she imagined, that they now considered themselves cargo. Even though she herself had been described as real estate (i.e., "Christ, you're as big as a house!"), Mrs. Rodgers didn't want to think of herself as cargo.

The clinic's sections were color-coded, an orders-from-headquarters setup that made Mrs. Rodgers think of the lousy trip to

Disney World she'd made with that Foster Grandparents outfit. In Disney World you checked your brain at the parking lot, where the sections are named after Disney characters, and for some reason Mrs. Rodgers expected the same logic to apply at the clinic. If the cardio unit is Goofy, neurology must be Donald Duck — Minnie Mouse for female problems (but then nowadays even men seemed to have female problems). Three-purple, four-yellow, two-blue. "That's my problem," thought Mrs. Rodgers. "I'm too blue. Send me to purple. Wheel me to yellow." All the people in the waiting room looked like they belonged there, as if waiting in a waiting room was why they were born. Most didn't seem to be reading anything, and some were in various stages of outpatient recuperation. All of them were big, so big that on those space-age white swivel chairs soldered to the floor they seemed to Mrs. Rodgers like livestock — livestock that were trained to be indoors, like the horses that wore party hats and braids on *The Ed Sullivan Show*. She wondered who those skimpy swivel chairs were made for anyway. Healthy Finnish people probably. Made in Finland for healthy Finns who never got sick.

The nurse doing the ultrasound rubbed the paddle on Mrs. Rodgers's neck like she was a barber giving a shave. "Leave the sideburns," Mrs. Rodgers said, although her comment was inaudible to the nurse squishing Mrs. Rodgers's mouth to the right side of her face. "OK there, hon?" the nurse asked. "Just a lil' bit more to go."

While her mouth was being squished to the right side of her face, Mrs. Rodgers saw a man walk past the doorway; then he came back and picked up and opened the folder in the trough on the hallway wall. "For the love of Mike" was all Mrs. Rodgers could think, because this is what her sister-in-law always said whenever she saw a person she didn't understand, a person who seemed out of his element. Dr. Jay was young; he had a shaved head and an expensive suit. "They must be trying to make this hospital something else," Mrs. Rodgers thought, "like the modern world with all those different types of coffee." On all the TV shows, the doctors were young and didn't have acne, but in real life most of the doctors she's seen have looked like the actor Karl Malden. Karl Malden up close—that's what a real doctor looked like to Mrs. Rodgers.

"Why do they shave off their hair these days?" Mrs. Rodgers thought. It's the ones going bald, so they figure no pretense. Maybe her poor husband should've done this, rather than grow his hair long at the sides and comb it over with Vitalis. Maybe her poor husband was born at the wrong time; he probably would've opted to shave his head if he were young today. Like he always said, "The only way out is through." But then he never said that. It must've been some other husband, some husband on TV, whom Mrs. Rodgers heard say that. If her husband had a hair motto, it was "The only way out is to comb it over with Vitalis." Before that it was Brill Cream—she could still hear the jingle as clear as day: "Brill Cream, a little dab'll do ya, for men who use their head and not their hair"—and after that it was Grecian Formula 19 that came off on the pillowcase.

Here at the color-coded clinic was a man who obviously used his head and not his hair. "I'm Dr. Jay," he said in a soft, almost muffled voice, yet the tone suggested to Mrs. Rodgers "Hold your applause till halftime." Mrs. Rodgers sat in a chair; he sat on an examining gurney that was high, but he used a footstool so that he wouldn't look odd sitting on this too-high gurney. The way he moved the stool into place while he was listening to her describe her symptoms made Mrs. Rodgers think of a priest on an altar. When you watched most people do things with their hands, you thought of cooking shows, or of Martha Stewart making a patio lantern using a tin can, a hammer, and a really big nail. Or maybe you thought of Martha making Thanksgiving dinner for eighty-five people and sixteen dogs. But this guy made Mrs. Rodgers think of a priest. There was solemnity in his placement of the footstool, as if somebody were about to make a confession. To Mrs. Rodgers, the gesture said, "Pay no mind to this gesture (but only a fool would pay no mind to this gesture)." Dr.

Jay positioned the footstool like he'd had some experience with swinging a canister of incense. He asked Mrs. Rodgers questions and nodded when she answered. She had the feeling he was being deceptively kind. She had the feeling there was a shtick—mainly on account of the ends not matching up, the incongruity of the modern world with all those different types of coffee and the footstool ritual that seemed older than the hills.

From the ultrasound, Dr. Jay estimated that Mrs. Rodgers's right carotid artery was 95 percent blocked with plaque, mucked up with the crud of life. All those doughnuts consumed around the age of thirteen, when she was skinny as a rail, her half-slip always slinking down ("A family without elastic," thought Mrs. Rodgers, "that was us"), and now everything that had ever been slinking down was catching up with her. The surgeon called the blockage "stenosis," which sounded to Mrs. Rodgers like a cramp you'd get by taking dictation. Also from the ultrasound, however, he saw that something was wrong with the blocked artery for a good four inches. He called the situation something that Mrs. Rodgers could not remember—she hoped it wasn't "diseased." Maybe he said it was "squirrelly." But then she doubted a man like him would ever use the word "squirrelly"; "squirrelly" was her word—really her dead brother's word. A car goes squirrelly on the racetrack if you don't accelerate before the curve.

Dr. Jay had told his secretary to make an appointment for Mrs. Rodgers to have an angiograph the next day. The secretary's name was LuEllen, but the way the surgeon said "LuEllen" gave Mrs. Rodgers the impression that he did not think of LuEllen as a person but a job title. Mrs. Rodgers figured that if LuEllen's husband got transferred to a ball-bearings plant in Georgia, Dr. Jay would have to advertise for another LuEllen. Because the doctor's LuEllen couldn't get the person on the phone to give Mrs. Rodgers an angiograph until next week, the surgeon grabbed the receiver and started negotiating. He wants it tomorrow, he wants it today, he wants it yesterday. "I'm admitting her," he kept saying. It seemed to Mrs. Rodgers to be some sort of game, hospital politics. From what she could tell, if she was admitted she could have the angiograph tomorrow. She half expected the surgeon to cover the mouthpiece and say, "Pretend you're sick—here, cough into the phone."

Two or so hours later she called her sister to say, "They've finally admitted me."

"I didn't even know you were waiting to be a member," her sister replied.

"Just get down here and bring me my denture cup."

Mrs. Rodgers, her sister, and her sister-in-law all lost their husbands at the same time—stomach cancer, heart attack, bridge freezing before road surface. "Bad things happen in threes" is what everyone said, as if this was the right answer that you said on TV and won a million bucks. But there they were, three medium-old sadsacks in black—"I'll weep at your wake if you weep at mine." At least Mrs. Rodgers's sister and sister-in-law had children—grown children with children of their own. And her sister had the bakery and her sister-in-law had something going on in Florida—a doughnut shop on a golf course, maybe some beachfront swampland with a gambling parlor—something anyway; they didn't talk much these days. Mrs. Rodgers had had none of these things—no commercial property and faulty fallopian tubes. She and her poor husband tried and tried to have babies until he called a time-out for good. Of course this was way before sticking test tubes in the freezer and way before there were ads for Viagra behind home plate at Yankee Stadium.

Even though it seemed to Mrs. Rodgers that she was only in the hospital because of hospital politics, the nurses kept calling her "sweetheart," like she was an old lady who needed to be spoon-fed sugar-free custard. Just a few months ago Mrs. Rodgers had visited just such an old lady at the Catholic hospital—someone who, on top of everything else wrong with her, needed her cataracts removed so that she'd be able to describe the color of her urine to one doctor after another. Mrs. Rodgers wanted to tell the nurses, "Call me that again and I'll sock ya in the kisser," but she decided instead to call them "sweetheart" right back, even though most of them didn't get the drift, didn't get that she was being a wiseguy. "How's thaaat, swee'heaaart," one screamed while rigging her up to a heart monitor that she probably didn't need, "aw-wright?" Mrs. Rodgers figured that the correct response was something like "Yes, dear, that's just fine." Instead she shouted, "Thaaat's aw-wright, swee'heaaart!"

"These nurses," Mrs. Rodgers thought, "how do they know what to wear?" It's like when they took away uniforms at the Catholic schools—total chaos. Now all the kids have their pants falling down. She made the mistake of calling one such kid to task on this issue in the drugstore parking lot. "Hey, kid, haven't you ever heard of a belt?" "Hey, grandma, haven't you ever heard of my fist?" At least Mrs. Rodgers could be relatively certain that the nurses weren't going to mention their fists to her. They all wore flowered blouses like they were a team of Japanese flag-twirling girls. Or was it the Chinese who were always twirling flags? "You can't lump together all slanty-eyed people anymore" Mrs. Rodgers had been told by some droopy-eyed Seventh-day Adventist who looked a lot like her dead brother-in-law. This was on a religion/shopping station way up there where she hardly ever went, way up where you had to pay or get the V-chip for the kids of the kids you never had.

The next day Mrs. Rodgers had the angiograph, a process in which they put dye in your veins and take X-rays. After the procedure she had to lie flat on her back for six hours—lie flat with weights on her stomach, like she was a fish drying in the sun. She was waiting for the six hours to be up, but she was also waiting word from the surgeon. She assumed that he wanted to operate, but she didn't know when. He needed to look at her big picture; he needed to "confer" with his "colleagues"; then he'd decide what to do about her squirrelly artery.

Mrs. Rodgers's sister and her sister's two grandsons kept her company some of the time she spent on her back. The boys kept running off, going down to the vending machines.

"You shouldn't keep giving them dollars," Mrs. Rodgers told her sister.

"That's what you have to do with kids these days—buy them off."

"I guess I'm lucky my days are numbered."

"No they're not," her sister said, not looking up from the brochure she was reading—*Carotid Endarterectomy and You*. "Listen to this: says you're supposed to 'refrain from sexual intercourse' for one week after you're discharged."

"So what do they expect me to do instead?"

"Have regular bowel movements."

"How do they do it?" Mrs. Rodgers asked her sister.

"Prune juice."

"I mean how do they keep cutting people open?" Mrs. Rodgers continued. "They must make mistakes. On some days they must make mistakes."

"Maybe nowadays they don't make mistakes."

"How can they never make mistakes?"

"They must get themselves all relaxed. Maybe they listen to classical music while they wash their hands."

"Classical music?"

"Look at it this way," Mrs. Rodgers's sister advised. "You've never listened to classical music, and you've made all kinds of mistakes."

Mrs. Rodgers's sister had intended to be there when the doctor showed up to talk turkey, but she and the bought-off grandsons got tired of waiting. "Just don't take anything with bad odds," she advised, "and find out what you're supposed to do while refraining from the intercourse."

At half-past ten Dr. Jay appeared in Mrs. Rodgers's room; he was followed by a little crew—boy-girl-boy-girl. More of the residents—people who lived at the hospital, too tired to read a thermometer let alone sew an arm back on or find themselves a tube of acne medication. She wasn't surprised at the residents, but she did have to blink a few times at what the surgeon was wearing with his surgical getup—a gold chain. The doctor wore a braided gold chain like he was an NBA player or a drug dealer. This is what Mrs. Rodgers heard Charles Grodin once say about men who wear gold chains, as a joke, to a couple of basketball players wearing gold chains. Or maybe the lily-white Dr. Jay was compensating for the hospital's having no black surgeons like they have on all the TV shows. That's what the protesters on TV would've called the Dr. Jay types in the sixties—"lily-white," because even though the sixties were gone and would never come back, he was that type. And this was the type of hospital where people—the livestock people sitting on the swivel chairs made for the thin and healthy Finns—would have conniptions about a black doctor. Still, in this day and age, with the hundred-kinds-of-coffee mentality going full throttle, Mrs. Rodgers figured that you could sneak in a doctor with a shaved head and a gold chain, but he sure as hell had to be as white as Dr. Jay's lab coat.

"We got some good pictures," Dr. Jay told Mrs. Rodgers, who was now fixated on the lab coat because he had his "Dr. Jay" embroidered in perfect cursive script. "How like him," she thought, "perfect cursive script." She wondered how she could think "how like him" without even knowing him, but when she looked at the blue embroidery again she swore she saw "Dr. J." Her poor husband used to talk about Dr. J. Her poor husband liked to watch the basketball games on television. Her poor husband would've had conniptions if they made him see a black doctor with a gold chain.

Dr. Jay told Mrs. Rodgers that she could either have the surgery to repair her carotid artery tomorrow or go home on a blood thinner. He gave her the odds—35 percent chance of a stroke on the blood thinner, with no surgery; pretty much smooth sailing with the surgery, but a 10 percent chance of a stroke during the operation. The hitch with the surgery was that Dr. Jay had to replace the squirrelly artery with an artificial artery or else graft a vein from Mrs. Rodgers's leg.

"So the fat guy was right," Mrs. Rodgers mumbled to herself.

"What?" Dr. Jay said.

"What the fat guy said," she repeated loudly.

"What guy?" he said, irritated, wiping his palm over his bald head. Then he sighed and told Mrs. Rodgers that she should think about it and decide in the morning.

"I don't want to think about it," Mrs. Rodgers said. "My sister told me not to take anything with bad odds. So I'm going with the surgery behind Door No. 2."

"Ya wanna watch your soaps, swee'heaaart?" a nurse asked Mrs. Rodgers two hours before her scheduled surgery. "They're not my soaps," Mrs. Rodgers thought. And what was this "soaps" business anyway? Mrs. Rodgers's sister called them her "programs." Her sister watched her programs on a thirteen-inch set in the kitchen at the bakery, two hours' worth. According to Mrs. Rodgers's sister, Procter and Gamble was nowadays keen on sponsoring murders, homosexual relations, and terrorists' bombs going off during what people used to call the ironing board hour. Mrs. Rodgers had watched only one such "program" in all her life, *The Doctors,* which the announcer would always describe as "dedicated to the brotherhood of healing." All of the doctors in that show were white, some even lily-white; all had good manners and wore long gowns for surgery, things that looked like the aprons that meat cutters wear, but there was never any blood. Everything these doctors wore in surgery looked spanking clean and just-starched, which, Mrs. Rodgers guessed, made you think of the ironing you were supposed to be doing. There was one "lady doctor," the beautiful wife of a surgeon who was graying at the temples, but you never saw her doing any doctoring. She just cried a lot about whatever candy striper her husband was running around with. In those days, the healing racket really was a brotherhood.

If there still was a brotherhood of healing, Mrs. Rodgers thought, it was probably still a racket—healing for dollars, sort of like bowling for dollars. Healing for dollars to golf with. Even with the HMO mess, Mrs. Rodgers knew that surgeons made a lot of money. *Ka-ching*—there's the addition to the kids' bedroom. *Ka-ching*—there's the six-car garage. "Who knows what they spend their money on nowadays?" Mrs. Rodgers thought. "Sex-change operations for their boyfriends in Singapore." She knew about these things; she watched Montel every day—a black man with a shaved head. One time at her sister's bakery she'd heard the fat contractor and another fat man discussing whether Montel was a homosexual on account of his shaved head. "Them bald faggots make my skin crawl," the contractor had said, to which the other fat guy replied, "Lots of 'em have big dough though." Someone else in the bakery had noted that Montel had a wife and multiple sclerosis, but the fat guys insisted that a bald faggot was a bald faggot.

Some gal who wasn't quite a nurse—a junior nurse—came in and said, "I'm going to have to shave your groin." Mrs. Rodgers thought it sounded like something a cop would say when he caught you speeding. "I'm going to have to ask you to step outside the car, ma'am, so that I can shave your groin." Soon after that, some guy who wasn't quite a doctor—a resident, or maybe a doctor who just wasn't Dr. Jay—came in and said that Dr. Jay would make the incision high on Mrs. Rodgers's leg so that the scar wouldn't show when she wore shorts. She hadn't worn shorts in thirty years. She can remember the last pair of shorts she bought, seersucker shorts at Sears. Mrs. Rodgers imagined that Dr. Jay would be appalled at this pair of size sixteen shorts—that was a good word, she thought, "appalled." He was probably appalled at a lot of things.

Mrs. Rodgers's sister and sister-in-law would certainly have been appalled at Dr. Jay's gold chain. He had it on again with his blue outfit when she was wheeled into the operating room. He told her things about the procedure that she didn't understand;

he spoke slowly while nodding: "First, we're going to *blah-blah-blah*, 'kay? Then we're going to *blah-blah-blah*, 'kay? Then we're going to *blah-blah-blah*, 'kay?" Mrs. Rodgers felt like he was calling her Kay. "I'm not Kay," she wanted to say, "and I'm not 'kay." Then someone wheeled her back out into the hall because there was a delay with the anesthesiologist. "Delay-shlemay," she thought. He was probably stuck at the end of a long line of cars in the Dunkin Donuts drive-through.

It seemed to Mrs. Rodgers a long time that she and the gurney were abandoned in the hall. It was very quiet; all you could hear were the elevator bells. From her experience with her husband dying, she knew about "the elevator law," that people weren't allowed to ask doctors questions about patients when the doctors were held captive in the elevator. This is why doctors usually took the stairs. "It's good that you doctors take the stairs," she had said to her husband's doctor on the day her husband died. "That means you'll live longer." "Longer than what?" her husband's doctor replied. He was Pakistani; he liked riddles. Or so he said. "What part of India are you from?" Mrs. Rodgers had asked when she met him, to be friendly. "I'm not from India," he said. "I'm from Pakistan." Mrs. Rodgers's husband said with a laugh, "What's the difference?" He was in a funny mood that day, probably because he'd just been told he was dying by the minute. The doctor looked at Mrs. Rodgers, not at her husband. He was sitting on a stool; he had leaned back. The nametag on his lab coat was upside down. "What's the difference?" he repeated. "I'll tell you the difference, Mrs. Rodgers. Indians like jokes; Pakistanis like riddles. That's the difference."

If the anesthesiologist is Indian, Mrs. Rodgers thought, maybe she should tell him a joke. She tried to think of a good joke to tell the Indian anesthesiologist who'd been detained at the Dunkin Donuts drive-through, but she also wanted to make sure that he didn't forget to give her the full dose of anesthesia. She knew a joke about a man who is rejected by the woman he is courting. He tells her, "It's just too much for me to bear that you don't love me, so I'm going away, far, far away, to forget—to forget you, to forget everything." And the woman replies, "Well, just don't forget to go away." Mrs. Rodgers wasn't sure if this was really a joke, but it might remind the anesthesiologist not to forget to give her the full dose of anesthesia.

Mrs. Rodgers tried to kill time by thinking up the top ten reasons why Dr. Jay would wear a gold chain with his surgical getup. Reason No. 10: He couldn't wear a wedding ring when he did surgery, so the gold chain was a proxy for the wedding band. Dr. Jay wore a gold chain because he was a devoted husband. Reason No. 9: The gold chain was given to Dr. Jay by a grateful patient whose life Dr. Jay had saved by grafting some veins onto some arteries. From that day forward, Dr. Jay always wore the chain during surgery to remind himself of his duty to save lives. Reason No. 8: Dr. Jay had left on the gold chain once by mistake when he was called in to perform a difficult emergency operation at ten o'clock on a Saturday night, and because this emergency operation was miraculously successful, Dr. Jay always wore the gold chain when he operated, as a lucky charm. Mrs. Rodgers didn't like this reason because it meant that Dr. Jay was wearing the gold chain in real life, which somehow seemed worse than his wearing it with his surgical getup. What was he doing wearing the gold chain in real life? Did they have to go fetch him off the disco floor? Mrs. Rodgers skipped ahead to Reason No. 1: Dr. Jay had operated on an NBA player from Philadelphia who insisted on wearing his gold chain during the highly risky surgery because this chain had brought the man so much luck on the court. During the operation the man died; it was a national tragedy. The man's fiancée later threw the gold chain at Dr. Jay, shouting, "You killed him!" From that day forward, Dr. Jay always wore the chain during surgery to remind himself that he was not God, that he sometimes made mistakes, that a lot of people died all the time, that life is sad.

"You got any more jokes?" Dr. Jay was saying to Mrs. Rodgers. The surgery was past—it was a success, because she wasn't dead.

"You were telling us jokes before the operation." Dr. Jay was leaning over Mrs. Rodgers. This time she did not focus on the gold chain; instead she was trying to get a look at his face. He really did look lily-white, like a blanched almond. If he was the blood man, she thought, where the heck was his own blood? He even looked a little sick himself, like he was having chemotherapy. He looked young, too—too young to have cut into her squirrelly blood vessel, even younger than the resident with the acne. He looked like a kid on a St. Jude's poster, a chemotherapy kid who had no hope. She couldn't see that well, but the skin around his mouth looked funny, like he'd broken out in a rash, a purple rash. It had a definite shape, this rash, and then she realized it was from wearing the surgical mask. His face, despite the rash, felt intensely familiar to her. "I know too much about him already," she thought, trying to resist the way that fear can make us resort to pretend affection, and for some reason she told him, "I'm not afraid to die."

"You're not going to die."

"I mean I'm not afraid of it, when it happens."

"You're doing just fine, 'kay?" he said, holding her hand. She knew he was holding her hand because she had a sensation of something soft but cold, very far away.

"It smells like iodine in here," Mrs. Rodgers's sister said in the ICU after Mrs. Rodgers was wheeled in from recovery. "You're lucky you're half-asleep, or you'd be sick to your stomach."

"It hurts in different parts," Mrs. Rodgers told her sister.

"That must mean the parts are working."

"Or that they're not working."

"I just saw Kojak," her sister whispered conspiratorially. "He shook my hand."

"Maybe he's running for office."

"Him? What would he have to say to people?"

"I dunno," Mrs. Rodgers muttered. "'Who loves ya, baby?'" She thought for a moment, feeling too groggy to even swallow. "He told me I wasn't going to die."

"I guess that means he really does know everything."

"He's not God," Mrs. Rodgers said bluntly, even though her voice was hoarse. "He makes mistakes."

"What do you mean he's not God?" her sister replied with hushed alarm. "How can you rain on my parade like this?"

Mrs. Rodgers scrolled through all the stars and bit players she remembered from heaven; she thought of Dr. Jay reminding her of a priest in his suit; she thought of an Oprah show in which a woman with big frizzy hair, a woman who looked like she'd just come back from a few rounds of electroshock therapy, babbled on about angels.

"He's an emissary," Mrs. Rodgers told her sister, because this is what the frizzy-haired woman had told Oprah when Oprah asked what, exactly, is the point of an angel: "They are emissaries," the woman had said, making her eyes bug out toward Oprah. "Sometimes they arrive on the scene wearing suits; sometimes they wear overalls." Mrs. Rodgers could feel that now it was her sister who was holding her hand, and she felt obliged to clarify, "But not the kind in the overalls."

Because Mrs. Rodgers's blood pressure would not stabilize, she was kept in the ICU overnight. She could administer morphine to herself by squeezing the button on the cord taped to her left hand—cheap fun, she thought. Whenever she squeezed for the morphine, she was able to isolate one sound from the ICU's beeps, blips, and alarms. Sometimes it was a voice. She heard someone say that all the fish in the pond were dead. It was a child's voice, probably someone's bought-off grandson; she'd heard this as the child was being ushered out of the ICU; she heard a nurse say that no one under eighteen was allowed. "I was just tellin' him that all the fish'er dead," the boy argued. "The fish'er just floatin' there." He was just a boy, but already he had the voice of what he would become—a big guy who ran a business using his truck, probably a tree and stump removal service, or a fat contractor who'd sit for hours at the counter of a bakery eating apple fritters and

French crullers. Probably this kid's name was Bob, the soon-to-be-famous Bob of Bob's Tree and Stump Removal Service.

She didn't even know that the hospital had a pond. Apparently the senior shuttle had strategically avoided the scenic route of dead fish just floatin' there. She kept thinking about her sister's grandsons running down to the vending machines with their dollars; she thought how nice it would be to be a kid, to run down to everything, even though you never wore a belt and your pants were falling down to your knees. She pictured Dr. Jay in his surgery duds and gold chain running down to some vending machine. He must've been someone's little boy once, even though now he was either a devoted husband and pillar of the community or else a bald faggot rolling in the dough. That thought struck Mrs. Rodgers with great heft: every vascular surgeon was once someone's little boy — or little girl. Someone's little fussbudget, someone's little widget, someone's little who's-it.

Mrs. Rodgers was sent to a room on the ninth floor so that she had a good view of the hospital's pond. Every morning when he made the rounds in his expensive suits, Dr. Jay called Mrs. Rodgers "Kay": "We're going to start you on one hundred milligrams of Atenolol, 'kay?" It seemed to Mrs. Rodgers like "Kay" was his secret name for her, and she found that she didn't even mind it. He also told her she was doing "fantastic." All of his terms of praise seemed to have at least three syllables. It struck Mrs. Rodgers that nowhere else in the world could she be praised three syllables at a time for just lying there as her cells grew back together like mold grew on cheese. And the more Dr. Jay praised her for just lying there like a moldy piece of cheese, the more ashamed Mrs. Rodgers became of her life in relation to his.

The nurses in their flowered blouses had lots to say about Dr. Jay — he was a "saint," a "wonderful saint" no less (as opposed, she imagined, to the un-wonderful kinds that nobody bothered to put on the Mass cards); he worked all the time, like a resident himself; he always talked to the families, always returned their calls; he was often in on the weekends in his jeans and sweatshirt. Mrs. Rodgers became ashamed of her life in relation to Dr. Jay's because she knew quite well that her life was a mistake, what doctors nowadays were not supposed to make. No, it wasn't really that. Not a mistake, because that would imply she at least attempted something else. Her life was more like a firecracker that didn't go off. That resident with the acne didn't know diddly-squat. She wasn't a walking time bomb; she was a dud firecracker. "Who is it that makes the firecrackers," Mrs. Rodgers asked herself, "the Chinese or the Japanese?" But then she remembered the warning that "You can't lump together all slanty-eyed people anymore." Nowadays firecrackers were probably made by Seventh-day Adventists in St. Louis. Wherever they were made, Mrs. Rodgers was sure that she was an old one that didn't go off, because if a firecracker never goes off, you can't tell what it was supposed to look like — its shape or its colors, whether it would fan out like a giant dandelion tuft or give off a boom like a speedway light hit by a shotgun bullet. A firecracker that doesn't go off was probably less than something, less than even a tree falling in the woods.

Every time Dr. Jay came near her, Mrs. Rodgers wanted her look to convey, "I am going to try to be a better, stronger person from now on. I'm really going to try to be Kay for you, Dr. Jay." She knew that if her poor husband had heard a spoken version of this thought, he would've waved his hand in front of his face and said, "That don't mean shit." Like a lot of people in these parts, Mrs. Rodgers's poor husband didn't worry about using the right verbs. She imagined Dr. Jay being appalled at the way her poor husband didn't match up his verbs. She also wondered why her husband always came out of her mouth as "poor." He wasn't financially poor. He wasn't much of a success in life, and he had the hair issue to contend with, but he wasn't any worse off than most men she knew. He would criticize people he saw on TV; he hated most Democrats. In what way was her husband poor — just because he was dead?

And what did Mrs. Rodgers really know about Dr. Jay? He

was a slow talker, a fast thinker, a sharp dresser. He had no hair and sensitive skin. But like her poor dead husband or somebody else's poor dead husband always said, "Ya never do know." How could she have known that one day he'd stop at the doorway of her room, read from her chart, and then shout at her from across the room? Coldly, abruptly, he asked her, "How'd you like to go home today, right now?" He seemed to be dismissing her forever from his life, from any proximity to his profession of healing, by reciting the script of the three blood pressure medications she would take. Something happened—she was suddenly poison, a leper. She was suddenly no longer his Kay. "He wants me out of his hair," Mrs. Rodgers thought, almost bitterly, "even though he doesn't have any hair." She kept thinking of all the things he wasn't saying. *Who loves ya, baby? Who loves ya, sweetheart? Not me, Kay. Not me, 'kay? And by the way, Kay . . . thank YOU for shopping at Sears.*

He was gone, gone for good it seemed, when Mrs. Rodgers felt imperiled, when she thought, "Don't leave me, Dr. Jay!" She had not thought about the time when he would not be around. No one's being around or not being around has mattered to her in years. She had not known there were things she wanted out of him. For instance, she wanted him to tell her husband's doctor that she wished her husband never said "What's the difference?" between an Indian and a Pakistani doctor. She had wanted Dr. Jay to find this doctor and tell this doctor that it was because her husband didn't have children; it was because he didn't have hair; it was because he didn't have good odds. She wanted Dr. Jay to tell the doctor that it wasn't her fault, that she wished her husband were another way. She had thought that Dr. Jay truly was an emissary; she was sure that if Dr. Jay had said this to the Pakistani doctor, the doctor would believe it was true, because both this doctor who liked riddles and this doctor with the shaved head were dedicated to the brotherhood of healing.

By coincidence, the Pakistani doctor was present when Mrs. Rodgers's husband died. Mrs. Rodgers thinks of it as a coincidence because everyone says that you can tell when a doctor's patient is going to die because the doctor is never around—off skiing in the Alps, tagging turtles in Costa Rica, murdering his mistress in Barbados. The doctor had stopped in between operations he was performing that day. He took Mrs. Rodgers's right hand and held it to his forehead, like he wanted her to feel for a temperature. He held her hand there for what seemed like a long time. When he released it, he said, "This is so I never forget sadness." "Did he still never forget people's sadness?" Mrs. Rodgers wondered. She also wondered what her hand had felt like when he held it to his forehead, because she wasn't at all sad in the several minutes after her husband died. She wondered if the doctor was looking for sadness but found something else. She remembered thinking, at this very dramatic moment, that the doctor must've kept his nametag upside down because he figured "Why bother?" Why even bother with people who don't care about the difference between an Indian and Pakistani doctor? She was sixty-two then but looked much older. Maybe everything about her said to him "sadness." This dead man was all that Mrs. Rodgers had in common with the Pakistani doctor, and now she would never see him again. This had seemed to her the saddest thing. "Do you really never forget?" she longed to ask him, again and again and again.

Mrs. Rodgers had to wait for her sister to come and claim her, and her sister wouldn't be there till well past five, till her sister had finished watching her programs. "What is it we're all chomping at the bit to get back to anyway?" Mrs. Rodgers asked herself. "Do we really want to be out there with the dead fish?" No, she thought. Most people would rather stay here; they'd rather be called "swee'heaaart" by nurses in flowered blouses. She walked over to the window because she realized she was lucky to have had such a pretty view for a full week. The thought of dead fish reminded her of her poor husband, of meeting her poor husband at a tavern, just like in the song that goes "there's a tavern in the town," only the song they were playing when she met her husband was "Little Brown Jug." When she met her poor husband at this tavern in the town, when he was still a stranger to her, she should have asked him, first off, "Why do you think it's OK to marry someone you won't care to ever know?" It struck her that perhaps her husband always came out of her mouth as "poor" because she knew the truth: he was not a man to be loved. She was too stupid at that tavern in the town to have said no to anything; there was nothing she could've done to change her life, to make it a working firecracker. She started to sing that song they were playing: *My wife and I live all alone in a little log hut we call our own.* If you live for forty-odd years all alone in a little log hut, why is it surprising that you're not afraid to die? Maybe living is what you were afraid of. Mrs. Rodgers looked down at the pond with its own little marsh, a special feature of this world unto itself, this world with its own exit on the highway. *Ha ha ha, you and me, little brown jug, don't I love thee! Ha ha ha, you and me.* "I love thee," thought Mrs. Rodgers. Now that was certainly a good joke to tell a doctor.

Rabbit Punch

The face on the front page of the morning paper belongs to a teenager and not the president, and for this reason you know the kid did something nationally bad. His photo abuts a pretty sensational image, a companion to the story, but the face is what disturbs me. I know him, or knew him, five or so years ago, when he really was just a boy. I've thought about him from time to time, but of course my thoughts don't account for the aging process, let alone growth spurts. Everything about his face seems swollen, as if his skull were a big, hyperactive gland. His mouth hangs open; his eyes slant downwards on the outer sides, as if for drainage. His unfortunate nose hasn't been mitigated much by puberty. On the contrary, it has grown to make him look sinister, villainous — like the boy who cuts the grass, or the former best friend of my eldest nephew, or the son on that movie I tried to avoid watching on a flight back from Seattle. In short, he looks like every other kid you see.

The time that I knew this boy was probably the worst period of my life — one during which I might easily have opted out of the whole dog-and-pony show altogether, probably with the aid of benzodiazepines. The image from that period that springs most vividly to mind is not the boy and his nose but the Drug Czar and his shoes. "How apt that you think me manic-depressive," I told the Drug Czar at our first meeting, "because I've been trying to finish writing a book on Virginia Woolf for ten years." He gave me a look that I came to know as his default expression — scorn verging on disgust. "I mean," I said, hedging like a teenager, "*she* managed to finish it—you know, the living thing—because she was manic-depressive."

"Bipolar affective disorder," the Drug Czar said, as if correcting my grammar. His hands—the long, well-tended fingers interlaced in a manner that reminded me of a painting of St. Jerome—rested on his lap; it seemed a great effort for him to pull the edges of his lips into a smirk that I (as the patient) was expected to accept as a smile, a gesture he felt obligated to perform every now and then. In profile he looked just like the etching of Rousseau holding a walking stick that serves as the frontispiece to my copy of *Emile*. At this point he decided to again seize the opportunity to glance down past his crossed legs, toward his expensive shoes, even leaning some to get a better view. The Drug Czar's shoes didn't look anywhere near the lamentable JCPenney and Sears styles I imagined running amok within managed care, and perhaps this is why he seemed to enjoy them so much.

"I'm all for calling a spade a spade," I told him, thinking how, if I really were a teenager, I'd have added my own obligatory smirk to indicate "As if." *As if anything I said to this guy even mattered to this guy.*

"You can call it anything you want," the Drug Czar replied as he wrote out my prescription. "Whatever you find apt, Miss Camden." No one had called me "Miss Camden" since before I was in college. "Miss Camden," for almost anyone, was not apt. Guadeloupe Kumner, the therapist my HMO assigned to me, called me by my first name and liked to dwell on "rejection," "esteem," and "women with attention-deficit disorder," whereas the pharmacologist in his pristine clothes had no time for hardluck tales: he just wanted me to keep having my blood tested at the lab so that he could prescribe higher dosages of different drugs.

My encounter with the Drug Czar was a latent effect of getting fired. I had taught twentieth-century British literature at a women's college that turned into a university; when this metamorphosis occurred, they let me go. Quaint term, that—*let me go*. Like I was freed from an arranged marriage to a duke and allowed to run off with the livery boy of my choice. I wasn't on a tenure track at the school, and as everyone admonished, it was my own damned fault—barely publishing a paper let alone a shelf of books. Teaching was just a pretext for not finishing my "provocative and insightful" study of Virginia Woolf, which I imagined would make me famous once it was shelved amongst the dozens upon dozens of provocative and insightful studies of Virginia Woolf that have been rolling off the presses in the half century since her death. I was well aware that as a "Woolf scholar" teaching at a women's college, I wasn't woman enough—or perhaps womyn enough—so when they sacked me I wasn't surprised.

I just didn't care, hadn't been caring for a long time. "Waiting for fries at the Beckettian drive-through" is how I thought about my life as I graded essays in which outright stupid girls were unable to apply the term "Beckettian" to their Nokia-accessorized lives. Mine was a story of "unrealized potential," a term my colleagues were wont to use on anything from nonoverachieving preteens to Airedales that could not be housebroken. I was so promising when I started out; people had such high hopes. But then my academic wonder years turned out to be years of deplorable stagnation—a condition only exacerbated by the degenerative lifestyle of my substance-abusing husband. I was unhappy and isolated even before I got fired, but getting fired made me crazy—or else made me stop pretending that I wasn't.

After I lost my job I started having anxiety attacks that prevented me from looking for another job. This transition period—what, had I been more of a womynist, I'd be calling this "interstitial zone"—would've been the ideal time to finish writing the book after ten years of anguished procrastination. But the anxiety attacks prevented me from turning on my computer let alone looking at footnotes on a split screen. I drank a lot, ordered cases of expensive wine from the place around the corner, had it delivered even though the place was around the corner, and somehow out of all this drinking came the idea that I would start painting the walls of my apartment—not just to cover them with new colors but to create murals, *trompe l'oeil,* a whole lot of contrived whimsy. I was already in a lot of debt before I lost my job, so this period of limp-wristed bacchanalia didn't help matters much. And then after a couple of months it got to the point where I couldn't sleep—two hours a night was the best I could hope for—so I made the temporarily sane gesture of visiting the mental health floor of my HMO—first Guadeloupe, then the Drug Czar.

For the anxiety, the Drug Czar prescribed Valium, which caused me to fall down some stairs but didn't help me to sleep, so then it was Klonopin, which is the wrong benzodiazepine for wanting to sleep; he finally hit on Ativan, which helped me sleep some of the time. Because he thought my fast talking meant that I was afflicted by what he referred to as a "soft bipolar condition," he prescribed Depakote, an anticonvulsant, to keep my moods from jumping the track. I also had just-in-case prescriptions for the wide-open field of depression—Zoloft, Wellbutrin, and Desyrel (he had no name-brand partiality).

"Have you always spoken this rapidly?" the Drug Czar had asked at that first meeting. "Yes," I said without pause for reflection, "so that I can squeeze more cruelty into one sentence." Aside from the fast talking, the grandiosity, and the scattering of thought, a classic symptom of the manic state is a spending frenzy, though my own frenzy, aside from the cases of wine, was limited to acrylic and oil paints, all sorts of brushes, linseed oil, and Benjamin Moore eggshell enamel, flat latex, and semigloss. But even though I wasn't charging Mark Cross luggage and Mont Blanc fountain pens on the one Visa card that hadn't been rescinded, the paltry cash of my adult life was nonetheless dwindling in my checking account. Also dwindling were my relations to the handful of people I used to call friends. My caring less and less for them had become almost palpable, like some embarrassing case of early hair loss. This, incidentally, is one of the side effects of Depakote—hair loss and weight gain. Can you imagine telling a thirty-three-year-old divorced woman that? "You'll feel better, but you'll get fat and your hair will fall out." That's why I called him the Drug Czar.

A month or two into the pills I felt no different about my moods, which seemed to run into each other like paints on a palette. But then I never bothered to stop drinking—a detail I neglected to share with the Drug Czar or Guadeloupe, although I have to admit that the pills did limit the quantity of alcohol I was able to consume. After a few glasses of one Tuscan Syrah or another I'd pass out wherever I was painting and wound up with a lot of fossilized brushes. But whereas before the pills everything in my life had seemed a paradoxically urgent muddle of regret and paralysis, now everything that constituted my shrink-wrapped life felt doused, saturated by neutrality—a neutrality that on some days felt almost perfect. I remember getting up in the morning, standing under the shower for an hour, until the hot water ran to a perfectly neutral cold, and for the rest of the day I'd feel like a head of lettuce at Stop and Shop being perpetually misted to the tune of "Singing in the Rain." On one of these perfectly neutral days I shocked myself by pulling my provocative and insightful manuscript out of a drawer and trying to locate the files on my laptop. When I started scrolling through the text, however, all I could think about was the neutrality, the equanimity perhaps, of Virginia Woolf putting stones in her coat pockets so that, when she was in the process of drowning herself, she'd sink like a witch rather than float like a duck—or maybe the logic went the other way around. In any case, stones in your coat pockets seemed more pathetic than anything, and the dozens upon dozens of Post-It notes curled like Dead Sea Scrolls on the manuscript's sides seemed as pathetic as the contents of Virginia's pockets.

I had always thought it was the life of Woolf's sister, Vanessa Bell, that would drive one to suicide—married to a philandering bore and coupled up for life with a sexually active homosexual, using up your life to paint the utilitarian objects in a summer home that turned into your permanent residence but was still merely a rental. "The house wants doing up," Virginia wrote her sister in 1916, urging her to take Charleston Cottage, which at that time was covered by Virginia creeper. Vanessa signed the lease and hit the ground painting. "Bowls of apples and marble-ized circles" is how she described her handiwork, but of course she wasn't alone; Duncan Grant was the more known artistic quantity, and he probably painted more surface area at Charleston than she. In the parlance of psychobabble, *folie à deux* to the max—only it was more like *folie à deux* and one of his boyfriends named Max. *How could she do it?* you had to wonder. How could she be happy with this rental cottage and this dead-end sexual situation, not to mention the incessant painting of walls and fire-places and bedsteads and window frames and lamp shades and folding screens and bathtubs?

But this is exactly what I started doing to my apartment in lieu of tampering with all that had come before the moment of stones sliding into Virginia's pockets. I painted the walls and then murals on the walls and then pictures on the doors and then pictures on the kitchen cabinets and then pictures on wooden tables and chairs and bookshelves. Before Charleston, Vanessa and Duncan had lived and painted things at a place called Wissett Lodge, but when they realized that the owner was going to have zero tolerance for their artistry, they painted it out. According to Vanessa's son, "The history of their work as mural painters is one of enthusiastic painting followed by ruthless obliteration." I was intrigued, almost seduced, by the phrase "ruthless obliteration." When I asked the Drug Czar if he thought what I was doing to my apartment was crazy, he laughed and said he'd begin to worry when I started painting it out. But I'd had this very idea crawling up my sleeve all along—that when I was "done" I was going to paint it all white and move out and far away, thus performing my own ritual of ruthless obliteration.

The only non-Bloomsbury image in the place was on the closet door of my bedroom—a super-enlarged photograph of a smiling angel on the cathedral at Reims. Everyone takes her snapshot—perhaps because of her assumed beneficence, her beatific smile. My ex-husband the photographer took the picture with a telephoto lens. He said she looked like me, except that she was "opalescent." I varnished the picture to the closet door and put on so many coats of polyurethane that you couldn't even shut the door. I don't know how many times the photo was enlarged and its enlargements enlarged. The kid at Kinko's felt compelled to comment at each stage of the excruciatingly expensive reprographic procedure that I was allowed to observe. "You sure must like this angel," he said every two minutes or so, and I distinctly remember longing to be him—this kid whose shaved head made him indistinguishable from the bumper crop of shaved heads currently his age. "I don't like angels, as a concept," I told him. "That's cool," he said, tapping numbers into the machine's keypad and nodding. "Whatever."

"So why do you glue things to doors?" Guadeloupe had wanted to know after a few sessions.

I laughed and said, "Because I am unhappy, I guess."

"You find it funny to be unhappy?"

"'Nothing is funnier than unhappiness,'" I said. "I'm quoting from *Endgame*."

"You like games?" she asked.

The eighteen visits I was allotted with Guadeloupe were grueling. She kept forgetting which of the sisters my book was about, so that I kept having to inform her that I was writing a book about the writer who killed herself, not her sister the painter who didn't kill herself. It would be nice to think she was pretending to forget, as a way to present to me the apposition of life and death, as part of the therapy to repair me, but I knew that she didn't know who the hell I was talking about; she simply couldn't keep track of the names. Guadeloupe dressed like a high school cafeteria worker; she wore those wavy-soled hospital shoes, and hers were filthy and cracked in parts, just like the ones I wore for my high school job at Kentucky Fried Chicken.

One day well into my new system of carrying on, I was surprised to be visited by Cathy and Bill Hazell, who stopped by to see if the pills were helping me any. This couple, the most enterprising of my dwindling acquaintances, were really friends of my ex-husband, with whom they'd done a lot of coke years ago. Cathy used to teach at the college with me, but when she cleaned up her act she went to law school and became a self-employed legal consultant with a current best-seller (tax fraud for idiots—something like that). Bill the bond trader never liked me, even during his drugged-out days—I think he considered my ambition to publish a provocative and insightful study of Virginia Woolf a heinous conceit given my limited capabilities.

"You didn't do too good of a job on those fruit things over there," Cathy said after I gave them a tour of my work, taking care to explain the Bloomsbury relevance of bowls of apples and marbleized circles.

"If it's worth doing, it's worth doing badly," I said with a shrug.

"Know what it's like?" Bill said as he surveyed the walls and ceilings and ignored his wife as usual. "It's like in every town at Christmas there's the one house where the guy's ten times over the top with the lawn decorations—electric bill of three hundred bucks. And everyone in town drives by to get a load of the place. He becomes famous every year for the decorations."

"You know," Cathy added, staring at her husband, "Putney might get a kick out of this."

Bill shrugged and put both hands in his pockets, continuing to look up and around as if he were a mason checking out plaster cracks he had no intention of fixing.

"Would you babysit?" she shouted at me.

"I did that once," I said. "It didn't work. Putney hates me."

"Putney hates everyone," Bill said. "Quid pro quo."

"He's different because of the therapy," Cathy explained.

"You're being shrunk. You should know how it is. Plus, we pay forty bucks an hour."

"Do I have to do meds?" I asked.

"No drugs!" Bill yelled. "We just took him off clonidine."

"Does he still pull that rabbit punch routine?" I asked.

"Unfortunately, yes," said Bill. "Even Freud couldn't yank that one out."

The Hazells had constructed an elaborately mordant running joke about Putney, their nine-year-old son. "He's the Omen — what can we do?" was Bill's stock response to any public debacle involving the boy. Putney had been seeing some famous British psychiatrist at Harvard for a while, but his parents never discussed any kind of progress — not with me at least. Putney was notorious among former (and one-time) sitters such as myself for demanding that his arrival be met with a drink he called "rabbit punch." He'd never tell you what this drink was; the test for the unfortunate adult was to read his mind. I didn't like him, and I didn't feel sorry for him. I didn't feel sorry for his parents either, and I don't know why I agreed to babysit again. I doubt it was for the forty bucks an hour, even though I was broke. "Babysitting," if anything, was the path of least resistance, acquiescence akin to a perfectly neutral lily pad floating off in any direction where another lily pad happened not to be. Pretty image, that, but I think it attributable to Proust's association of lily pads with the souls in hell.

Before Putney was dropped off on the following Saturday night I did exactly what I'd done for my babysitting venture two years before: I mixed Hawaiian Punch with raspberry sherbet in a punch bowl borrowed from the people downstairs and used Redi-Whip to draw a rabbit's silhouette on the surface.

"That's not rabbit punch!" he shouted after rushing to my kitchen table and spitting in the bowl. "This," he said, striking me in the arm, "is a rabbit punch."

"I knew you'd do that," I said. "I knew you'd say that. That's why I borrowed a martini set."

"A martini set?" he shouted. Then he used an index finger to push up his nose like a pig's.

"Sure," I said. "We can throw back a few while watching *Wall $treet Week* on Channel 2."

"You're a freak," he said, looking around, "and this place is a slum."

"That's exactly how I feel by living here," I said. "That I'm slumming it."

He wouldn't quit running around the apartment, knocking things over and shouting, "Houston, she's got a problem!" He demanded that I take him out to get something that would serve as an antidote to the ersatz rabbit punch, so we went to the sleazy corner market that specialized in "party trays"—foil platters with all kinds of luncheon meat in concentric circles and snow-flake rolls suggesting a garden's cobblestone perimeter. Sitting on the counter at the register was a Saran Wrap–covered party tray in the shape of a heart. The three kinds of spiced pimento loaf, the sliced American cheeses (both yellow and orange), and the snowflake rolls were all tracing the shape of a heart. For some reason, I pointed at the tray and sang to Putney, "Everybody loves somebody sometime." He reached over and with both hands quickly squished most of the snowflake rolls through the Saran Wrap. "Get the fuck outta my store right now!" the cashier yelled, snatching away the bottles of soda we had intended to buy. "Get that fuckin' kid outta my store!"

"You blew your soda," I said as we stood on the sidewalk; I was frustrated but not at all angry. "The wine store across the street only sells mineral water, and I told you I don't want to drive anywhere."

"We can go there and get beer!" Putney shouted. "I want beer!"

"You can't have beer."

"I want microbrewed beer! I can have it. I drink Honey Porter Ale at home."

"You're nine years old."

"I want beer!"

I ended up driving to the White Hen to get IBC root beer because, according to Putney, any other kind of root beer was "deer piss."

"So you've tasted deer piss?" I asked him on the drive back.

"You don't have to taste to know."

"That's true. I hear that taste is all in the imagination."

"I ate dog food once!" he said, defensively.

"My little brother liked to eat Bonz—B-O-N-Z, Bonz."

"You don't have a little brother!"

"Yes I do, only now he's not so little. He's twenty-nine."

"That's old. You must be so old. I couldn't stand being that old."

"I am old," I conceded, "and I'm also not supposed to drive while I'm on medication."

"If we get hit my father will sue!" he shouted.

"Yeah," I agreed, "but he'll sue the guy who hit us for not hitting us hard enough."

"Houston, she's got a fucking problem!" he shouted.

"Don't say any version of 'fuck' in my car, Putney."

He rolled the window all the way down and stuck out his head: "Fuck, fuck, fuck!" all the way home.

I recall the dusky sky looking like a Thomas Hardy novel, which made me want to stay outdoors so that I could absorb the abundant sadness suggested by such purple clouds. The sky looked bruised where the sun was going down; the atmosphere felt to be pressing in on both of my ears, like what happens when you run in January, though I was only standing and it was July. To Putney, however, I maintained a cheerful façade. "It's nice out," I said. "Let's sit on the steps."

"*Let's sit on the steps*," he said with a lisp, snapping off the lid of the root beer bottle and throwing it into my neighbors' yard.

"You must really dislike me," I said.

"You're just like everyone!" he bellowed. "I hate them all."

"Who are 'them'?" I asked, trying to sound sincere in the way I thought children read sincerity.

"I need to write a poem for summer school!" he shouted.

"Writing a poem can be hard," I said, "especially if you care about poems."

"I don't write on the lines!" he shouted even louder.

"You're going into the fourth grade," I said, pressing the base of a sweating root beer bottle against my forehead. "You should write on the lines."

"I don't want to write on the lines!"

"You have to."

"Why?"

"I don't know why, but when they asked Charles Manson for a handwriting sample he wrote right off the paper and onto the table."

"Who's Charles Manson?"

"Ask your father that the next time he gets mad and says 'What are we going to do with you?'"

He scowled at me. "You're weird. My father says you're crazy."

"And you believe everything your father tells you?"

"He tells me to write on the lines!"

"I guess that means I'm crazy."

"Why don't you have a job?" he shouted at me.

"When I was your age I wanted to be an artist—a painter, a drawer. I wanted to stand at an easel all day."

"I want to make bombs!"

"Why not be an artist instead?"

"I want to make bombs and sell them."

"Listen, Putney," I said in the concerned voice I used to be good at, "by the time you get out of college everyone's going to have a degree in either bomb-making or bomb-selling, and it's going to be hard to find a job with an internationally recognized terrorist organization. So maybe you should seriously think about being an artist, because by then no one will want to be one."

"I'll be the only artist in the world?"

"Sure, and you can paint pictures of bombs going off."

"That's what I do!" he yelled.

"See? By the time you're grown you'll be so good at it nobody will bother to compete."

He shouted "Houston!" and before he could get out the rest I shouted, "No, I don't have a problem!" Then he laughed and wouldn't stop laughing; tears appeared from nowhere, and his eyes looked almost rheumy. After a few minutes of his uncontrollable laughter I got nervous, but then he was so intoxicated by the episode that I could easily usher him inside, where he soon regained his toxic disposition. We tried television, but the fact that I didn't have cable made him want to punch things, throw magazines, and say "Fuck you, asshole!" He wouldn't play any of the games he'd brought to install on my computer. The one thing he liked in the apartment was my bedroom closet door; he thought the enlarged photocopy of the smiling angel looked like Darth Vader. We wound up sitting on the bed, and I was amazed that he'd accepted sitting on my bed as something to do.

"I'm so fucking bored!" he yelled.

"We are bored when we don't know what we are waiting for," I said. "Of course I'm quoting Walter Benjamin."

"It's Benjamin Walter, jerk!"

"You're right, Putney," I said, as if snapping to from this self-induced trance in which I quote anything that pops into my head. "Benjamin Walter is your therapist, right?"

"What's in all those bottles?" he asked, pointing to my cluttered night table. He obviously didn't want to talk about his therapist.

"Medicines," I said.

"Why aren't there labels on them?"

"I don't know," I said. This was the truth: I had no idea why I did this, took all the prescriptions out of their brown plastic bottles and put them in brown glass bottles I'd purchased with my painting supplies. "I like it that way. They're like unmarked cars—you know, like troopers out to get your father on the turnpike. I know which is which."

"How do you know which ones to take?"

"I just know."

"So what are they?"

"Let's see what we have," I said. "Here we have a run-of-the-mill decongestant, an antihistamine, a nonaspirin pain reliever, some ibuprofen, some Valium, some Klonopin, some Ativan, some Zoloft, Wellbutrin, and Desyrel—at five bucks for everything, how could I say no?—and of course Depakote. You know, as in 'And of course Chekhov.'" I shook the Depakote bottle and told Putney about what happened to certain people who didn't take it: "There was a guy in my college dorm who went off his nut, threw everyone's stereo out the window, and then asked people to cut his eyes out. He was manic-depressive and refused to take his medicine, which wasn't Depakote but worked in the same way. I, however, am boring. I'm the same whether I take the pills or not."

"So why do you take them?"

"The doctors think I should."

"Why?"

"Because I talk fast and don't want a job."

"Everybody on TV talks fast and doesn't want a job!"

"I always knew I ought to be on TV."

"You have to be good-looking to be on TV," he said, in a surprisingly contemplative tone.

"Well maybe I can do voices for cartoons. I can be a schoolteacher with blue hair and eyes like saucers."

"A fat one everybody hates!" he proposed with renewed excitement.

"Yeah!" I said, aping his enthusiasm. "Because her blue hair is falling out!"

"She's bald!"

"Yeah! And they can put me on a space shuttle and it'll blow me to smithereens while taking off!"

"Yeah!" he said. But then he thought to add, "But why do you need all those pills?"

"To relax," I said. "Didn't your doctor ever give you pills to take, like Ritalin?"

"My dad won't let me take that. He doesn't want me to be a junkie."

"Bananas and lavender; they relax you," I said for some reason.

"You could've made the punch with those."

"With bananas and lavender?"

"Bananas and stuff. You should've used a blender, or a juicer."

"That root beer made me thirsty," I said. "I sure could go for some of that rabbit punch right now."

"That's what Bowwow says to me."

"You mean Benjamin Walter?"

"Bowwow!"

"You don't like Bowwow, do you?"

"He thinks he knows about the punch."

"But nobody knows about the punch?" I ventured.

"Some people do," he insisted.

"Some people know things," I agreed, nodding. "Some people do. I guess I just don't know that many people who know things anymore."

"What happened to that guy you were married to?" he asked.

"What guy was I married to?"

"Houston!" he shouted, hopping on the bed.

"OK," I said, trying to get his feet off the comforter. "One day we realized we didn't like each other anymore."

"Why?"

"He accused me of not wanting to change anything. He said I was afraid to change anything."

"You changed everything in here," he said, looking at Darth Vader.

"Yes, I changed everything," I agreed, nodding at Darth Vader.

"You changed yourself. You used to be a jerk, a real asshole."

"You shouldn't call me an asshole, but thanks for indicating improvement."

"Asshole!" he yelled, leaping up and then falling back down on my bed. "But you're not that bad now."

"Does that mean you won't punch me in the arm again?"

Of course he punched me in the arm harder than before. I just said, "Ow."

"That wasn't a real punch," he said with a laugh. "That was a pussy-whip punch."

"And don't say that word either."

"Pussy, pussy, pussy!" he shouted.

"OK," I said. "Whatever kind of punch you want."

He'd been lying on his back, but suddenly he bolted up. "Want to hear?" he said, a bit conspiratorially, sounding more like a naughty little boy than this thug with his dirty sneakers on my bed.

"Sure," I said, "I always want to hear."

It turned out to be a recurring dream, a dream that Putney said he wouldn't tell Bowwow. Putney said he started having the dream when he was in kindergarten, that it was caused by a song that the class used to sing. Of course he wouldn't sing the song for me, but it was one I remembered well from the repertoire of childhood:

> In a cottage in the woods,
> there was I by the window stood,
> saw a rabbit hopping by,
> knocking at my door.
> "Help me, help me, help me!" he said,
> "or the hunter will shoot me dead!"
> Little rabbit, come inside,
> safe where you can hide.

Putney said that he dreamt he was in the auditorium at school, watching a play about the rabbit and the hunter, and all of the kids in the auditorium were given a cup of rabbit punch, and they started jumping like rabbits, so they jumped out of their seats, out of the auditorium, out of the school. "They can get away," he told me, "but no one gives me the rabbit punch, so I can't."

"You can't get away from the hunter?"

"No!" he shouted. "Away from the school!"

I used two fingers of my right hand to make a rabbit, or else a peace sign. "When we sang that song," I said, "we'd always do this for 'saw a rabbit hopping by.'" My hand went up and down, right to left, and we both watched it, my stupid paint-stained hand. This seemed to contribute to Putney's drowsy consternation. He snarled his lip, said something under his breath, fell back on the bed again, and rolled on his stomach. Soon he was asleep, and as I watched him I felt no affection whatsoever. I lied when I said everybody loves somebody sometime. Thinking about this everyday lack of affection for a sleeping child made me appreciate the great burden Putney must bear for being so universally disliked. He was just starting out, and already his path was a deep rut—no friends, always belligerent, always unhappy. Nobody would want to be lolloping along Putney Hazell's path. I was struck at that moment by a revelation: he wasn't a physically ugly boy, as I'd previously thought. My memory of his pushing up his nose like a pig's had been conflated with a conception of him actually having a face like a pig's—all nostrils and beady black eyes.

Guadeloupe had told me that many people who seek therapy complain of not feeling "real," but what do you know about feeling real when you're nine? With me, the being real was what I couldn't take—I felt so real all the time, because being real was the everyday curse of doing the exact same thing. The way your legs looked when you were sitting down—that never seemed to change. What I always wanted was to feel transcendent of what for me was "real"—I wanted to feel the fantastic illusion of someone else's reality. I wanted to feel opalescent, like that smiling angel on the cathedral at Reims. *Isn't that what antide-*

pressants were supposed to do for you? I wondered. "Why the fuck aren't these drugs making me opalescent?" I said aloud, as Putney slept. I again did the rabbit hopping by with my hand, moving it back and forth, staring at my fingers, and I thought how this boy and I were very much alike—not just in our nicknames for the mental health professionals in our lives, but also in the degree, or perhaps the perfection, of our alienation. No friends, always belligerent, always unhappy. *"Help me, help me, help me!"* he said.

When Bill arrived, Putney remained asleep during the literal pickup. "Christ," his father said. "Out cold. This never happens. What'd you do—feed him all those drugs over there?"

He paused, holding the sleeping boy in his arms—paused to get a better look at the bedroom walls. "You know," he said, tempering his voice to a whisper, "I sort of get everything else—the circles and flowers and all that Martha Stewart stuff. But that," he said, lifting an elbow toward the closet door. "What about that?"

"Your son thinks it's Darth Vader," I said.

"I guess it takes one to know one," he said.

"Maybe Putney will grow up to do something artistic," I said. "He's really a smart boy."

"It doesn't matter how smart you are," Bill said. "In the end, if you got a problem, you got a problem." He looked thoughtful for a minute. "It's bad when you don't like your own kid," he said, now somewhat dragging the body like it was furniture he'd been roped into moving for a friend of a friend of a friend.

"It's a problem," I concurred, although Bill was already lugging away the body, the rabbit that couldn't escape. *Why not carry him by his ears?* I thought as Bill thudded down the stairs; why not carry him by the ears like game? Why not carry him like game considering it's all a game anyway—*him son, you father?* "Tastes just like chicken!" I hollered as Bill slammed shut the front door.

I went to the window to watch the Hazells' Saab drive off; then I sat on the bed and looked at Darth Vader. I now felt hungry as well as thirsty, but I didn't know what I was hungry for. I wanted to do something, and yet I had nothing left to do but swallow a bottle of pills or paint out the entirety of my folly. If I opted for the Virginia route I'd be using my rabbit hand to unscrew the white lids on the brown bottles and eat different colored pills as a late-night snack. If, on the other hand, I decided to live like Vanessa Bell and Duncan Grant, I'd be painting it all out starting now, painting it all out my entire life, erasing the past before I went ahead and made the same mistakes all over again.

During the next few weeks I painted everything in my apartment using seven gallons of Benjamin Moore Atrium White. Layers and layers and layers. When the paint was finally dry I moved away, to the hinterlands of New York. I got a better therapist, a bona fide psychiatrist, borrowed the money from my family. Of course this is the time-lapse photography rendition of events; arrivals and departures were not clean and orderly but sloppy and ambiguous. Five years is five years. Still, the overall direction was toward the kind of life that garners applause on the daytime talk shows. For a few years now I've been living in a farmhouse in Nowheresville — the worthless property inherited by my brother's wife, and I rent it from them for practically nothing — teaching freshman English at a state ag-tech school an hour's drive away. If I look at my life in the context of my peers, my life feels a syndicated-TV-show level of tragic. But living the life I've stapled and Scotch-taped together here in the boondocks, focused on the minutiae as we are meant to do, is not so bad. I don't mind doing it.

I haven't been cured of my Vanessa Bell compulsion, however. The day after I moved in here I began to do the same kind of painting, although this time around I was neither frenetic nor drunk. The place is a sunken-floor dump, and after all this time I'm still painting things. I like referring to the house as a work-in-progress even though it's merely a rental. My psychiatrist thinks my project a healthy one; he likened me to the cave painters at Lascaux — early man trying to make sense of the world and all that. Most people get a kick out of it; even my nieces and nephews and their elementary school friends have good things to say. Everyone but my ex-husband, that is. "It embarrasses me," he said during an unexpected visit awhile back. He was in transit from one high-end detox clinic to another, and his parents thought it would be a good part of the therapy to see me. They'd recently rescued him from the junkie life he was living in Antwerp, taking pictures of very expensive, very depressing clothes that happened to have people inside them. After his visit with me and after the second clinic, he moved in with his parents in Virginia and was said to have gotten better, was said to have adopted a blind dog. But last fall he moved back to Manhattan, and now he was said to be doing the same bad things all over again.

I am still unhappy and still take a variety of prescription drugs, although, in cahoots with my shrink, I am forever halving and quartering pills with a paring knife on the island in the kitchen, "playing with the dosages" as they say, in my ongoing attempt to figure out what's what and hopefully hit upon that brilliant combination that will lead to ever more "breakthroughs." I would like to say that I've arrived at a sophisticated attitude toward my emotional illness, but all I've come up with is this: it's something that conceals itself from your hyperactive mind and then stages an ambush when you're thirty-three, so that suddenly your role in life seems to be a conduit for everyone's unhappiness, not just your own. It's just fate that happens to you, and you can't escape it, can't drink the rabbit punch and hop away.

The photo next to Putney's on the front page of the paper looks like those pictures of Dresden after the Allied bombings. Putney had managed to pull off what so many "troubled teens" in states in every time zone have been attempting for years—he blew up his high school, but just himself and the school. He broke into the building the night before last and placed seven timed explosives around the premises, but despite the brilliance of his plan, the timers malfunctioned, and all seven bombs went off at 5:45 rather than 8:45. Amid so much destruction, "miraculously" there was just the one death—that of the perpetrator. Not even a stray custodial worker or an insomniac algebra teacher. Considering that it was just one kid acting alone, the investigators pieced together quite a lot about the logistics—like that the powerful bombs were made of army explosives, containers of oil, and propane cooking-gas cylinders. The paper mentions a Darth Vader poster in the boy's bedroom, and there is the obligatory sidebar exegesis on the connection between troubled teens and the *Star Wars* movies. Still, the students, parents, and teachers interviewed can cite nothing out of the ordinary in the boy's behavior, though most had nothing to do with him. A guidance counselor mentions recurring truancy and insolence but is careful to qualify that this could apply to one-third of the student body. A total of one post-punk and two goth bands are alluded to in passing, though nothing is said about the famous British psychiatrist. No mention is made of Bowwow.

That last time I saw Putney, after his father had collected his body and I was left wondering what to do next, I decided that Putney wouldn't want Darth Vader to be painted out of my apartment, so I got a screwdriver and removed the door from its hinges. I decided to give Putney the door as a souvenir. I decided to leave it on the Hazells' front porch, leave it leaning against something. I affixed the door to the roof of my car with clothesline. I tied the thing so that Darth Vader was appropriately facing the stars—or, apropos the angel within, facing the heavens. I had not been so decisive in a long time, and I can still remember how good it felt.

Driving through Cambridge at three in the morning with a door tied to the roof of my car, I kept thinking of something Rodin wrote about the cathedral to which the smiling angel is attached. He was talking about the effect of Reims at night: "I cannot distinguish it, but I feel it. Its beauty persists. It triumphs over shadows and forces me to admire its powerful black harmony." I had read that only once, and I remembered it for years and years. It was a gift I had, this photographic—or xerographic—memory.

And what was it good for? Nothing but enlarging and distorting reality, identifying and translating for innocent bystanders the dimensions of my psychosis, which at that moment felt defined exclusively by its powerful black harmony. How Woolfian that phrase, I thought; how alike we all are, us crazy chickens in this big-ass Western Civ henhouse. This made me laugh—laugh uncontrollably to the point of tears, just like Putney had done earlier on my front steps—and while I was laughing I remembered the line, from one of Woolf's novels, on which my entire ill-fated career was based: "I behold the moon rising, sublimely, indifferently, over the ancient chapel—then it becomes clear that I am not one and simple, but complex and many." How true, I thought, wiping the tears from the dark circles under my eyes, for at that moment it seemed I was both Virginia and Vanessa, both Darth Vader and Luke Skywalker, both the wretched Putney and his wretched father, the pristine Drug Czar and the slatternly Guadeloupe, the tragic rabbit and the indifferent hunter. I was everybody for whom things could go blessedly wrong in one way or another, and it seemed a shame that I had just the one door to give away.

The Send-Away Girl

The afternoon's snow still had the lift of an infant's blanket—or teased hair, maybe a spongy Orlon sweater, the bed of cotton under jewelry. *Jewelry.* The girl couldn't even think the word anymore without feeling the lot of the hopelessly cheap crawl into bed with her, every last scallop of "let's pretend"—let's pretend at midnight trysts, at cabs from here to there, at ocelot clutch bags with their own matching lighters. This is why she never attempted jewelry: she couldn't stomach "let's pretend" for a lime rickey with the girls in offices down the hall and up and down the stairs. Stupid girls, nauseating girls—she herself just one more, an advert repeated all over town: Earnestly seeking security; will cross legs for early dinner and Gregory Peck picture.

This particular picture was Copley Square at dusk, lit the way only January can do—Trinity, the library, black cars moving like beetles in a box of baking soda—and beyond that row upon row of pinkish stone, with people inside, living their foreign lives. Her boss had called her attention to the blood-tinged rosiness of the sky, and as they stood in the window of his seventh-floor office, stood side by side before the limp glow, she thought that maybe what he wanted to share was the shameful innocence of this intrusion upon the most cheerless part of his day, this serendipitous injection of radiance into his seventh-floor view of the world.

In theory it made no sense to specify this part of her boss's day as the most cheerless, as he always seemed to derive some vague satisfaction from the activity known as getting ready to go home. But he was an unhappy man getting ready to go home, and that was different from a man stuffing his hat on his head and dashing to get the 5:45 from South Station. He'd leave the office never wearing his overcoat; it would be slung over his arm, like something dead he was taking to a funeral parlor to have pressed out and made to look momentarily good. He'd pause at the threshold between her office and the shabby reception area that was shared by several businesses in the suite. He'd look at his hands as if waiting for them to say something, to break into conversation like a couple of stocking puppets, a snake and a weasel who hadn't seen each other in ages. At one time she had thought he might make a pass at her, slide his hand up under her skirt with a sly silence, a cunning absence of narrative. She had no idea what she'd have done if this kind of thing happened, but she couldn't help forever taking inventory of the lost benefits — credible jewelry, nice pairs of shoes, twenty-dollar bills — anything to make up for the monotony. She took inventory but was certainly wise to the fact that the sun never shines where the sun never shines, especially in the dead of winter.

She used to work for a jeweler, as the girl to fetch things. Initially the fetching was from the counter to the vault out back, but for some reason this fetching grew into transporting thousands of dollars worth of merchandise from the store downtown to the one in Central Square, via bus, right before closing. "Send the girl," they'd say, and she'd be out on the street with precious commodities in her handbag, out on the street with her pair of dime-store nylons doing the work of Wells Fargo tires. They paid her next to nothing, and she was always afraid she'd accidentally drop the cache into some dark hole — a sewer drain, for instance — and be arrested without mercy, for being idiot enough to trust that the Johnny to whom she'd handed the stash would wait around to collect her as well. This conveyance went on for several months until early December, when it began to get dark before five. She'd got off at Central and noticed that the man in the black overcoat who'd crushed up next to her on the bus was now following her. For a split second it struck her as highly comical—this being tailed, like in the movies—but then her scant allotment of prudence kicked in, and she panicked, out and out panicked on the slushy street amid the rush-hour pedestrian flow. She walked briskly in the direction of the Baptist church at the intersection, which was difficult given the cheap construction of her over-the-shoe boots. She walked briskly but in slight hops, like she'd seen Chinese women do in the newsreels. She knew she was slopping up the backs of her nylons, and she knew the black overcoat was right behind her. Would she seek sanctuary in the church? This was indeed a solution, but only if your pursuers happened to be a hoard of toothless peasants with burning torches—like she'd seen in a picture after the newsreel.

Her disorientation suddenly seemed ludicrous, as ludicrous as running in those boots, and the thought of being ludicrous shortened her temper. She turned around to go back past the bus stop and on to the store, and when she turned she smacked directly into the chest of the overcoat. "Aw, honey," the man said in a snide way as he gripped her shoulders, "I just wanted a little kiss." He turned out to be the jeweler's brother-in-law, and his following her was a test of her mettle, to see if she'd take note and proceed in a levelheaded manner, soliciting an officer, seeking refuge in a well-lit store along Massachusetts Avenue. "We thought you weren't just another skirt," the jeweler said, counting out her midweek settlement in singles. "We thought you had some moxie."

In her next job she resumed with the fetching, but there was little risk of being followed and tested by a sinister-looking brother-in-law. She'd got so adept at spending her work time in transit that she became the girl for a dressmaker and a milliner who shared an atelier in the Back Bay. She delivered hats and taffeta and tulle ball gowns to ladies out in Brookline or just up the Hill. Sometimes she'd be left waiting for an hour outside the building, in a narrow brick pedestrian alley where she'd pace, smoke, and pinch at invisible ash specks on her teeth as she'd seen Ida Lupino do in some picture. Eventually the door would open and there'd be a hatbox shoved in her face: "Here, do something else with it. It's complete rubbish. Tell Irma it's rubbish." Sometimes she'd be invited into the sanctum, the fussy boudoir of a hapless woman who was momentarily all the more flummoxed over how she should look, what would make her husband the most terribly happy man on the East Coast. "Tell me honestly what you think. This is an important party for Arthur. He must make an impression. I must make his impression." Or else she'd have to assist some shapeless woman with hoisting the stiff artfulness of stays and plastic buttresses around her boxy midriff, the bulge of her breasts displaced in all directions, the red moles looking nothing like the moles on the Mesdames de Pompadour painted on the screens at the atelier of Mesdames Helena and Irma.

On a bus to Brookline she'd sit in one seat and have the dress under its encasement sitting next to her, like it was the ghost of a former companion. Her most robust ghostly companion was a beaded ballet-length gown with layers and layers of organdy; its destination was a house in Chestnut Hill—a mansion really—up beyond the reservoir. This gown was what the dressmaker called her chef d'oeuvre; she'd hired four Armenian girls to sew the beads, and she'd gone down to Providence herself to select these beads. The woman for whom the dress had been made wore slacks and smoked with the aid of a short cigarette holder. She had a drink in her hand and a sister in from Florence. She spoke with the cigarette holder in the crook of her mouth and called herself and her sister "girls," even though the sister's husband in Florence was said by the two of them to be "an ancient gasbag." "Embassy, you know," the sister explained, "but then I don't expect you'd know anything of embassy, would you? I don't reckon you'd know anything of anything, would you, Patsy?" They seemed to find it a laugh riot to address her as Patsy, and she tried to ignore the tight midday gaiety of the Chestnut Hill world, figuring that it was some sort of trend among the drunkard wives of Florence to call the shopgirls Patsy. On the woman with the cigarette holder the dressmaker's chef d'oeuvre looked somewhat silly, but on her younger sister it worked as a passable barometer of strained opulence. She distinctly remembered the two of them half-dressed, brassiere straps falling down, pressing their foreheads together, giggling and whispering: "Who'll ever see you? Who'll ever know?"

When she got back to the atelier Helena shouted, "But where is the dress?" She explained the situation of Mrs. Rahill's sister, that Mrs. Rahill's sister had decided to take the gown. "But Mrs. Rahill only just telephoned! She told me the dress was sent back with you, for adjustments to the length! What have you done with my dress?" By the next day Madame Helena well understood what had happened, but at the base of this shock and embarrassment was the messenger, the girl, and there was nothing to do but quietly bury the evidence, like a cat patting soil over its droppings. The girl scolded herself for being so stupid; she knew something was up when she left the house and Mrs. Rahill had urged, "Here, take the box. We don't need the box." She refused to take the box, saying that Madame Helena would consider it improper. When she said "improper" Mrs. Rahill had laughed through her nose, and the sister chimed in: "You don't even know where Florence is, do you, Patsy?" This was a moment indeed, for in it she considered all the options open to her on the earth of her own access, and she said, "Isn't it in California, where they grow the oranges?"

Because of this brief history she could not help but think of herself as someone you immediately sent away — "the send-away girl," like it was her role in the school play. Getting out of scrapes had become a way of life — small, tedious scrapes, gauche situations. She had come to Boston from nowhere, only because there was an elderly cousin of already old relatives who thought this elder cousin would never tire of her own company. But suddenly she did this at eighty-four — tire of her own company. This cousin, Lucile, had a badly papered flat in the West End—five cramped rooms, pipes running along the baseboards in full view, pipes surrounded by the brown aura of wasted hours flushed past, hours and days and months and years. The girl couldn't help but dwell on the sadness of Cousin Lucile's pipes, the way they sullied the rose and peony wallpaper that reminded you of how people used to want to see flowers all the time. The room out back allowed a subtle and handy escape route for a lodger, kin or no—through the kitchen and onto the landing of the back stairs. The girl spent no time in that kitchen beyond this split-second transit. She took her meals at luncheonettes and often skipped dinner. If a date was enacted, meal-worthy packets of oyster crackers and roasted peanuts might find their way into her handbag. On random evenings and Sunday afternoons she'd sit with Lucile as Lucile rocked in her rocker. She gave the old woman more money than the situation was worth, but she knew that without the old woman she would never have arrived in Boston, because in the nowhere from which she came there lacked gumption on the part of the locals to make anything happen.

The man in the flat upstairs was said to be an actuary, although she did not want to think what being an actuary meant. She had never seen him, only heard his footsteps cross the floorboards overhead. When the record was over he'd walk to the phonograph and put the needle back to the start, to play "The Rose Room" yet another time. Some nights she'd lie in bed on her back smoking, unable to sleep even though she'd contributed to the ruin of cheap shoes by walking all over town that day. Hearing the same song over and over from start to finish made the world seem stuck, not spinning happily away on its axis as they'd once told her. The music wasn't loud enough to justify her screaming out the window that people were trying to get some sleep around here and that wasn't he a funny one with his one song. And the repetition wasn't at all soothing, lulling her with the cadence of sheep hopping a low fence. "The Rose Room" dozens of times seemed an oblique message, come to her in the middle of the night, while the decent world was ensconced in slumber: *nothing is ever going to change.*

Her own room contained nothing to suggest the brassiness of modern times except a paper-covered book loaned to her by one of the girls who worked in the building, a file clerk. The book's cover depicted a woman collapsed at the side of a bed, crying into her elbow. The woman wore a clinging negligee, and though you could not see her face, you could tell from the wave of her shiny auburn hair that she was beautiful in the customary way. The bedroom was of a chic style of some years past, with an ornate white telephone on the bedside table and a frilly lamp and shade suggesting a poodle with a ruff. The book was called *Bleak Teardrops,* and the file clerk had been given it by her cousin so that she might have her heart broken just as her cousin's was. The girl didn't even have to open the book to know the manner in which her own heart was slated for demolition; she only had to read what was written on the back of the cover showing the woman crying into her elbow: "The Other Woman—tormented by a love that is above all love, yet bound to secrecy, to the mercy of the whispering night. Will *she* do What Is Right? The Man—handsome, dashing, chained within a loveless marriage. Will he do What Is Right? The passion! the anguish! that causes such bleak teardrops. Read for yourself this riveting tale of lustful desire and tremulous Fate!"

A lucky girl was she to have been made the secretary of a successful man, even one so unhappily successful—unhappy and quiet and admirably regular. She had waited in a tiny reception lobby like any other, sitting in a worn leather chair that sunk at that exact place where her behind was wedged. It was right after Christmas, when the murky scent of wet woolens and warped floors blended in with the cigar smoke that seemed to live in the building. The hiss and clink of radiators could be heard up and down the stairwell to many other places of employment as she sat sinking, her knees pressed tightly together, a dainty puddle of the expired outdoors forming around her cheap boots. She flipped through an issue of *Collier's* from the year before, vaguely noting how these men's every whimsical conjecture had already been proved wrong—these men who wrote *Collier's*. The advertisements for brands of cigarettes all seemed to show the same man enjoying his smoke. That he was so everywhere made him all the more elusive. He'd wear a hat but you knew he wasn't balding; he'd wear an open-neck shirt but you knew that on most days he was buttoned up with a suitable tie. Her idle mind had been following this man like a hesitant child would an older playmate when she heard a voice that seemed, quite mysteriously, to match this persona that skittered across the pages of *Collier's*. It was a voice youthful but certain, direct but considerate; what this voice was saying did not even register, but later she figured that it must have been "send her in." She was sent in by a pretty secretary, and she got this woman's job, even though she had no secretarial experience. It was for this reason that she anticipated an overture; perhaps her hairstyle, the fit of her sweater, was what he'd fancied. Perhaps it was that, of the many applicants who'd sat with their behinds wedged into that worn leather chair, her proportions had, by luck of the draw, dovetailed with what he imagined he needed.

In the small anteroom to her boss's front-window office the implements of paperwork and perfumed toil were deemed hers and hers alone. She started off with "let's pretend"—let's pretend at shorthand, at the proper forms of business address, at inserting carbon paper into the cylinder of the typewriter, at stapling Exhibit A to Commensurate B. "Good morning, Mr. Perkins's office" she'd rehearsed at night in her room out back, with a delivery so melodic as to be a caricature of rosy efficiency, a tone she'd once heard a nightclub entertainer use to impersonate a voluptuous receptionist. She spent a month of after-work Mondays through Thursdays at the library across the square, poring over the manuals and grammar books she'd never much bothered with in school, because every day at Mr. Perkins's office she was happy not to be sent away after something, and she'd been out of regular work for several months, smoking in her room late into the morning, making Cousin Lucile nervous. She soon found that her physical attributes—what she so assiduously worked at maintaining—were not at all what Mr. Perkins had in mind when he hired her. She turned out to be a serviceable secretary, which, to her amazement, is what he had uncannily perceived.

She was not and had never been a bad sort; she had come from a brood of bad sorts but was conscious of striking this aspect of her history from public view, like a string of Xs over material that her boss decided he did not want said. She had never become jocularly familiar, let alone intimate, with a married man, even though this is what all working girls were said to do. The rationale was that you had to, really, if you wanted to keep your days and nights from running into a slurp of melted hopes, like the two soupy spoonfuls that remained of your Bailey's sundae. She worked on being good, however, as if virtue were a wood-burning hobby or a regimen to correct splayed, bleeding cuticles. Still, there was the matter of his voice, as well as the matter of his signature. She'd been oddly enamored since the first she saw of this signature—the graceful swoops, the careful slant, but also the stress that removed any undertone of femininity. "Why'd I have to see his handwriting?" she asked herself, not bothering to blanch at the absurdity—that, as his secretary, his handwriting was practically all she got to see. And she never saw him slouch at his desk or heard him get angry on the telephone or speak in incomplete sentences. He would dictate slowly and carefully with that voice, and everything he said beyond dictation seemed to register with a period, a comma, or a semicolon. Only once did he specify that she use an exclamation point. It was in a letter to a client who was wintering on one of the Keys: "My envy to you in sunny Florida!" He had paused after that sentence to ask her, "Envy—is that a bad choice?" She hadn't even bothered to ponder the issue: "Of course not. Everyone wants to be envied. It's highly flattering." Then he proceeded along in a weighty tone with what ought to have been a frivolous letter, taking care at the end to reiterate, "And just one exclamation point after *Florida,* not two."

It had been a satisfactory year of employment — no moments of duress, no predicaments involving breeches of etiquette. Before Christmas he had handed her an envelope on which her name was written in his hand. The envelope contained twenty-five dollars in five-dollar bills. This was the only bonus she'd ever been given, and she was not ungrateful, but there remained a discomforting feeling about the envelope, perhaps because he had written her first name without the last. He called her by her first name, which most girls' bosses did not do, fearing suspicion of things that might or might not be happening. She attributed this openness to the fact that her Christian name was hopelessly traditional; spoken in full, it sounded like an homage to a long-dead grandmother or a beloved old schoolteacher got up like a Gibson girl. The girls, her own breezy pool to pal around with, had shortened her name, played with it like taffy, coming up with a panoply of perky identities. When you were single and went to work in zipped-up skirts, it seemed that you could be loose with your name, pass it around like a toy that was amusing only when handled by grown-ups.

There was another reason for the envelope's instilling a discomforting feeling, however: she had done her boss a personal favor, and he probably felt that he owed her. It was sad to receive an envelope of cash — a payoff — under the guise of Christmas cheer, especially when it was handed to you by a man whose unhappy presence provoked such sympathy. One afternoon at the start of December he had asked her to have a seat in his office without her steno pad. "Just please sit down there," he said with a motion of his hand, as if she were the wife of a wealthy client. He moved behind his tidy mahogany desk and opened a lower drawer in a manner that suggested he'd often done this before, whatever he was about to do. He placed in front of him a large jeweler's box, lifted its lid, removed the contents wrapped in a thick burgundy cloth, and carefully set back each of the four flaps. "This belonged to my wife's late mother," he said, "and my wife doesn't at all favor it. In fact, she dislikes the lot."

He informed her that his wife's mother had "passed on" in the fall and that the estate consisted of some rather fine jewelry in horrible settings and amalgamations. Mrs. Perkins had been quite distressed with the contents of her mother's jewel box—the gems and stones and braids of gold and silver all in a tarnished, tiresome heap. "What do you think I can have done with this?" he said courteously, neatly clasping his hands as if he were a jeweler himself. "I'd like to have it made into something she'd like, as a Christmas gift, but I haven't a clue as to how to proceed. You worked for a jeweler, didn't you?"

From the jewel box her boss had taken a gold necklace saturated with black pearls—pearls set as droplets all the way around, with tiny diamonds at their bases. This was the item he'd selected for reconfiguring, as representative of his dewy love. He didn't say this—"dewy love"—but this was the language buzzing about her head since she began dawdling around various cosmetics counters decked out for the holiday season.

She leaned forward on her chair to peer at Exhibit A. "You might have difficulty getting anything done so soon before Christmas," she advised, pretending to have some professional instinct in the matter. She studied the necklace but was really marveling at how this was the first time in nearly a year that he spoke of his "wife" versus the staid, distant "Mrs. Perkins" who was often wanting him on the phone. "Oh, yes, he speaks about you," Mrs. Perkins had said to her the first time she rang him up, feeling no obligation to expound on the matter, to indicate whether he spoke about her in a positive or negative way. The girl immediately realized that there was to be no infantile chatting with Mrs. Perkins, no cute teasing about reducing regimens, no comparisons of hairdressing, no pretense about the elusiveness of one's age—the very game the wife and the secretary were expected to play.

"Do you have any kind of 'in' with that jeweler?" he asked.

"Not really," she said, reaching a finger toward her throat, as if there were pearls there to fidget with. "I was fired by that jeweler."

He looked dismayed, and she wondered whether it was because she didn't have an in with the jeweler or because she hadn't told him that she'd been fired by that jeweler.

"I do have a friend whose fiancé is an apprentice to a gem specialist," she said. "That's what my friend calls this man — a 'gem specialist.' He does this sort of thing, and I could ask her tonight for you."

"Would you do that?" He perked right up, something she'd never seen him do. "That would be ideal."

"I'll ask her to have her fiancé phone you tomorrow."

"Perfect," he said officiously, placing his palms flat on the desk surface, on either side of the necklace. "But what do you think? What would you do if this necklace was yours?"

She wanted to say, "Hock it and buy a pair of fur-lined boots that I wouldn't even need to wear in sunny Florida," but she knew his feelings would be hurt. "I'd take just one of each for a pair of earrings," she said, "one teardrop with a diamond at the base. That would be nice. That would look lovely with a strapless gown."

"And would you have a necklace made up to match?"

"No — no necklace. That'd be too much. You'd want just the earrings, the black above milky skin. That's the effect a woman would want. At least that's what I would want."

It was painful in an unclassifiable way, having Ruthie's fiancé pick up the necklace in a parcel that contained typed instructions, her instructions, for producing teardrop earrings for the optimum effect. The earrings were delivered to the office on December 23, and on the 24th the envelope addressed in her boss's hand was presented to her, in her boss's hand. For Christmas Day Cousin Lucile had bought a hastily plucked chicken from some dicey butcher in the North End. She insisted on doing all the cooking, so everything came to the table blackened in some way. Two elderly strangers joined in for the holiday meal—a lady and a gentleman whom Cousin Lucile had known of. The three of them seemed unperturbed at the somber table of burnt food, so busy were they being shocked at how they'd lived to see the day when a divorced man believed that he might run the country. She'd look out the window and then back at the singed feathers affixed to the drumsticks, and once during this routine she wondered what Mrs. Perkins was making of her Christmas gift, her husband's objectification of dewy love.

Even on Christmas night, when she'd gone to bed ridiculously early, the man upstairs was playing "The Rose Room" over and over on his phonograph. Every night of the year it was with him. She had already begun to imagine his flat as just one room, one big room that was all rose. Not a pale rose but a thick cantaloupe shade—the rose of a harsh cologne, the kind of cologne that broken women use to douse the pain of broken hearts. She had heard the man upstairs early that morning say to a fellow tenant on the back landing, "Nobody talks of the war anymore." It was a guttural voice, almost severe, and she could tell by his tone that he was a veteran. The other tenant on the landing sounded like an old fellow: "I was talkin' 'bout the one just was, mister. Read the papers once in a while!" Part of Cousin Lucile's tepid Christmas dinner conversation had consisted of stories she'd heard circulated about this actuary. "He's a Swedenborgian I'm told," Cousin Lucile informed her guests, "and we all know what that means." Then the three of them nodded. She herself did not know what being a Swedenborgian meant, but she assumed that whatever guided the man was based on a nostalgia for something he no longer had.

It was at a point into the New Year when "winter wonderland" seemed like a tedious old joke that the girl stood next to her boss, looking out her boss's window. "It makes the world seem easy," was all she could think to say, "like we all could get what we want." What did she want but a decent pair of boots, a cab home, a bed more comfortable than an army cot? It was hypnotic, the silence, this muffled score to the Cinemascope view of row upon row of pinkish stone with people inside living their foreign lives. As she envisioned a bed more comfortable than an army cot—perhaps a giant cradle filled with cotton balls and skeins of angora yarn—it struck her how at odds everyone was in his or her desire to get what he or she wants, even (and perhaps especially) within this office of two.

"Can I show you something?" her boss proposed in a low voice. She watched him go to his desk and open a drawer and then lick an index finger to ruffle the pages of *Vogue*, stopping at a spot marked by a ripped-off envelope flap. "This dress here," he said handing her the magazine. "Do you like that dress, that color?"

It was satin, off the shoulders, like the Edith Head number on Bette Davis in *All about Eve*. Here it was a pale orchid, and the mannequin's shoulders stuck out like powdered chicken bones. All in all, however, a gossamer rendition of radiance. "This is a beautiful gown," she declared.

"I am thinking of having a similar dress made up for my wife, for Valentine's Day, to wear below those earrings, as you said. Do you think that color's correct?"

"I haven't met Mrs. Perkins."

"Chestnut hair, not black as this girl here. And of course the frame isn't the same—Mrs. Perkins has had three children."

She didn't care about Mrs. Perkins's frame or Mrs. Perkins's chestnut-out-of-a-bottle. "I would make it the rose of that sky out there," she said with a nod. "A heady rose, for Valentine's Day. And the bow, the corsage, should be in the back, in the small of the back. I can't tell what's going on back there, but I would have the decoration there, and the front plain and smooth."

"You worked for a dressmaker, didn't you?"

"Madame Helena. She's the best, they say."

"Would you phone her for me, and send this picture?"

"But she would have to fit your wife. You cannot make a dress like this without a fitting."

"My wife is the same shape as you."

So, I have the frame of a mother of three, have I? Bitterly was how she wanted to think this, but she could not be bitter toward him. "Well, that doesn't help you much, does it?"

"But couldn't you be fit for the gown, at Madame Helena's?"

"I would feel terribly uncomfortable with that."

"Oh, but I'd have the dress delivered right to Mrs. Perkins. There would be nothing untoward."

"What I mean is, I was fired by Madame Helena."

She ended up standing like a doll in the salon of Mr. Praeger, "the second best" in the Back Bay. "Ees for wife but he fits to you?" a heavy woman named Mathilde said, laughing like Maurice Chevalier. Mathilde seemed to smoke, talk, and laugh like Maurice Chevalier all at the same time, fussing under the armpits of Mrs. Perkins's proxy. The girl thought of how Mr. Praeger was often shown in the *Herald-American* pulling at the delicate white cuffs under his tuxedo, but in reality this Mathilde with the fingers like sandpaper created all the gauzy hoopla and dazzle. "He'd rather have her surprised than sitting pretty and comfortable in her gown," the girl told Mathilde, who just grunted. She went back a second time to be set into the gown, and the vision of herself in the arc of mirrors elicited no emotion whatsoever. Mathilde used the pad of her fist to pound at the center of her mannequin's back. "You must always stand straight inside these gowns!"

Valentine's Day came and went, but the winter stayed on, like a drifter allowed to sleep in the barn. Her boss didn't bother to mention how the gown was received by Mrs. Perkins, as had been the case with the earrings. On the phone Mrs. Perkins's voice remained exactly the same: "My husband, please." These two situations involving the procurement of surprise gifts for his wife were the only indications of life she'd witnessed in her boss, and one day at the start of a leonine March it occurred to her that maybe it was Mrs. Perkins who was failing to love her spouse—that maybe she was the kind of woman a man would walk the earth for, even after her frame had been compromised by the delivery of three children. All that year she had assumed, as most girls would, that her boss's unhappiness stemmed from disappointment with his home life. His desk supported no pictures of the chestnut-haired Mrs. Perkins or their probably blond little angels. That her boss's unhappiness could have stemmed from his wife's disappointment with him was a new thought, and pondering it seemed to open up another world of possibility—to this and every situation. For everyone who no longer loved there was someone who was no longer loved, and she saw the world as consisting of these people interleaved with people such as herself, the blanks to separate the two kinds, to buffer these strong ways of feeling.

"Don't you want to get married, to be taken care of?" This is what all men asked her, and this is what a man named Harvey asked her on a first date, at a tavern where men ate oysters and steamers while standing up in their coats and hats—the men, that is, not the clams and oysters. Harvey had hollered for chilled mugs of ale, and when hers came she felt too cold to even touch it. "I was born on a Saturday," she said in reply, no longer finding any novelty in this practiced quip, for it was the punch line to a joke she'd heard long ago, a joke about a lumberjack and a prostitute.

"But still don't you want to get married?" Harvey asked. His hand was locked into the mug's handle as if the mug were a machine he was operating, as if this were the way he'd been taught to grip artillery in the war, something he did in the turret of a tank. She'd heard so many stories on so many dates that were like the fine print in those ads in the *Combat* comic books you could at one time find lying around everywhere—ads for things boys would want to send away for. The serial numbers of guns and bigger guns and how to take them apart to clean and then put them back together; the types of land mines you never mixed up, no siree Bob. "I'll never forget those numbers," they'd say, "scratched right into my brain they are." And yet they all recounted to her the procedurals of their soldier identities with apprehension, as if once they forgot the sequence of numbers it would come to be that it all never really happened; they were never battalions with rifles but actuaries with phonographs, Swedenborgians with one-room flats.

Harvey was a new chum of Ruthie's fiancé. He kept books for a shipping firm on India Row, and Ruthie had fixed them up with the grave warning, "Don't let this one get away!" Because of this gravity, the girl had the sense to eventually chill her hands around the ale, to forget the sawdust floor and the coats and hats slurping their oysters and beer. She told Harvey, "Of course I want to get married. I don't look like that much of an idiot, do I?" Later that night Harvey touched her all over on the back landing, making sounds the neighbors should not hear. During all this touching a very thin moment elapsed as her nose was pressed into the thick of his smoke-doused overcoat: the awareness that this could be it, that all she'd have to do was be the girl he could phone at the number he'd written into a matchbook.

Dates with Harvey went on for the month of March without her boss knowing of the sudden liaison; she'd wait at the office for him to pick her up at six, when her boss was long gone with his overcoat. A few days before Easter, however, the presence of Harvey made its way into office hours in the form of a skimpy bunch of daffodils.

"What are those?" her boss asked after lunch, pointing to the bouquet on her desk.

"Daffodils."

"Did you go out and get them?"

"They came for me."

"Who brought them?"

"A delivery boy."

"Who sent them?"

"Harvey."

"Who's Harvey?"

"My boyfriend."

Her boss moved closer to her desk and pinched one of the petals like he was trying to make the flower cry. "I didn't know you had a boyfriend."

"Of course you didn't. I didn't tell you."

He shut his door slowly, with a ka-clip, and she pressed her fingertips into her eyes; this is how, she was told, nurses prevented themselves from crying over the children who wound up dead on the operating table.

On Easter Sunday Harvey took her to dinner at the Parker House and gave her a diamond in a box that said it was from the gem specialist who employed Ruthie's fiancé. "If you say no I'll shoot myself," he said. It was Easter—cold enough for wool coats but with a sky the blue of a robin's egg, the satin insides of a music box—and he was serious about deciding she should marry him. Harvey was a big man, and his elbows on the table crowding out the plates suddenly made her nervous. "We've only known each other a month," she said. "I'm flattered, Harvey, but it's one month."

"You said you wanted to get married, that you didn't want to be an idiot." His face was red; she took note of this because the little dab of mint jelly on his plate was such a manly green, like shaving gel. His face was red, and she could smell his perspiration.

"I'll have to sleep on it," she said with a horrible little laugh. "A girl's got to sleep on it!"

"I've got to go up to Portsmouth tomorrow," he said, "and I'll be back on Wednesday. You can sleep on it for three nights." They got drunk as usual, and he touched her all over on the back landing as usual, but he hadn't let her leave the table at the Parker House without her taking the velveteen box, which fell to the bottom of her handbag like an anchor, not a package of oyster crackers.

What she slept on that night was a bed like an army cot, although she slept wide awake, with "The Rose Room" to keep her company. The next day it rained buckets, so that when she got to the office her hair was as much of a mess as her nerves.

"Has something happened?" her boss asked as he removed his galoshes, just as bosses all over town were probably just then doing. He shed his outerwear in her tiny office, not his own. The coatrack was there, next to the rubber tray that fit only his galoshes. She waited till he'd tugged at his jacket, was all ready to greet this exemplar of cheerless days.

"Harvey wants to get married," she said.

His eyes fell to the floor, as they often did during certain conversations. This habit reminded her of a doll going to sleep without being put down. His eyes came up a bit to the dead daffodils on her desk and then to her hands at the typewriter, to the spot where a ring ought to be.

"What will you do?" he asked.

"I ought to get married, don't you think?" she said.

"It's a decision to make," he replied, turning to look at the coatrack as if it were someone he'd forgotten was in the room.

"I don't love Harvey," she said honestly, "but I ought to get married."

"Miss Cumberland worked even after marriage," he offered. "The former Miss Cumberland, I mean—Mrs. Tallady. But then Miss Cumberland was married in a compromised position."

"I didn't know that."

"Of course you didn't," he said. "I didn't tell you."

Much later in the day, before her boss commenced with the ritual of getting ready to go home, he asked her into his office. "Look at that," he said of his seventh-floor view of the square. "My mother called it the dismal wearies, days like this." Within the gray there seemed no third dimension, and she felt her sleepless face, her whole presence, as flat as a board, a board propped up next to him. He had one hand in the pocket of his trousers; the other he lifted to the back of his neck, to begin a tired rub that continued on over his face. "I have to show you something," he said. He walked over to the old walnut credenza that he never seemed to use for anything. There was a key in the lock, and he turned the key, opened the doors to three shelves filled with nothing much but a dress box. He took out the box, and squarely in the center on top of it was a brown velvet jewelers' box. "Here," he said, moving toward her, "you might as well have these. After they were done, I could not see them as separate from you. I saw the picture, but the picture was of you." There was no decision to be made whether to extend her arms, for the box seemed to be already in her possession. He set it onto her arms like a fireman she'd once seen in a picture, a fireman setting a child's limp body into a woman's arms.

"I'm feeling ill," she said. "I have to go home."

It rained hard on the dress box, and when she got "home" she threw it on her bed, and then she changed her mind and threw it on the floor, so that she could throw herself on the bed. The rain kept on with the metal tinking sound, like the world to be rained on was all made of tin; it was the time of year, the time of day, when you had to decide if the lights should be on. On or off? On or off? It was a decision to make, and it put her to sleep, so that soon she was inside that shamelessly rosy gown, with the pearl earrings dangling above, and she was in an empty room, an enormous empty room. She swirled around and around as if she were dancing, but she was all alone, and as the gown flared out she could see it was segmented like petals, and she could see that the distant walls of the enormous room were rose. As she twirled and twirled her skirt got thicker and thicker, with more and more petals, and she could feel the thickness getting tighter and tighter at her waist, so that her waist was up to her throat, and she couldn't breathe.

She sat up in the dark, all wet, even though she wasn't out in the rain. The terrible clanging on the tin matched the terrible banging of her heart. As she pulled the damp sweater over her head, she realized that it wasn't raining, that the sound was a voice, a hacking sound, coughing and gagging in the midst of "The Rose Room" from above.

Cousin Lucile had collapsed between the kitchen and the dining room so that the swinging door was closed upon her, like it was a toothless mouth biting down on her. The old woman's terrible sounds had ceased almost the instant the girl flicked on the kitchen light. Despite all the small ugly things she'd seen, she had never witnessed death. Cousin Lucile's eyes were half open, and her jaw jutted out. The girl had to step over the ghastly picture to get out the front door and to the phone on the landing on the floor below. She knocked awake the Winslows, the busybody superintendents, who scolded her to "get back up there with the poor soul." She scampered around like somebody's child, and by this time she could tell the whole building was up and busily dressing for the arrival of the ambulance. She forced herself to stare at the body of the poor old soul, out of respect, and she found herself looking for something to wedge into the door, to keep it open, to keep it from biting down onto Cousin Lucile. She grabbed the unread book in her room and stuck it into the door's crevice. She stood guard with her arms folded, only once cocking her head to read the words "tremulous Fate!"

The men who came to take Lucile away in an ambulance asked after "next of kin." "I don't know," she said. "I'm only just a lodger." Then the busybody superintendents took over, as apparently Cousin Lucile had at one time specified that indeed they should. Mr. and Mrs. Winslow went with the ambulance, and before she pulled a silly Easter hat over her half-set hair, Mrs. Winslow warned her, "Don't go pinching things. We know what she had." The motley array of tenants who felt entitled to be in Cousin Lucile's flat glared at her as if she'd done something wrong, as if she had caused the old woman's death. After getting quite used to shivering it occurred to her that they were glaring because she was only wearing a slip and a skirt. She recognized the faces of all these tenants except one tall man with an extremely large white forehead and only one arm. He stood by the back door and looked at her sympathetically, not as if he wanted to help her but as if he was sad that there was nothing he could ever do. When he saw that he'd been acknowledged, he moved closer, at the same time moving his stump of an arm a little behind him, so that from one angle you couldn't even tell. The book that had kept Cousin Lucile's body from being bitten was lying face-up on the kitchen table. The man nodded at it with his extremely large white forehead. "Are you fond of the novels?" he asked.

The book suddenly seemed to her like some kind of filthy evidence: did they all think the woman on the paper cover was her? She felt cheated, and she was almost ready to cry in front of these strange people, but then she heard something equally strange. What she heard was the noise of the street, the noise of the building at its nighttime repose: there was no "Rose Room." She looked up at the wide face of the one-armed man. "Where do you live?" she asked. "Up there," he said, lifting his eyes. How could she cry? How could she even think about crying when this was the Swedenborgian actuary? Here he was, yet another someone who either no longer loved or was no longer loved, and she felt, sadly and coldly, that she'd been right about the world, had been right all along. She was the person interleaved between her boss on the seventh floor and this man from upstairs; she was the blank to separate these two kinds, or maybe these same kinds, of strong feeling.

A pink-haired woman from some other flat had her by the shoulders. "Hasn't anyone bothered to get you your robe, dear?" She hadn't the mind to explain to this woman that she owned no robe, that because Cousin Lucile could barely see she'd felt comfortable walking around the flat in her underwear. Finding no robe, the woman gave her a pill to make her sleep. As she was put down on her bed like an army cot, she could see the actuary's hulking frame taking up most of the doorway of her room, and she had to whisper to the pink-haired woman, "Make him go away."

Early the next day she took the dress out of the box and wound the ribbon stirrups around the neck of a wire hanger; then she looped its petticoat around as well and hung the affair on the nail on the back of the door to her room. The dress had been stained by the wet tissue, and the weight of the gown was already causing the hanger to bend. She lit a cigarette and observed this odd ghost, this bus companion who'd made the journey all the way home with her. The more the hanger bent, the more the gown resembled a lynching victim. She left the dress and its petticoat hanging on the back of the bedroom door when she left Cousin Lucile's flat. She did take a cameo owned by Cousin Lucile, the only item of value from the premises. "Who'll ever see you?" she said to herself. "Who'll ever know?" Only she knew that Cousin Lucile always kept the cameo right on the collar of her blue Sunday dress in the closet, not in the locked treasure chest next to her bed.

During these two and a half years out in the world she'd never gone anywhere that required a fancy dress, and after she'd hocked Harvey's diamond and her boss's pearl earrings and Cousin Lucile's cameo she tried to remember back to when she was young, if she ever imagined herself going somewhere in a satin gown. She got the train at South Station—not to sunny Florida but to windy Chicago, where one of the girls had just moved and was pleading for company, as the man this girl was slated to marry had skipped town, and the girls in the rooming house where she lived were resentful of new arrivals from the East Coast. She thought about her boss in his office, dialing up the employment agency for another bunch of girls to be sent over, so that each could wedge her behind into that worn leather chair. She thought about her boss in his office with the old walnut credenza temporarily empty, her boss waiting for the moment he could get ready to go home. This friend in Chicago had complained that the girls in her rooming house wore completely different shades of lipstick and called everything that was got at a soda fountain by different names. This, anyway, seemed much preferable to a city full of ghosts, dead or alive. For the moment, being someone you immediately sent away seemed preferable to being an apparition of loveliness, someone you might cry over but never bother to touch.

Risk Merchants

Of all the boys and men whose names I've committed to memory since kindergarten, none was really a boyfriend. With me, exaggeration for comic effect is a way of life, but this is one instance in which I'm not distorting the truth. The closest I got to a boyfriend was that lawyer with the house on the Vineyard who didn't like the way I used chopsticks and stopped calling me after seven months. Seven months was also the young age at which the beloved gerbil of my childhood passed away. I usually think of my short-lived gerbil when I think of my short-lived boyfriend, because it seems to me highly ironic that the gerbil's name was Anthony and the lawyer's name was Snickers. Although I still mourn the loss of Anthony and can remember that he loved to eat Bacos, I can't even name the town in Maryland where Snickers was from or anything on his long list of food allergies. There was also that boy in junior high school. All we did was kiss for a while in the movie theater parking lot, to see what it felt like, but he considered me his girlfriend even after he moved to Shickshinny, Pennsylvania, and sent postcards twice a year ("your boyfriend, Kevin"). Aside from these two people, however, I've never had a boyfriend in any official capacity.

It's not that I'm lonely or bemoaning my unmarried status, but who'd want this kind of relationship history? All of these scattershot, half-ass affairs have only been a smoke screen for this chronic deficiency of mine, every choice a reinforcement of the status quo, which in my case is wrongness. The guy I was most recently involved with is a shining example of this lifelong streak. For starters, he believes that the Midwest should be given back to the Indians. I don't know how he feels about the Far West, but more important, I don't know why I became involved with him. His name is Devon, which I try not to think about. I have a keen sensitivity to names because mine is Imogen Diffendorfer, though everyone has called me Peachy since I can remember being called anything. People Devon's age don't think there's anything wrong with his name, which is probably why people tend to get along with people their own age. But then Devon gets along with everyone—he goes through people like they were ibuprofen tablets. He's not mean or arrogant; quite the contrary. He's terribly nice, yet he nevertheless goes through people like they were ibuprofen tablets. Lots of openness, no strings and no baggage, just like that old Sonny and Cher song: "we'll sing in the sunshine / we'll laugh every day / we'll sing in the sunshine / then I'll be on my way."

Despite my shortcomings in the boyfriend arena, my best and oldest friend happens to be a boy, Teddy, like the peanut butter or the president chiseled onto Rushmore. Teddy is a music critic—brilliant, renowned, and steadily getting fat. You'd never know he's the guy we all wanted in college, although anyone with eyes could've detected his genetic predisposition to fatness even then. His first phase of weight gain (onset: immediately after graduation) gave him the bad-boy appeal of the young Orson Welles, the postwar Hemingway, or maybe the painter Francis Picabia. This phase of managed robustness lasted for about ten years, but then subsequent phases suddenly came piling one atop the other, so that now I'm not quite sure what kind of appeal my overweight friend has for the objective observer. Underneath all these phases, Teddy was another in that select group of guys who weren't really boyfriends but whom I nonetheless slept with, hung out with, fought and made up with. Teddy and I understand each other in the way that only people who graduate from the same college the same year are able to. Or maybe it's just me who understands Teddy and his cultivated obscurity. Like when he says, "Your problem is that you keep hooking up with those godawful pantywaist types," I know that he doesn't even know what "godawful pantywaist types" means, so I don't worry that I don't know what it means.

I have to take back what I said about not knowing why I became involved with Devon: I slept with him because he's so damned cute, acts bouncy and even younger than his youthful age, sort of like Tigger. We met at the organic bakery where he used to work; I told him, "Everyone calls me Peachy." He thought that was neat—me being called Peachy. He said he was a composer; he said he hiked the Appalachian Trail; he said he didn't have a middle name (which I thought good—damage control). When I told Teddy about Devon, I avoided the name thing as long as I could. When I could avoid it no longer, Teddy started calling him Derwood or Dagwood or Dumbo—anything that Endora from *Bewitched* called Darrin Stephens. He asked me, "Why would you want to go out with someone named after a cheese?" I tried to talk the guy up; I told Teddy that when Devon was eleven he formed a band called the Risk Merchants. Teddy told me I should've sent him home with a note to his mother pinned to his jacket. Now, in addition to calling him Derwood, Dagwood, Dumbo, and even Ranger Rick, Teddy calls Devon the Risk Merchant, and though I hate to admit it, I do too.

If there was ever any potential for Devon to evolve into a bona fide boyfriend it's pretty much been shot to hell. Since my refusal in May to be on the softball team of the organic bakery where he used to work, he's been pulling the wounded-puppy routine, which consists of snapping, "There's nothin' the matter with *me*," and sleeping with an array of Appalachian Mountain Club–type girls with names like Heather and Bree. I can't give him anything that will prolong the novelty of dating what my mother calls "a younger man." ("He's not a younger *man*," I tell her; "he's just younger.") And besides, he doesn't even consider what we've been doing "dating"; to him we've been "hanging out." Of course

I was a more-than-willing party in this initiative from the get-go, from the day he asked me, "Do ya wanna hang out tonight?" I hadn't received a hanging-out invitation since high school, and as I tried to picture myself playing Scrabble in someone's carpeted bedroom I made the casual observation, "You're wearing a windbreaker." "It's windy," he said with a shrug, and bingo!—I fell hopelessly in love with him for the entire afternoon.

For the summer Devon signed himself up to work on a farm, a sanctuary farm where yuppie schoolchildren come to learn that, yes, we still have farm animals like they had in the olden times, that these farm animals still eat and shit and produce the artisanal cheeses that their parents buy for parties at Whole Foods, and that although cleaning out the stalls would seem as despicable a job as cleaning the subway, it's cool for white kids to do this for any length of time when they get out of college. Devon doesn't particularly care for children, but like Thoreau he doesn't want to have a checkbook or a wallet, and within this falsified farm environment he doesn't need to carry a wallet. In a sense, Devon is all over the board with his life—composer, aspiring musician and/or music teacher, but he also wants to do something ecological, wants to call himself a "naturalist." "The Trail" was the defining moment of his life, and the few people whom he hasn't seemed to have gone through like they were ibuprofen tablets were alumni of this experience—people with "Trail names" like Hickory, Cirrus, and Lichen, all of them guys.

Devon had been working at the farm for two weeks when he called to invite me out for Cow Day. "Does that mean cows get in free?" I asked him. "I dunno," he said—his stock response to just about everything. "What if I bring a cow as a guest?" I suggested. "Do I get in free?" I think he thought I was hedging on the visit altogether, so he asked, "Well, do you wanna come out for Sheep Day then?" When I asked if I could bring Teddy with me for Cow Day, he was the one who seemed to be hedging. "Whatever you want, Peach," he said. "It's your call." He hadn't met Teddy and seemed in no rush to do so. You'd think that he'd be impressed by Teddy's being a brilliant music critic, but then Devon doesn't read magazines or newspapers—he just reads books by people whom he's first heard interviewed on NPR. He'll buy the book of someone whose NPR apologia strikes a chord—buy it secondhand and online, but because he doesn't have a credit card, he has to have his mother place the order. And because it's his mother using her credit card, she never bothers to ask him for the money. So basically what Devon does is get his mother to buy him books—just like he did when she was still retrieving the notes pinned to his jacket.

For the drive and in honor of Cow Day as an event, I brought the box of chocolate cows that someone had just sent me from Zurich, on account of the art cows that had been installed all over that city. I knew that sharing the box of Zurich cows with Teddy was probably not a good idea, given his genetic predisposition to fatness, but lately Teddy's been depressed—something to do with the lyric "all alone is all we are"—and I had three tiers' worth of chocolate cows to get through.

"Do you want your cow in milk or dark chocolate?" I asked Teddy as I opened the box with one hand.

"How can a cow not be milk chocolate?" he asked with a philosophical air, taking a piece from each tier.

"I dunno," I said. "But let's not think about that. Let's eat like there's no tomorrow."

"That's how I eat every day."

It was a hot afternoon to be eating chocolate in the car, but we persisted—persistence being a trait Teddy and I share, though compromised by cynicism on his end. Thus our conflicting mottos—persist and prevail (me) and persist and endure (him). Although I rarely seem to prevail in my endeavors, I've always been a reader of horoscopes and fortune-cookie ticker tapes. I generally come across as sanguine-verging-on-banal; people seem to want to talk to me. As a teenager I could always find a midrange clique within which to be subsumed. Although I like to think myself the captivating kind of "quirky" and idiosyncratic, in a slasher movie I'd be the girl who gets killed exactly halfway through.

"You know, Teddy," I said, trying to sound earnest and forthright and all of those other things I rarely am, "I've been thinking a lot lately about how I've never had a real boyfriend."

"Neither have I."

"I'm serious about this," I said.

"Oh, come off it," he said. "Have we ever stooped to 'relationship problems'—and in the car no less?"

"It's not the single-woman complaint about all the bad relationships I've had," I continued, "but that my relationships aren't even what most people consider relationships and yet I'm nonetheless compelled to keep having the same kind, which makes me feel even worse than those women who've never had any relationships, because at least they have a clean track record."

"Why are you complaining to me?" he said. "You're always going on these *dates*. I go to shows alone."

"You like going to shows alone. And after fifteen years, who wouldn't?"

"It'd be nice to bring a *date* with me once in a while. She could give me cute little blow jobs during the opening acts."

"Why are we talking about you, Teddy? Why does this always happen? Why are we talking about *your* love life?"

"My *love life*?" he said. "What the hell's got into you?"

"At least you had Robin," I said. I knew I wasn't supposed to mention Robin, especially now that Teddy was self-diagnosed as depressed, but I was pissed that he wasn't even letting me start to talk about myself.

"I told you never to talk about Robin," he snapped, and I could tell he was particularly irked that I mentioned her name so soon after the word *blow job*. Then he decreed that there was to be no "Jan Brady wingeing" until we hit the farm. This is how it was with Teddy—your problems were Jan Brady wingeing, whereas his were of Grand Guignol dimensions.

The farm had a massive parking lot filled with hunter-green

Subaru wagons—Legacy, Legacy, Legacy, Legacy, like it was senior hat day or something. We found Devon in a barn surrounded by a hoard of kids. He was giving out little plastic cows to stick to the dashboards of their parents' Legacies.

"Devon hiked the Appalachian Trail," I said to Teddy as an introduction.

"Really?" Teddy said, though he knew this fact quite well. "I saw *Deliverance*."

Already it was starting—Teddy's nasty habit of insouciant derision. Fortunately for my position as mediator, Devon had no time to kavetch with us because of his farm duties. He kissed me on the cheek when I gave him the last three chocolate cows, and for some reason this embarrassed me in front of Teddy, although Teddy hadn't even noticed. And then there were larger and larger swarms of children around Devon wanting their free merchandise, so Teddy and I got to roam the property as unchaperoned greenhorns.

That this was your classic Gen Y hippie land was beyond contestation. One of the twenty-something farmworkers we encountered at the first milking station was wearing a T-shirt that said "Raw milk cheese doesn't kill people, people kill people." We soon learned that the guy was a member of the Slow Food Movement—"fighting against the bland, the bad, and the boring," he told us. Apparently, this is an international movement with more than sixty thousand members in dozens of countries. The guy with the T-shirt was involved in the Ark of Taste campaign, which, as he explained it, "seeks to draw attention to regional and local foods that are endangered by a globalizing economic world of mass production." Some girl within earshot immediately shared with us the long and drawn-out story of how she became a member of the Voluntary Simplicity Movement, "launched in 1981." She said "1981" in a way that suggested that anything that came before was antediluvian. It went on like that all through our barnyard encounters with cows and pigs and sheep and chickens and yuppie schoolchildren having hissy fits about being forbidden to torture certain animals by pulling at their ears and tails. One farmworker guide is a member of the blah-blah-blah, another a member of the blah-blah-blah. After a while Teddy began introducing himself with "I'm a member of the Pee-pee in Public Pools Movement."

On the drive home that day we had to stop at Osco Drugs for a bag of Biggy Bee's mesquite barbecue potato chips, as an antidote to the Ark of Taste campaign. Eating the chips, Teddy seemed even more depressed than he was before we hit the farm. "He's too young for you," he said like a brooding child.

"That's a moot point," I said, "considering that we're not even officially hanging out anymore."

"Yeah, well just don't take up with any of his fellow Farmke-teers," he warned me. Then he gave me that knowing look that indicates a mental ellipses followed by the unuttered exclamation "Kids these days!" Teddy and I do a lot of talking about "Kids these days!" because his profession and my predilection for the likes of his profession put us in venues where kids-these-days tend to congregate. According to Teddy, the problem with today's young people is that nobody understands where he belongs. This is what most pop songs are about; they're not about love, because love is cheap and easy. Today's pop songs are intended for young people who know too many people — *there's this guy . . . there's this girl.* The girls and guys can relate to each other mighty fine precisely because they all don't know where they belong. They're waiting in the wings for their cues, waiting to be told when it's time to grow up — just like they waited for the teacher direct-ing the third-grade production of *Willy Wonka and the Choco-late Factory* to signal the arrival of No. 11 Oompa Loompa. It's not like when we came out of college. Not only were college graduates expected to look for jobs then, but they also had real names then — their fathers' names, their grandmothers' names. Nowadays people come out of college as nonaccidental tourists, breezing through the Appalachian Trail and organic bakeries, yuppie farms and summerlong nonviolent conflict resolution consortiums; nowadays people are named after cheeses or car parts—or the plantations in Taylor Caldwell novels.

"Who knows who I'll take up with next?" I told Teddy, disenchanted with the whole thing—not the process of entering into relationships but the one in which you attempt to talk about yours to someone who cares. "This is why I wanted to talk to you about my boyfriend problem, Teddy—my problem with being fatally attracted to godawful pantywaist types. I think maybe I don't want any relationship to work. I think there's something wrong with me."

"I need to learn how to be outdoors," he said with a great sigh. Of course I immediately wanted to be pissed at him again for being such a terrible friend, but I was too exhausted from having seen the future and realizing that the future is ten-year-olds with Palm Pilots.

"What's there to learn?" I said with resignation. "You just remove yourself from the indoors and then exist like plankton or fungi. There's not too much skill involved."

"I have problems with open spaces," he said, "nature, wild animals."

"Cows aren't wild."

"To me they are. Everything's wild compared to me."

I looked at his chubby cheeks that were flushed from the heat, as if he'd planned that they do so to match his red ears, which also seemed chubby to me. I reminded myself of how much Teddy's been through in the past few years—he had to have back surgery when his legs collapsed, and during this operation the surgeon nicked a valve to his heart, so he had to have six blood transfusions. I reminded myself that Robin dumped him when he really started to gain weight, right after his brush with death and his months-long convalescence (ironically, the time when most people tend to lose weight), and that life was shitty for him even though he was a celebrity within the magazine world, with kids in Iowa and Georgia creating Web sites of his aphorisms and synopses of his twenty-five-hundred-word bitch-fests.

After Cow Day, things happened pretty fast. Devon called to say that he'd been wanting to drive up to Acadia for a camping weekend and was wondering if I'd like to drive him given that his truck had just failed to pass inspection. I took this to be an invitation to go camping with him and not just act as his chauffeur, but maybe I was being presumptuous. In any case, when I mentioned this to Teddy, he said, utterly uncharacteristically, "I want to come, too."

"You've got to be kidding."

"Why would I be kidding?"

"This would involve being outside, Teddy—on dirt, the ground, with bugs."

"Don't you ever listen to anything I say?" he asked, irritated—maybe theatrically and maybe not; I couldn't tell the difference with him anymore. "I need to learn how to be outdoors. I told you that when we went to see the cows."

"With the Risk Merchant?" I asked, legitimately shocked. "You'd go camping with the Risk Merchant?"

"And you," he said. "The Risk Merchant and you. I'd go if those were the odds, because I know you're gonna end up playing on my team."

I knew that driving to Acadia with these two people would be a mistake, but most Americans make these kinds of mistakes by the minute. The pretext for the excursion was to teach Teddy how to be outdoors. The subtext was for me to forget about my life and my boyfriend problem while learning to identify a wide variety of trees. And of course Devon needed a ride.

Surprisingly, things started out smoothly on the drive because Devon sat in the back and basically ignored Teddy's nonstop ranting. It was agreed that Teddy would get the front on the ride up, Devon on the way back. I wanted to joke "age before beauty," but I felt that this would certainly enhance Teddy's depression. When we hit the Down-Easterly zone, however, there was a lull in Teddy's ranting, so Devon said something about how many times he's read *The Maine Woods*.

"Here's my take on Thoreau," Teddy bellowed, shifting his butt in the seat as if preparing to pass gas. "One, he was a fag; two, he was uglier than sin; three, he made his sister order him cookies from Boston. And that's a fact, Jack. If he were alive today he'd be an interior decorator."

"Interior *designer*," I said, though I had no idea why I was pushing semantics.

"What?" Teddy said, squinting as he moved the visor down and then up again.

"They call themselves interior *designers*—people who like to decorate rooms with obelisks and orbs."

"Ha!" Teddy yelled. "Sex toys! They're all fags."

"Thoreau wasn't gay," Devon declared sternly.

"How do you know?" Teddy asked. He was mirthful but in full attack mode. "How do you know for a fact that Thoreau didn't decorate his cabin with obelisks and orbs?"

"I'll bet he decorated it with pine cones," I suggested, attempting to inject some levity into this topic I planned to deep-six posthaste. "He probably glued them into shapes. For Christmas I'll bet he made a nativity scene out of pine cones."

"Just like Whitman," Teddy continued, completely unreceptive to my proffered tangent, "our first national Male Nurse."

"Really?" I said. "I thought that was Gertrude Stein."

"Whitman, Thoreau, Emerson," Teddy said in perfect Dan Rather crescendo, "all fags."

"Thoreau wasn't a fag," Devon shouted, "OK?"

Teddy was already engaged in another strand of Thoreau-bashing when I felt up to my ears in homophobia. "Shut up about Thoreau, Teddy!" I yelled. "I don't see why I'm being forced to witness this staged reading of *Midnight Cowboy*."

"Midnight what?" Devon asked.

"She's making an allusion to the golden age of contemporary American cinema, Derwood," Teddy said with a snigger. "Start taking notes."

"Why are you being so belligerent toward me?" Devon asked.

His composure under the circumstances I found highly admirable, and for a moment I felt proud to have hung out with him for as long as I did.

"SAT word!" Teddy yelled. "Somebody give this man a cigar!"

"Come on," Devon persisted, "tell me."

Teddy turned around to look at Devon. "Because you've got a bull's-eye painted on your forehead, my friend."

"You've got a lot of hostility to deal with, *my friend.*"

"Why, thank you very much, Master Freud," Teddy snapped. "Now can I have some of your Zoloft?"

"You work out hostility by getting off your ass and doing things—ride a bike, take a hike."

"Did you hear that?" Teddy asked me, feigning disbelief. "He told me to take a hike—me, a convalescent!"

"C'mon, Teddy," I said, "that was two years ago. All your doctors told you to exercise. What about that chiropractor you dissed? He even gave you his old set of golf clubs."

"He's a fucking doctor! Golf's a theological issue with him."

"Even so, you're a classic Type A lard-ass personality heading for a quadruple bypass. And you're very hostile."

"We're not in Cambridge anymore, Dorothy. You're not allowed to say *hostile* in these here he-man states."

"OK then you're a mean motherfucker."

There was a pause, which made me apprehensive, because pauses rarely happen with Teddy. "I'm a depressed motherfucker is what I am," he said. "Maybe I do need his Zoloft."

"Everybody's on antidepressants," Devon declared loudly; his bitter tone reminded me that he was the one who brought to my attention the Web site www.antipsychiatry.org—this and www.roadrage.com. "It's not helping anything."

"Not everybody's on antidepressants," I argued. Although I'd never been in therapy, I knew quite well that I only persisted with the option of prevailing under the assumption that most of these drugs would be available over the counter by the time I'd need to be popping them like Tic-Tacs.

"A lot of people are then," he insisted.

"There are thirty million Americans on antidepressants," I said, "and most of them probably need them." I recognized Devon's cynical tone as the one he uses when preparing to segue into Indian territory, and I wanted to head him off at the pass.

"Yeah, well, what kind of country is that?" he asked. I could feel his irritation—that he was sensing what I was sensing—so I decided to change the subject to trees. Devon had been feeding me directions onto these back roads so that I would see more trees that he could identify for me, though we had not yet achieved the bucolic atmosphere for this to happen. "Here's something to ponder," I said. "Trees represent freedom; they stay pure and absolute forever; they symbolize unconditional love. Every tree is the same, hence a tree cannot disappoint you. *Discuss.*"

The minute I decided on trees, however, I feared that Devon would start talking about The Trail, because whenever he did he'd end up confessing to how he felt a genuine connection with the Unabomber.

"On second thought," I said, "don't discuss." And with this I hiked the volume on the CD I was playing.

"I want to discuss," Teddy insisted, jabbing his fat finger at the button to turn the volume down again. He'd been turning off the CD player or skipping tracks since the start of the trip, and I didn't know why I kept letting him do this. "OK, so everything I know about trees I learned from watching the weekly deforestation on the opening credits of *Here Come the Brides.*"

"What is it with you and seventies kitsch?" I yelled. "It's really lame, and it's really bugging me."

Just then we encountered a long line of cyclists—Hell's Angels would be an Altamont overstatement; this outfit consisted of fat guys blubbering along on machines as wide as side-by-side refrigerator-freezers.

"Whoooa, partners!" said Teddy. "Looks like we got us a convoy."

"Can't you get your brain out the seventies for even a minute?" I yelled, irritated by the bikers and Teddy in equal measure.

"What are they doing up here?" Devon said. "They should be in Laconia."

"Who comes to fucking Maine in July anyway?" Teddy snapped.

"Stupid people and flies," I said, using all my concentration to avoid being run off the road.

Teddy sighed dejectedly and reached over to turn off the music altogether.

"Stop doing that," I said, slapping his hand.

"Too bad this isn't Sunday," Devon said. "We could listen to *This American Life*."

"Why the hell would I want to hear that guy always swallowing his spit?" Teddy snarled.

"OK," I said, ejecting the CD, "we'll listen to Radio Free Acadia."

"What the hell's that?" Teddy asked.

"The local pirate radio station," I said, trying to regain some degree of equanimity. "I read about it in *Let's Go*."

"*Let's Go?*" he said with a contemptuous laugh. "What are you trying to do — *bridge the gap?*"

"Oh, just cut it out, Teddy," I said, my voice now limp with more of that resignation.

Teddy seemed to sense my resignation like it was barometric pressure (or lack thereof), which led him to really light into Devon. "Speaking of the Gap," he said turning to the backseat, "I hear that members of your generation feel angry, pathetic, and alone."

"Fuck you," Devon said.

"Let's just stop this," I said.

"Fuck you and your 'generation' hang-up," Devon said, much louder.

"We trick-or-treated for Unicef," Teddy replied, apropos of nothing. "It was all about starving children in Africa then."

"Could we stop this?" I said. "Could we all grow up?"

"Can't we all just get along?" Teddy mocked.

"Fuck you!" I yelled.

"I *was* trying to get along with the Risk Merchant here," Teddy said.

After an agonizing pause, Devon asked me, obviously hurt, "What do you do, report to him on everything, every little thing people tell you about themselves? What is he, your Stasi? That's fucking great, Peachy."

"I'm sorry," I said, which was the truth. I was sorry about Teddy's big mouth, and I was sorry that Devon referred to Teddy as being my Stasi, because what he meant was that I was Teddy's Stasi, if this in fact were even true. I was sorry about my dishonesty, my lack of fidelity to my so-called friends, and I was sorry that we had to listen to this kid on Radio Free Acadia: he sounded like one of Devon's farm friends or else a budding ecoterrorist, someone whose mother let him charge his terrorist matériel on her Visa—cartons of Silk Chai and pipe-bombs by the six-pack.

"You know something," Devon declared with uncharacteristic profundity, "you're afraid." I glanced at the rearview mirror to see his eyes moving from the back of Teddy's head to the back of mine, like he was identifying assailants in a police lineup.

"OK, so now *I'm* the one who's afraid?" I yelled, turning off the radio. I was now quite hostile in all directions. Even though Teddy was my best friend, I didn't want to be placed in the same category as him—even a category as all-encompassing as "fear."

All through this bickering the car kept being surrounded by swarms of bikers, or else we passed groups of them on the side of the road. The last roadside contingent contained a gaggle of chicks in lacy and gauzy halter tops, and despite the harsh words just uttered, Teddy and Devon gleefully hollered in unison for me to "Slow down!" None of the girls was a beauty, not by a long shot, although collectively they seemed happy to be ogled by the fat lounge lizard and the buzz-topped Tigger riding in my car. The girls waved and laughed; a lot of them gave us the finger; most of them looked prematurely aged on closer inspection. They seemed to me fearless, the kind of girls you'd worry about beating you up when you were in seventh grade, although I doubt that any of these girls would waste her time beating up people like me. They were too busy jumping on the backs of bikes and chewing off their ice-blue nail polish.

Devon was probably right about my being afraid. Things do scare me. Teddy scares me with his multitasking brain—the number of CDs he owns, all the movies he's seen, his vast library, his DVD collection, and now food—he was eating like he was also collecting food. And Devon scares me with all the people he knows, with his unwavering enthusiasm for enlarging his social circle, for exploiting Emerson's open field of possibility in each and every human he encounters. My friends in their twenties who think oral sex is a good way to break the ice on a first date—these girls who inhale technology, who've seen every teen movie made since 1979 at least twice, who pride themselves on being able to spend whole days in video arcades, knowing which evil robots to beat; they scare me, too. Where do they find the mental capacity? How can they accommodate all this? How do they come up with these extra hours in any given day? It's like when I go to the newsstand and encounter whole sections of one-word lifestyle magazines: I'm paralyzed by fear.

Suddenly I had to slam on the brakes because one of the biker chicks had strayed into our path. Actually, she wasn't astray; she was standing in the middle of the road, waving her arms like she constituted a police barricade. When the car screeched to a halt, she let her arms drop; then they caught her as she fell forward toward the hood of my car. "Ha ha!" she laughed, both palms securely fastened to the vehicle. From the car you could see everything remotely related to her cleavage, maybe even the light on the other side. In my mind I heard Teddy shout, "What is this, a fucking Drew Barrymore picture?" But he didn't say anything besides "Holy shit!" when I slammed on the brakes.

She looked like the kind of girl who was always carrying on in a public place—either fighting or making out with her boyfriend. She looked young, maybe even seventeen, but she had that wizened smoker quality that can mess up the whole youth package. Her long, stringy hair was several shades of blond and at least two of tangerine.

"I need a lift to a bus stop in the direction I'm going," she said, already opening the back door, getting in next to Devon. "That OK with you folks?"

"Sure," I said, staring at her in the rearview mirror. I could see that she had some bad acne that she didn't bother concealing like most girls do—lots of eyeliner though, and purple mascara. Not "pretty" and barely "cute," but her body was round and fleshy and busting out of everything, as was the style. If anything constituted a *pièce de résistance* it was her belly—gelatinous rolls hanging over her low-rise jeans. I was disconcerted by the girl in her entirety but especially by her feet. She was wearing different sandals, each a different caliber platform, and because she limped when she walked, I surmised that one leg must be shorter.

"OK, so let's rock here!" she said, writhing her torso forward like a trained seal hankering for a fish, or a child who'd been buckled into the back seat of her parents' Legacy and was desperate to make the vehicle go already.

I turned the key in the ignition, unnerved by having brought the car to a screeching halt but also by the Darwinian qualities of my new passenger. I mean, how could a biker chick have uneven legs? This seemed to me an incredible survival instinct—quite on par with growing another kind of finch beak.

"I'm sorry," she began, digging into her macramé shoulder bag, "but I was with Randy Nyes? I thought he was cool. All my cousins—they used to go with him—all over, to Arizona and shit like that. But then that bastard slapped me. OK, so nobody hits me. You hit me and I'm gone—I'm, like, so bloody-fuckin'-your-mother's-ass yesterday. Lucky I don't come back and blow your goddamned brains out."

I could see in the rearview mirror that she was still feeling for something inside her bag, and it reminded me of a cat frantically shoving its paw under the door the minute you closed yourself in the bathroom.

"Can I smoke in here?" the girl asked after placing a cigarette between her lips.

"Not really," I said, hiking up my shoulders like a squeamish ten-year-old.

"Yah!" she shouted, spitting out the cigarette and catching it in her bag. "Guess I'll need to chew me some gum then." She recommenced with the rummaging.

Being so preoccupied with this backseat view, I had to swerve to avoid hitting a guy on a tractor. This time there was no "Holy shit!" from Teddy, though Devon did venture a tepid "Watch it, Peachy!"

"Your name's Peachy?" the girl shrieked, bouncing on the seat. "Holy fuckin' no shit! So's mine! Like, is yours Peachy for real?"

"My real name's Imogen," I said, still sounding like that squeamish ten-year-old.

"That's not a name!" she hollered. "Christ, that blows. Peachy's a lot better, let me tell ya."

"I think so," I said. I had been afraid of this girl, I admit, but now I was trying to think outside the car that constituted my demographic box. Teddy and Devon were so quiet that their silence, rather than the presence of a second Peachy, is what should've scared me. I suppose they were afraid as well, though I couldn't conjecture what they feared more—Peachy and whatever else was in her bag or Randy Nyes and his ilk coming after us.

"So what's your real name?" I asked her.

"I just told ya: it's Peachy. Peachy's what's on my birth certificate.

My fuckin' mother named me, the moron bitch. Like, couldn't she think up a real name, like Samantha or something?"

I glanced at Teddy, expecting him to comment on "Samantha" as a theoretical construct, but his eyes were riveted to the road ahead. I even flashed him that comic expression that says *I'm dyin' here—help me out!* But he was refusing to acknowledge mine or anyone's presence, just like the guy in that old rap song who's "tryin' not to hear that, see?"

"No more boyfriends for me!" Peachy exclaimed. "I've had a fuckin' heavy-lay boyfriend since I was nine, and I'm tired of the whole goddamned thing. I need a breather big time. I need to go to fuckin' Arizona or something. I need space and shit."

"I often feel that way, too," I said and immediately felt like some stupid talk-show moderator.

"Ya?" she asked, kicking my seat. "So who's your boyfriend here, bitch?"

"I don't have a boyfriend," I said with a laugh.

"Whoo-hoo!" she yelled, pinching her Lycra tank right above her left nipple, her little-girl exaggeration almost sweet. "Two-for-one day for me!"

"You've changed your mind about the boyfriends already?" I asked.

"Noooo!" she crowed, and from the sound of this exclamation I decided that she was probably something like seventeen and a half.

I had no idea where I was driving because Devon had stopped feeding me directions. Teddy just sat there like a zombie or someone grappling with sudden amnesia. "Amnesia" is the word that sprang to mind because when Teddy didn't want to answer a question he'd feign memory loss and declare, "I am Elmer J. Fudd, millionaire; I own a mansion and a yacht."

"Christ, I can't believe Randy Nyes smacked me!" Peachy yelled. "Christ!" She punched the back of my seat, and for some reason it was Teddy who bolted upright. I'd never seen him remain silent through this many subject areas—at least not when he wasn't unconscious in a hospital bed. "Man!" Peachy shouted, and I swore I could feel her voice on the back of my neck. "I wish my dad was here."

"He has a cell phone," I said, tilting my head toward Teddy. "Do you want to call him?"

"Won't help," she said. "He's in prison."

"That's too bad," I said.

"My dad—man oh man!" she hollered, slapping the back of my seat again. "He's so goddamned smart it's scary. He scares ya he knows so much. People'll remember all kinds of things he says. He's always sayin', 'If ya go huntin' with a coon hound, don't be surprised to find yourself shootin' at coons.' Stuff like that. He's fuckin' brilliant."

"Is he getting out soon?" I asked.

"Nah," she said, waving her hand in front of her face. "He'll be in there forever. He killed my mom. She deserved it though." She was looking out the window when I caught her in the mirror; I guess you'd have to at this kind of juncture. "Shot her on her forty-second birthday. Can ya beat that? Best thing that ever happened to me," she added, "let me tell ya."

"I'm sorry," I said.

"Don't be," she said. "Sorry people always look like shit to me."

She seemed smart in a way I could not define. Smart and also very familiar—familiar in the long-ago Proustian sense. I could remember a girl from my junior high school (in the seventies, Teddy's seventies) who looked just like her—a vo-tech type I wouldn't be caught dead talking to, always smoking behind the bleachers with her male cohorts, maybe some girls with pregnant bellies popping out from their long dirty army jackets. Peachy was a dead ringer for this girl—probably right down to the number of inches by which her flared jeans fell below sole-level, scuffing the ground like a pair of minesweepers. Outwardly she was a pastiche of everything that was instantly popular, and yet there was this foundation, this historical depth.

Ahead on the left I spied something that looked to be a gas station but was essentially a place for some guy to take apart the engines of three or four junk cars. "I'll ask this guy about a bus terminal," I said, pulling over.

The guy taking apart the cars was about thirty-five, tan, oil-smeared, and fat, though not as fat as Teddy. He told us it was only five or so miles to the Trailways terminal. We had to wait for Peachy to go through what I took to be an autoreflexive flirtation routine, the rules of which seemed to be as follows: the more cretinous the specimen, the greater the effort. Half of her body was still out the window as I inched the car away. "I'd kiss ya, but I got gum" were her parting words.

When we pulled into the Trailways lot, Peachy turned to stare at Devon. "You're so hot," she said, grabbing his arm and stroking it. "Wanna come with me to Providence? We can stay with my sister. She's got pit bulls and waterbeds."

Devon blushed and pulled his chin down to his chest, like it was some instinctual response to a predator. "Thanks, but I don't think so."

"Christ!" she said, shaking Devon's arm. Then she rolled her eyes toward the roof of the car in mock-simpleton fashion: *"No, thank you, Mrs. Cleaver — no fucking before my homework's done."* She thought for a moment, making an elaborate gesture of relinquishing Devon's arm. "You're freakin' out about me, aren't ya?" she said with a gravely-throat snigger. "You're freakin' out 'cause of my dad killing my mom, right? You're havin' all these Bad Thoughts — boom boom, out go the lights. All of ya are freakin' out right now thinkin' I'm this trailer-trash baby."

Of course we were silent. "Probably," I finally said with a pathetic laugh.

"Well don't worry about me," she declared. "You don't know the size of it, you know that? You think you know, but you don't.

My dad's in a country club prison, OK? Christ, he's got a personal trainer! He's a doctor—was the head of a fucking cardiac unit."

She got out of the car and slammed the door. "You know," she said, giving the vehicle a lax kick with either the higher or lower platform sandal, "it just blows my mind how you people drive around in your little wet-nap worlds." Then she paused—reflectively I want to say, but I couldn't tell for sure. She was still idly kicking her sandal against the car. "You'd think my dad might've fixed up my leg," she said, "wouldn't ya think that?" She stared at her feet, waiting for someone to say something.

"He'd have to be an orthopedic surgeon, wouldn't he?" I ventured.

"Duh!" she shouted. "You're fuckin' right, you college-educated bitch!" Then she leaned down to my eye level to add, "I meant that in a good way, honey—*smooch, smooch.*" She puckered her lips toward Devon and was off. I opened Teddy's Arctic Zone bag and grabbed some ridiculous variety of Fresh Samantha. "Here, Peachy," I hollered after her, holding the bottle out the window. "No shit!" she said, returning to swipe the juice out of my hand. "Wait!" I yelled grabbing my bag, getting out some money. "For the bus ticket," I said, sounding like my mother. "Aw!" she said, snatching the bills, "you're such a peach!" We watched her limp off, past the sign that said "To Concourse." We watched as she turned and shouted, "Pit bulls and waterbeds! Your fuckin' loss!" For the fifteen minutes we sat there in silence I wondered if Peachy's father really was a cardiologist, and if so, why didn't he fix up her leg before he went to jail, the bastard? I wondered if he really killed her mother on her birthday, and if her mother really was a moron bitch. When a bus finally approached we watched Peachy and three other people get on. I've always made fun of the New Agers yapping about an "ageless soul," but as I watched Peachy disappear into the bus and the bus trundle away I was certain that she was among the chosen—this ageless hip-hugger soul, drifting amid the decades like the bouncing ball in those old cartoons.

"And the concourse is a Boreal shame," Devon finally muttered. I only made out what he said because I knew the song from which that lyric came. It's why we — all of us "you people" whom Peachy had so effectively fingered — get along; we've memorized the same scripts, like good little Unicef trick-or-treaters, like good little Oompa Loompas.

"Stop being fucking esoteric," Teddy said. His voice sounded odd to me, like the world sounds odd when you remove your headphones after an hour or so of incremental hikes in the bass and the volume.

"I guess nobody needs to teach her how to be outdoors," Devon continued, obviously on a pensive streak.

I glanced at him in the rearview mirror. He appeared as young as ever, but suddenly youth looked very wise to me — wise in direct proportion to my ignorance. It further disconcerted and unnerved me to think that I could be Peachy's mother, even without the qualifier "if this were Appalachia."

As I pulled out of the lot, I forgot what direction I was supposed to be heading. I forgot why we were here, why I thought there would be some sort of amusement in store for me in Acadia. Amid this quandary, nothing seemed funny to me — the plastic cow on the dashboard, my relationship problems. Why was everything always so funny to me? I seem to joke about everything that scares me, and I have already determined that it's everything that scares me. I felt I was living out one of those short didactic films you'd get in a South American convent school: Peachy the Fearful meets Peachy the Fearless. In a propaganda film I might come out as the model to emulate (I own a late-model car after all); in life, however, I don't think anyone would choose to be my kind of Peachy.

The rain that came from nowhere hit the car with a smack, like a bucket of water on *Laugh-In,* although with these manic wipers the precipitation was squeegeed away before I realized I couldn't see worth shit. Teddy turned on the Radio Free Acadia station; it was the Carter family. At least no one could object to the music. "Aw, Peeeeeachy," he cooed after a bit, like this was the part where we all hugged and went for a Schlitz Light.

"Stop saying my name like that," I snapped, but what I really meant was "stop saying that name." *That name belongs to Peachy with the limp,* I thought; *I'm not allowed to use it anymore.* Not that I wanted anyone to start calling me Imogen, the name of my grandmother's infant sister who died in the 1918 influenza epidemic. Funny how it never occurred to me that kids-these-days don't name themselves. It's their parents who named them. I seemed to have overlooked this salient fact—Teddy, too. I glanced over at him. *And Teddy, too!* my mind mocked. I kept thinking his name, thinking it over and over with each scrape of wiper. Teddy seemed to me the worst kind of coward, a fat coward. Fat cowards had to be the worst kind. How could he have said nothing during that whole encounter? From Devon I expected fear—crude, messy, marginal people didn't seem to gel with his Emersonian worldview. From Teddy, however, I expected a lot more—something like compassion, I guess.

I didn't know why I'd always thought so highly of Teddy. He was really a bastard. He'd party with the upstairs neighbors, and then after he'd gone home to crash and was woken by the noise, he'd call the cops on them. I knew every last thing he detested—post-punk/garage bands who sang songs about elevated trains and depressed waitresses, the phrase "infectious pop music," waiters who lectured him about how not to cook pork. He'd have big, indulgent, drama-king fights with Robin and then come over to my apartment with his bottle of Tanqueray. A few hours later when Robin showed up to pound on the door, he'd say, "Let the bitch beat her drums." The last time one of their fights dragged out into my apartment Robin was higher than a kite, and the pounding went on for well over an hour. "Tell him to get his fat ass out here," she yelled, "or I'll eat his firstborn . . . twice!" It was so ugly, and I was so complicit—smack dab in the middle, drunk on Teddy's gin.

"Stop the car!" Devon shouted, jolting me from this mental character assassination. "I think that's an American chestnut."

"You can't see anything out there, idiot," Teddy snapped. "You want to get us killed?"

"I see a tree," Devon persisted.

I pulled over and backed up; Devon had the door open even before the car stopped.

"You guard the food," I told Teddy as I got out. I didn't even look at him, and I didn't even flinch when pelted by the rain. I followed Devon as he waded into a wet thicket of thigh-high weeds and grasses. The sensation was at once terribly unpleasant but also somewhat pleasant; it reminded me of part of a song that went "oh, this mess we're in."

"Know what?" Devon said. "That's not an American chestnut."

"Let's pretend it is," I said.

We stood there getting drenched, like it was the cool thing to do, like all of the popular kids were getting drenched these days. At least he was wearing his Gore-Tex windbreaker. Everything he owned seemed to be Trademark Gore-Tex—and had a hood.

"How can you stand him?" he asked, chewing on one of his hood strings. "He's such a miserable person. Smart, yeah, but what a way to live."

I looked skyward in one of those asinine "Me so loco" gestures. The storm clouds were huge and black. "Where on earth did this sky come from?" I said.

He looked up from under his hood and sang, "All of my money skies, my last July." I felt a sharp jab to my heart—it was the reminder of how damned cute he was, the memory of him saying "It's windy" and putting this whole scattershot, half-assed affair into motion. He was always singing. Here Teddy was the music critic, and he'd never sing out loud in someone else's presence. He wouldn't be caught dead singing, whereas Devon here, whereas the Risk Merchant to my left, was spontaneously singing in the rain. After the recent sudden onset of nothing seeming funny to me, this struck me as hilarious—Devon singing in the rain, this guy I had associated with the lyrics "we'll sing in the sunshine / then I'll be on my way."

"What was that you said about trees?" he asked.

"Trees represent freedom; they stay pure and absolute forever; they symbolize unconditional love. Every tree is the same, hence a tree cannot disappoint you."

"True," he said, "but a tree can't give you a hard-on either."

In my mind I could hear Teddy's reply: "No, that would be a bush, my friend," and the thought of how thoroughly Teddy had occupied my brain made me feel even sorrier about my dishonesty, my lack of fidelity to people like Devon, and I wondered if standing out here with Devon meant that I was now playing on his team—or if this were even possible. Anyone with eyes could see that I really wasn't much different from Devon, that I, too, went through people like they were ibuprofen tablets. *There's this guy . . . there's this girl.* Not too long ago I was at the Harvard Square Starbucks and saw a guy I slept with a few times some years back. I asked how he was doing; "Still just hanging around," he said. When I paid for my iced mocha he said he came to this Starbucks every day to claim the mistake beverages that the counter people would call out for takers. *Clever or pathetic?* I wondered at the time, but now I didn't feel much different from him in the way I entered into relationships. Hanging around Starbucks waiting for the five-word rejects—it couldn't possibly get any simpler.

Devon asked if I wanted him to drive, and I said that would be OK even though I was conscious of the risk. It seemed that the safest thing for him, Teddy, and me to do would be to go our separate ways at this random juncture, each of us heading off in a different direction, lighting out for the territories in search of pit bulls and waterbeds and chestnut trees. Off to Arizona and shit. The risky thing, by contrast, would be for us to drive to Acadia and try to teach Teddy how to be outdoors. The risky thing would be to let Teddy have the front seat again on the drive home, even though it was promised to Devon. The risky thing would be to forgive Teddy for being a bitch today and every day for the past ten years and try to get him to be nice to Devon. Hop back on the horse, jump back into the bull ring, run straight back into the lion's den—and do it with a song in your heart if not on your lips: *Look out, here I come again, and I'm bringing my friends.* The risky thing would not be fun or fast or easy, and there was always the danger that you'd die of irritation or exasperation or a surfeit of seventies kitsch or, worse, that you or someone you love might actually find out where he belongs.

The Empire of Light

He was reading in the Wegner chair that the owners had placed to the left of the purple fox painting when she realized the solution to her problem about him. He hadn't moved from the chair for hours, since midafternoon, so absorbed in his book that he probably couldn't tell you what kind of fox he and the chair were next to. He was usually absorbed in whatever he was doing, but she had never seen him with this much idle time available at a single stretch. She'd walked back and forth through the room so many times during the day that she came to perceive him, the chair, the painting, the rug, and the floor lamp as an organic still life — *Man with Fox and Grapes* perhaps, though the grapes part you'd have to imagine.

She herself was anything but still — "ants in your pants" would've been her mother's prognosis. Her initial plan for the day was to become so absorbed in doing nothing that hours passed like minutes. But Real Time, even out here in the sticks, had a way of busting up the party. She wound up being antsy in the state-of-the-art kitchen, intermittently looking into drawers and cupboards and pushing the ON buttons of various inbuilt appliances to see what sort of sounds they made. The quiet was hard to get used to, but perhaps it was the afternoon's interminable silence that suggested to her a monastic retreat, thus providing the opportunity to disentangle thoughts, to finally see, after so much anguished deliberation, that he was as separate from her as was this house belonging to strangers, and that he would always be as separate from her as he was right now.

Maybe resolving this problem had been her subconscious plan all along. Maybe this was the reason they came here. Maybe there really were no accidents (though their being here was the unintended outcome of several layers of people — tenuous connections to say the least — having double-booked and then canceling plans). Two years she'd been with him, and last month they'd decided to get married, so she figured they were likely to be together for two more years at least. He had become a problem for her the moment she began to feel for him — which was probably the moment she met him — and now that the problem was solved, she wondered how she was supposed to feel about him forever, or at least for the next two years.

The house's owners had many things besides art, but their art is what gave you an Oklahoma welcome here in the heart of the heart of Vermont — the right ventricle to be precise. The house itself was modest in relation to its owners' net worth, though the pictures suggested bigness — big money and even bigger mistakes. These people had a penchant for animal imagery — monotonous equestrian prints; one mammoth, grimy oil painting of a mountain lion ripping into the flesh of a stag; a few water-stained Audubons; something by a Thomas Cole pretender featuring microscopic cows lolling near a waterfall; a sunny Santa Barbara-esque impressionistic mishmash of herons; and of course the self-consciously incongruous showpiece consisting of one purple fox, all twelve or so feet of him, just sitting there with his bulging orange eyes and green speckled snout, fanning out an enormous tail that was an even deeper shade of purple. When she began this house-sitting vacation and was confronted with all the animal art, she wondered if she'd have animals in her dreams, because this had happened to her before — although before it was the absence of certain animals that made animals what her dreams were about. The night they decided to get married she dreamt of a carousel with no horses (no wonder all the children were disappointed!). This horseless carousel continued for a couple of weeks, transmogrifying according to the day's events. First her sister sent them an engagement card with a woman, a rooster, and the salutation "I hope all your dreams come true." Then one of his colleagues sent them a case of bad wine, the label depicting George slaying the dragon. Consequently, the carousel contained intermittent roosters and dragons as stand-ins for the missing horses.

She could be just like him, she supposed; she could fetch a book and sit in the companion Wegner chair that the owners had placed to the right of the purple fox painting—settle into the wood and rush even though these were not the kinds of chairs meant for hours of occupancy. She could turn on the Castiglioni reading lamp because it was approaching dusk; she could be quiet next to him with her book and, if successful, give genesis to yet another still life—*Domestic Bliss with Grapes* (she'd have to have some grapes). Alternatively, she could begin making an elaborate dinner in the state-of-the-art kitchen, or she could go outside. Going outside seemed the better option, because earlier she'd had the inkling that this might well be the loveliest night of the year, like the song they used to play at roller-skating rinks: "when you are in love, it's the loveliest night of the year." Her outside agenda might consist of wandering around the property and making a mental inventory of the owners' flowers; this seemed a worthwhile enterprise since they'd hired artisan landscapers, had a Bucks County blacksmith do the front gate, put a lot of feng shui thought into the pond area.

Outside with the flowers, however, all she could think about was him. He was a composed individual—cool as a sea cucumber. The times he was reading were just like the times he wasn't: if you called out his name or an *Encyclopedia Britannica*–type question, he'd probably look at you and blink, look at you and nod, or maybe he'd look away from you and tilt his head as if to say "possibly." He was a man of science who never jumped to any conclusion. He was passionate about restraint—a very noble-sounding phrase that she got from an article about an obese shoe designer and his attitude toward the grooming of shitzus. Still, restraint was his passion. If she didn't find him, she thought, she'd probably have looked for someone not at all like him. There seemed a million other ways, in fact, for her life to have turned out without him but no other way for it to have turned out with him.

She met him during an occluded period in her personal history. She'd been waiting for several unrelated though contingent problems to clear up so that she could devise a new set of unattainable ambitions to daydream about when she was too tired to read on public transportation. He was initially someone who did her some small favors; she was going to send him a card or a book or both. Nothing, at the time, seemed appropriate. She had been seeing a man who drove a car with a broken speedometer; that's all she can seem to remember about the one who came before. She could remember the day, the very moment she realized that what she wanted out of him was exactly him, like he was a catalog item in a certain size and color. She remembered wanting to place her right thumb on his left eyelid as he spoke to her with profound detachment; she remembered thinking that he should have been wearing a better white shirt that day—a higher-count cotton weave. She had seen him wearing better shirts; she knew he was capable of this. On this day and on subsequent occasions he acted in a professional capacity and didn't seem truly cognizant of her, but she knew that if he had seemed truly cognizant of her she would not have wanted him as much.

His gray-blue eyes were like marbles—not stunning, mesmerizing, tradable marbles; more like marbles deemed special by a child prone to choosing a peculiar flavor of ice cream and immediately declaring it her all-time favorite. When she first knew him and he spoke to her about a serious professional matter—before she embraced him, had her doubts about him, and then became terrified of losing him—she'd had the keen sensation that she could take his eyes home with her. She envisioned popping them out of their sockets and into a tiny change purse—sable-lined calfskin or something equally impossible—and then later setting them on her night table and looking at them before she went to sleep. He was a sober man with a gravelly voice, but on the phone and in person he always said "bye-bye," like he was ending a game of patty-cake. He'd say "bye-bye," and this would be her cue to think about popping out his marble eyes and taking them home with her.

Each time she saw him when she hardly knew him, he shook her hand. His hand was always cold, which she half-expected, but usually it seemed to be more than just a regular handshake, which the other half of her began to hope for. It took a while, however, before she was able to distinguish the way in which his was more than just a regular handshake—whether it was a reassuring gesture of goodwill (he wasn't arrogant, but it was important for him to be admired and respected) or whether he was taking her hand because he wanted more. Right before every anticipated handshake she tried to remember what his previous handshake had felt like and, for the sake of comparison, what a handshake by a state senator or a Baptist minister felt like. She tried to objectively assess the varying styles of human contact. She also tried to prevent her hand from revealing to him the lack she was feeling in all parts of her body.

In his suits he reminded her of a Magritte painting—that ubiquitous *homme d'affaires* in the bowler, even though she hadn't seen him wear a hat of any kind. He had that stiff, carefully drawn quality, and it was the incongruity of this image and her messy passions that suggested the erotica of a Magritte landscape—one in which you had the undressed woman being observed nonchalantly by the stiff and carefully drawn man in a suit. After one of his cold handshakes, she wanted to say to him bluntly, "I have a new doorbell. Why not come over and try it out?" This was true:

her landlord had given her a new doorbell, but any overture she could think of seemed deceitful. Part of the situation's allure was the feeling that she was conning him. Who was the person she was machinating for him to perceive? "The ideal woman" probably, whatever his version of that entailed. She'd planned out her strategy down to the very postage stamp (she'd sent a card *and* a book), assuming that these calculations would not go unnoticed. She was sending signals that she was a person of enormous value, even though she knew her worldly accomplishments to be nil.

She had studied psychology and then quit what they call "the discipline" to do something intellectually menial for most of her adult life. He, on the other hand, did everything correctly from the get-go and in record time. "Driving straight through till we hit the beaches" is how she thought of his life. She was able to patch through a connection to people like him because she had consecrated her nonremunerable hours to edification. But rather than happily embrace what Plato designated as the highest form of human existence, she thought of it as a chronic, debilitating disease, this compulsion to constantly examine what seemed unknowable about life. The unknowability of other people had confounded her for some time—probably since the cradle. She didn't even feel close to her parents, her sisters, all of the people she was expected to love. Philosophy had infected her with the fatal virus of uncertainty, turned every desire into a problem to be analyzed into oblivion, prevented her from being spontaneous. A surfeit of philosophy, she thought, would surely be the death of her—a suspicion confirmed by Plato's contention that philosophers were half-dead already. By this calculation she was something like one-quarter dead, given that she considered herself a half-assed philosopher.

If she was the perennial student, he seemed the gifted teacher. Her rationalization for why a relationship with him might work came from the Buddhists: "When the student is ready the teacher arrives." But then maybe what she felt for him was the most ordinary thing—with the same format, the same intensity that the checkout girl at Wal-Mart feels for the stockroom guy at Wal-Mart. Maybe it was all just sex. Whatever the initial stimulus, after too much deliberation and despite her impairment when it came to spontaneity, her elevator pitch came out as "I have a new doorbell." He said, "That's nice." She said, "I like you." He said, "What comes next?" What came next was a "date," to stroll through an arboretum on a stormy Sunday in May. The episode later entered their discourse as "that cold, strange day of the coral azaleas." When the drizzle at the arboretum turned to a downpour, they sought refuge beneath a large azalea bush whose interior reminded her of a chapel. The entrance was an arch, and she suggested to him that the bush might well be a human-scale version of something that the bowerbird would construct to find a mate. The contrived romance of the situation was so sappy that sap is what she expected to feel falling on her through the chapel's branches. But he said nothing about birds let alone avian mating habits. All that day she'd found it difficult to extract a full-fledged conversation from him; as he considered his reply to a comment, she got the impression of a child running back up to his bedroom to get one more toy for the long car ride.

When the downpour let up, they ran to his car and drove to a Chinese restaurant where they ate salty food you could hardly see because the restaurant's interior was so dark, like a cave. "Viscosity" was the word that came to her mind to describe everything about the afternoon. Because they were the only patrons in the restaurant at midday, the waiter brought them complimentary plum wine in dirty glasses; he set the glasses on the table with a bored, exaggerated gesture to indicate that they were lovebirds. He also gave them a whole plate of cookies to crack open; the fortunes were alternately adorned with illustrations of roosters and dragons. All this wadded garbage was left on the table when his beeper went off, and he had to leave. They were silent in his car on the drive home; she felt that the silence meant error, which she despaired of but was prepared to stoically accept, like the sudden declaration of war by your country. But then he kissed her goodbye like the plum wine had been a portent, like there was somebody in charge who said, "OK, you two there will play the lovers," like the whole "date" had been a Pirandellian etude. When he was gone, she felt sad, not happy. She had the sense that the lonely, wanting part of herself that was so assiduously present had connected with a similar payload, so that her emptiness was amplified, no longer acoustic.

It was Freud who lured her into psychology and Freud who made her want out. *Beyond the Pleasure Principle* was why she quit the "discipline"—quit, like it was an after-school intramural sport. For years she'd managed to hobble along without the pleasure principle doing her much harm, but after that cold, strange day of the coral azaleas it all came rushing back to her. She had thought that she liked sex as much as the next person, but she was disturbed by wanting it so badly with him. Her desire seemed to transcend this person who was supposed to be the reason for her desire, which was immensely frustrating to feel let alone contemplate. Eventually her frustration turned to a mild terror, because her desire was something that possessed her; she couldn't possess it, couldn't take it home with her and place it on her night table to inspect and consider at her leisure.

"Terror" came into the picture because in wanting his body or the gifted teacher contained within (how could she tell which was the major draw?), she felt like she was desperately clawing to get somewhere—to some unseen "beyond," or perhaps to get out of a bad dream, like one in which you are on a carousel with no horses. The prospect of wanting to get *out of* rather than *to* this unseen beyond was yet more disturbing. "What if we desire to no end?" was her problem. What if our only purpose as humans was to desire, so that the objects of our desire were mere facilitators? The situation reminded her of that Marx Brothers picture in which Groucho has Margaret Dummont in a facetious embrace: "Hold me," she implores him, "closer . . . closer." He looks at

the camera and says slyly, "If I got any closer I'd be behind you."
Maybe being behind him is what she now wanted—that is,
maybe when we want someone so much we end up wanting to
be rid of him, as relief from such incessant, tormenting desire.
And maybe this compulsion to expel the offending desire didn't
originate in the sinkhole of the subconscious but was an autoreflexive mechanism, similar to the way you vomit your guts out
after ingesting a scintilla of bacteria.

"How is excruciating desire so different from excruciating
pain?" she wondered as she wandered the property, looking for
feng shui anywhere she could get it. Questions, she knew, are
what psychologists and philosophers have in common, but not
much else. Freud had a big problem with Plato's Cave of Ignorance, which is right where she headed when she'd had it with
Freud. If you stuck with the father of modern psychology, you
took it that the lonely, wanting part of yourself so assiduously
present was like a chip implanted in your brain as a sex-obsessed
infant, and there was nothing you could do but the best you can.
But this is not what she wanted. What she wanted was hope. The
start of philosophy for her was the search for an exit from this
Cave and its vasty depths of indiscriminate longing. This was
simple enough to conceptualize: all we want is to get out from
the darkness of the Cave, and Plato suggests that if we stick with
the difficult ascent we'll eventually be able to see the light, to bask
in the sun. In Plato's view, the sun, the light, was good—like one
of those crystal-clear early fall days when the sunlight hitting the
swaying trees makes the leaves shimmer like diamonds, when
every house on your street looks better than it ought. Were these
rare days the truth and all others counterfeit, or were they simply
aberrations not to be replicated in human endeavor? All she knew
was that she'd always been suspicious of the sun, the banality of
a clear blue sky, and she suspected as much of Freud. She was
certain he adored weather conditions—i.e., clouds, clouds, and
more clouds, as was the case on that cold, strange day of the
coral azaleas. True, one gray day was not much different from

the next, and yet it took a gray day to cast the gleam of a Dutch oil painting—*ceci n'est pas un Magritte*.

As the orange sun slipped into the pink of the clouds—slipped like the clouds were a set of honeymoon sheets—she laughed out loud to think that after all this philosophy hooey she'd come back to Freud. Despite his numerous sexual hang-ups, she thought, she should've stuck with the man and his motley downerisms rather than go for the codicils of "the good life." In *Beyond the Pleasure Principle* Freud hit a brick wall when this thought occurred to him: any "beyond" that we define as being the apogee of life can only be a fantasy that imposes limitations on our experience. She knew the truth: the Cave idea just wouldn't wash. Dark to light, ignorance to enlightenment, was just a Playskool ambition. But what was the alternative to philosophy? Back to the sinkhole of the unconscious?

The owners had told her that the house was built in 1939 by a Viennese violinist, a refugee Jew whose wife had been a patient of Freud's, but she found this hard to believe—the Freud part, the violinist part, the whole thing. It made no sense for the owners to lie, but she knew that lying was most often a nonsensical enterprise. The house looked vaguely European but was more of a pastiche of architectural clichés from the core members of the European Union—which in a sense made it very modern, something you might call The Euro. The windows were long and narrow and opened like shutters, like the windows you'd see on a villa in Torino. There were a lot of windows in this house—"seven on each side for good luck" they'd been told by the man who lived here, a former options trader who was severely ill, awaiting a kidney from anywhere in the world. She found it difficult to believe that a violinist forced to leave his beloved Vienna would be thinking about luck when he built his mock-villa here in the boondocks. She tried to envision this refugee violinist and his analysand wife trying to re-create their Viennese world in the Vermont of the forties, and she thought how it was the details that tipped you off about a lie—for instance, 1939 marked not just the start of the war but the death of Freud. This particular lie, she decided, was merely an exercise in free association—war, Jew, Freud, Vienna, waltz (hence violin).

Thinking about the war prompted her own mental volley of free association—OSS, espionage, saboteurs, spies, and with this she decided to spy on her betrothed through one or more of the lucky Torino windows, spy on him as he read in the Wegner chair. She walked along the curvature of the gravel path and then onto the plush, verdant grass; she parted some shrubbery with her legs and felt her feet sink into the spongy cedar mulch surrounding the house at its base. And there he was, cool as a sea cucumber, though from this angle she could not see the fox on the wall—not that the fox had anything to do with her clandestine surveillance, except that, being a fox, and such a large one at that, he was no doubt sly, and sly is how she felt spying on her fiancé. Did he really love her? she wondered. Was the way he felt for her the extent of his expressible devotion to anyone, or was she just a good-enough proposition for a man of science to accept? Was she simply the path of least resistance for someone so passionate about restraint?

He gave no indication that he was aware of being watched, even as she moved to the next window for a different view. "When the student is ready the teacher arrives," she thought, but what, she wondered, was their status now? According to Nietzsche, "One repays a teacher badly if one always remains a pupil." And here she was the perpetual pupil, gaping at the teacher through a window, always on the outside looking in, into the sanctum, the *sanctum sanctorum*. Passion, intellect, passion, intellect—which side was she on anyway? Somewhere she read that "passion precipitates the first marriage, intellect the second," but why couldn't you have both in one marriage?

The shed for which she had no key was her next destination. What the owners called a "shed" was in real-estate terms *an adorable little peaked-roof chapel with octagonal stained-glass windows*. This seemed to her further evidence for why the refugee violinist story was all bosh; she very much doubted that a Jew would have commissioned a private chapel—the bland gesture of an Indiana Methodist. You couldn't see inside the shed/chapel, couldn't see the presumed heap of rusting and soil-caked rakes and hoes and spades. What, after all, does one keep in a shed when one hires artisan landscapers to make the lawn plush even at the end of July? For some reason the options trader's wife had thought it important that they take possession of the shed key. Her name was Artemis, after the goddess she said, but then this woman was a known liar—blithe Botox beauty, willowy and well-meaning, but a liar nonetheless. Artemis said that she divorced her first husband because he did not believe in the big bang and used too much liquid soap. Of course those were not the real reasons; nothing is ever the real reason. "The pain rises to the surface" was one of the incomprehensible things she had said in regard to her first marriage, fishing in her Fendi bag for the key to the shed. The key to the shed seemed to be a catalyst for Artemis's buried feelings about this man. "Pain, pain, pain—pain is the scum of all passion," she finally proclaimed, declaring the key a lost cause, wiping tears from her eyes.

It was already dusk, twilight, what the French called *l'heure bleue,* though what grabbed you was the sky's pink and orange palette. This was indeed the loveliest night of the year, she decided, with or without the love part. The sky, the twilight, reminded her of something—something intensely. Of what though? Was it a dream or something less idiosyncratic? A diabetic Jungian once told her that "what your mind chooses to catalog and file as a 'remembered dream' is simply a duty-free wish." Perhaps this scenario reminded her of something she once wished for. Parts of the sky still seemed illuminated by sunlight, but the hills and woodlands were dark, a velvety indigo, suggesting to her the dense coolness of a lake amid heady pines. The white on certain objects refused to cede its brilliance amid the encroaching shadow—a lovely paradox everywhere she looked. What this reminded her of, she finally realized, was yet another

Magritte painting, *The Empire of Light,* a landscape tableau containing no people, dressed or undressed. Here it was the exterior of a bourgeois home—an estate by contemporary American standards—the kind you'd see in the thirties in a French prefecture or maybe the Belgium equivalent of St. Cloud. House, gas lamp, graveled roundabout, a little pond, natural or manmade, shrubbed and wooded backdrop. What made the scene surreal was the fact that the sky was a daytime turquoise but the house and it environs were ensconced in the pitch of night, the window aglow from within, the gas lamp a modest beacon. From the moment she saw this picture she was intensely drawn to the luminous quality of her favorite time of day, but it was many years later that she realized what made the picture a bona fide Magritte, the trope of day for night, or vice versa—so in that sense what she was drawn to was the illogical absence of her favorite time of day. The scene was seductive and familiar, and yet in no way did it seem absurd to her. The surrealists were said to have ransacked the concept of the Freudian unconscious for shock value, and Magritte's paintings were certainly in no short supply of Freudian iconography. And yet Magritte seemed to her more Platonic than Freudian. Freud was dark, hot, messy; Freud was the scum of all passion, not the empire of light.

Now, suddenly, the Magritte canvas was gone—disappeared as quickly as it had been dreamt up—and things were uniformly dark. The only visible light was that of his reading lamp shooting out the slits of the window at The Euro, and she was drawn back to the house like a moth, a fluttering moth at the window. There were no screens—too nouveau riche for Artemis and the options trader—so if she were a moth she could fly right in and clamp herself onto the stucco ceiling. Perhaps she'd be happier as a voyeuristic moth clamped to the ceiling—happier, that is, than being his wife. But then if she were a moth would she really opt to clamp herself to the ceiling? Would she be content with that? Wouldn't she be diving at lightbulbs, smacking against their hot surfaces, relentlessly pursuing the fire, the flame, to get to some unseen beyond? This, after all, was how she felt herself to be living already—him inhabiting Plato's empire of light, so composed and serene, and her the Freudian insect smacking against things hither and thither in a frenetic and futile effort to penetrate that empire. Was there any room in there for passion? she wondered. Maybe in the empire of light you checked your passion at the door. Maybe the lesson for the student to take away is that you should never be "passionate" about another person. Perhaps passion should be reserved for things and places and ideas—restraint, for instance, or Wedgwood and Limoges, Vienna if you were Mahler, Poland if you were Chopin.

Outside looking in—looking in at this motionless man amid so many motionless animals—she wished she could say she felt enlightened, felt some Platonic high from having tapped into this font of wisdom. *He was as separate from her as was this house belonging to strangers.* This was an airtight thesis; this was the way things were. The book he was reading bore the title *Short, Beautiful Things*—a Keatsian sigh, Blakean hiccup—but the words inside constituted a history of endoscopy. Was the title premonitory, she wondered, referring to their relationship? Or was it referring to this day, this evening, the twilit sky now passed into oblivion? It was the end of July, when, vacationwise, a lot of people make enormous changes at the last minute, August being the point of no return. But it was still the loveliest night of the year, and she was still the perennial student who would shortly enter the state-of-the-art kitchen and turn on the lights so as to begin making an elaborate dinner. She'd blink to accommodate her eyes to the harshness of the light, and once she was used to the light, she knew exactly what came next. She'd wash the vegetables, she'd cut the vegetables, and then she'd want the same damned things all over again.

Tenants

"This is his back door," my mother said, pointing and circling her yardstick like some kind of wizard—the disenchanted kind it'd have to be, one who moonlights on the Home Shopping Network and is forever driving off with her wand on the roof of the car. I bent down to where her yardstick wand grazed the earth, pretending to inspect the hole at a better angle, even though I couldn't see a thing in there. "As you can see," she continued, "it's not as wide as his main entrance." When I walked around to the other side of the shed to again inspect his main entrance I could see that she was right: his main entrance was definitely wider. His setup relative to his size made me think of the theme song from *Green Acres*—"land spreadin' out so far and wide." His spread was indeed a nice one. He was lucky for this but even more so for the fact that my mother had decided not to evict him, as she'd done with his forebears last summer and planned to do very soon with the skunks under her front porch. Last year's tenants were a big rowdy clan that climbed up my mother's beloved pear tree to gorge themselves on the fruit and the leaves and the bark, so that in the fall the lifeless tree had to be cut down. My mother alternately referred to last year's tenants as "the wild bunch" and "the marauders." The man who trapped the marauders and took them away in his truck commented that they were the heaviest woodchucks he'd ever carried. My mother said it was from the incessant snacking, just like with the 33 percent of Americans who were certifiably obese.

My mother has deemed tolerable the current inhabitant of this prime subterranean real estate given that her yard no longer contains anything that a woodchuck and his cronies could strip bare with their insatiable appetites. This guy was busy doing a number on the peach tree two houses away. My mother said she'd see him waddle off in the morning with a glint in his eye; then he'd waddle back after lunch looking ready to belch. Like his forebears, he was brazen — after his peach-tree conquests he'd doze in the sun just a few feet away from my mother as she worked in her rock garden. Various members of the rabbit families that live under the woodpile did this as well — dozed in the sun just a few feet away from my gardening mother — though I never heard her call any of the rabbits "brazen." In some respects my mother has acquiesced, has accepted the Peaceable Kingdom into her life, but there's still the problem of bees making nests under the house's cedar shingles. Bees of all stripes are my mother's enemies, with no exceptions. As she sees it, "Either you're with me or you're with the bees."

My mother claims that most of the human contact she's had this summer is in the realm of pest control. The bee man now comes twice a month to spray wherever there's a loose shingle. Usually this procedure is done once a season, but my mother has a lot of loose shingles and hence a big bee problem — on some days she'll kill forty bees in the kitchen alone. I'd been reluctant to visit her on account of the bees (I'm allergic and she's not), but guilt and family solidarity won out. Though I love my mother I hate where she lives. After my father died she sold our big, boxy two-story colonial and bought this bungalow ("gnome cottage" would be a more accurate description) with the mammoth yard — her logic running that it would be easier to clean and she'd have all this money to travel. Plus, she fell in love with the inspirational-greeting-card tableau suggested by the rock garden and overhanging pear tree. Three years later, however, she never goes anywhere. "How could I?" is her stock reply to any suggestion of a Royal Viking cruise. "I'm under siege here."

Traveling is not the only thing I pester my mother about; I keep coming up with compelling reasons why she should buy a condo or at least rent an apartment and get rid of this gnome cottage under siege. "Oh, sure!" she'll say. "You mean like one of Laura's apartments?" Some years back my sister and brother-in-law thought rental property would be a good investment, so they bought one rundown apartment house and then another right next door: in total, six apartments and one beauty salon. It was also an opportunity for Larry to use the huge garage that had been jointly shared by the two buildings for his summertime outboard motor repair service. They soon discovered, of course, what a headache it is to be landlords. People who rent non-prefabricated apartments in this part of suburbia tend to have bad credit histories and garnished wages and restraining orders against them. In the five years Laura and Larry have owned the property, not a week has gone by when they weren't in the process of evicting a tenant for nonpayment of rent. And it wasn't just that the tenants didn't pay their rent; as my sister put it, they'd "trash the place and behave like animals." Like the guy who kept his motorcycle on the front porch. When Larry told him to get the bike off the porch he moved it into his apartment, parked it in the bow window.

Oddly enough, I, too, have a tenant problem, just like the chronic woes of my mother and sister. I'm not a landlord let alone a homeowner; it's the fellow tenant in my apartment who's the problem—my ex-boyfriend, Augie. He refused to leave the apartment when we broke up three months ago. "This was my apartment," I told him, "so you have to leave." "This is the only home I've ever known!" was his irrational reply. "You've only lived here a year," I argued, "whereas I've lived here six years. Your name's not even on the lease." Of course this was the perfect segue into the broken-home spiel ("My name's never on any lease!") that he has crafted into a moving monologue much in the way those washed-up television actors get a second life on Broadway when they seize upon some colorful persona—Harry Truman, say, or

Bebe Rebozo—and actually grow to look like their characters because they've vowed never to go back to infomercials. Augie could easily do Broadway with this foundling-of-suburbia routine, especially with lines like "You'd do this to me twice in one lifetime?"

"I don't want this to get ugly," I could've said, but the situation wasn't moving in an ugly direction, just a crazy one. I couldn't believe I was having this kind of logistical contretemps after all the messy breakup stuff we'd gone through, but then sooner than I expected, talk turned to action. A few weeks ago Augie took a futon I had stored in the basement and put it down in the walk-in closet in the hallway; he moved all of my things out of the closet and left them in the middle of the living room. Now he sleeps there, lives in the closet with his cell phone and his two laptops and his stereo and his flat-panel LCD television and his halogen lamp. He refers to himself as "a breakaway republic" even though he's using my extension chords to extract my electricity and is using my kitchen and my bathroom—my food, my toothpaste. And he hasn't given me a penny in rent since the day we broke up.

I live in a city where rents are outrageous and people with bad credit histories and garnished wages and restraining orders against them stand little chance of renting a decent apartment. And musicians—ditto for them. Augie has a degree in music production and engineering from Berklee and a recording studio in Dorchester that he rents with anywhere from three to thirteen guys. Even though he thinks himself part of the counterculture (and he's not even embarrassed to profess his belief in such an entity), he is fairly typical of the local crop of going-nowhere-fast/ just-turned-thirty/don't-make-me-not-wear-a-T-shirt music guys. If life were a series of action figures, this is a category you'd get to sooner or later—like maybe in the aftermath of a skirmish in which, say, the Wellbridge Aromatherapists wiped out the Local 180 Pipefitters, you might place a couple of Music Guy action figures on the periphery of the carnage, and that would be it. Just standing there with their hands tucked halfway into the pockets of their pants would be the key component of their superhero status. If they had a string to pull they'd say only one thing: "Don't make me spill my beer."

Augie's excuse for everything is money — being that there is none for artists like him. He just can't understand why the world gives him such a hard time when all he wants to do is write and record love songs. "Yeah, you and about three hundred thousand other people" — say that to Augie and he is affronted. He has no postmodern irony when it comes to himself. "Why do you have to act like you're the First Man?" I was always asking him. "I don't go around acting like I'm the First Woman." And he'd usually come back with something like "Well maybe you should for a change — gimme an apple or at least some juice," acting like this was profound.

Lately Augie has been especially vexed by the elusiveness of money because his brother was just on a prime-time television game show and won a lot of money by identifying the napkins at Wendy's as being yellow: that was the million-dollar question. When this windfall occurred, Augie thought his brother would "share," like they did in the days when they got the Post Breakfast Variety Pack and both wanted the little box of Sugar Pops. But his brother said no way. Now Augie's brooding and hoping for his brother to change his mind and at least give him a sliver of the pie so that he can launch the record label he's been yelping about since I've known him. This is the same brother who'd been trying for years to get on the *Real World* and spent most of his twenties in denial about already being too old. You always think that these kinds of shallow, misguided people come to sorry ends, but Augie's brother has proved this theory wrong. Quite often shallow, misguided people win — and win big. They become your landlord or your boss or the president of your country.

"I wonder how he's got it arranged down there," my mother mused, tapping her yardstick on a rock. I knew she was seriously thinking about putting two little plaster of Paris lions on either side of the woodchuck's main entrance. Larry's brother the mason has miniature models of all kinds of landscaping adornments, like the New York Public Library lions, sitting everywhere in his little storefront, so this wasn't an unrealizable notion. I myself was picturing something like a penthouse-style bachelor pad—the playboy woodchuck ushering females in the front door and out the back, like a member of the Rat Pack, although it was hard to imagine woodchucks comparable (poundwise) to a Frank Sinatra or a Joey Bishop. I wanted to share this scenario with my mother—woodchicks slinking in the front door and scampering out the back—but I was afraid it would remind her of my father and all the affairs he had with unattractive women.

"There's probably a lot of garbage," I said. "Peach pits, guitar picks, toenail clippings."

She nodded appreciably. "Like someone we know."

I had to reciprocate her nodding, because how could I not think of Augie? If a wizard with a yardstick decided to turn him into an animal, it'd definitely be a woodchuck who slept through entire seasons, completely oblivious to trends in cargo-pant lengths and code-yellow terrorist alerts—which is basically the way Augie lives his life while awake. As I tried to imagine Augie sleeping under a shed I realized that the woodchuck's digs were larger than Augie's—the shed was at least twice the square footage of my walk-in closet—and I shuddered to think what he was doing to my apartment while I was visiting my mother. He claimed that financial destitution had him on the verge of putting his Pope-on-a-Rope collection on eBay, but that didn't seem to crimp his party-guy lifestyle any. Just last weekend, for instance, he was blaring music from his closet while I was in the kitchen making dinner for five people—new people, people from the outside world—and I thought I was going to lose it. I called his cell phone and threatened, "Don't make me come over there," and of course I ended up pounding on the closet door. He did turn off the music, but then he started singing loudly, over and over, "*I'm eighteen with a bullet / Got my finger on the trigger, I'm gonna pull it.*" I couldn't do anything rash (like force open the door) because he had put a deadbolt on the inside. Long story short: he ended up joining my dinner guests and having them like him better than they did me. They all went out to a club; I did the dishes.

However much charm Augie could unleash on five new people, he just wasn't the kind of guy who could be there for you even when he was camped out in your hall closet. "You need at least one reliable tenant," Laura once advised while discussing the fine art of landlording. She and Larry thanked their lucky stars that they had Jeoffry Thresher, who helped out in a superintendent capacity for a break on his rent. "Funny, isn't it?" Laura had said, showing me his security deposit check when he moved in. "I mean the way he spells his name." *Jeoffry* was spelled like the name of Christopher Smart's cat in the famous ode he wrote to this pet while in the loony bin. I know Laura didn't make this connection (she was the ceramic engineer; I was supposed to be the poet), and I doubt Jeoffry's parents did. Though I like to think that their choice of spelling reflected a fondness for Restoration-era verse, most likely they were part of that vast demographic contingent that Larry considers dumber than a sack of hammers. Jeoffry Thresher mainly did things for the girls at Beauty Matters, the hair salon next to his apartment—change sixty-watt light-bulbs and occasionally hang framed pictures of Jennifer Lopez's various hairstyles. He was what my mother called "a little slip of a guy" who worked at Red Lobster and drove his mother's old Mercury Sable. When he wasn't working he always wore "dress slacks and a belt"—this from Larry's mother, who went to the same church.

"What if he's fixing it up," my mother proposed pensively—I almost want to say winsomely—"getting it ready for a bride?"

I tried to imagine her tenant being industrious like Jeoffry Thresher and hanging pictures that a mate would want to look at—perhaps inspirational-greeting-card images of pear trees, whole orchards of them. I tried to picture him carrying his wood-chuck bride across the threshold—no, more like stuffing her into the hole after their orgiastic honeymoon at the peach tree. Stuffing her into the hole and then rolling her into the marriage bed to sleep until February 2, when one of them would have to get up to put out the cat.

"A bride?" I asked, scotching this imagery in favor of wood-chicks slinking in the front door and scampering out the back.

"The birds and the bees, honey," she said, snatching at weeds around her tenant's main entrance.

Hold your tongue, I thought; let her think that she has a woodchuck with the moral constitution of an Ethan Frome rather than a Frank Sinatra. After all, my mother truly needed to have her faith in the male of her own species restored. Even after three years, she can't go out for a cup of coffee without running into some woman with whom my father conducted a short and sloppy affair. For my mother, the real grief factor in my father's philandering was that all of his mistresses were dumpy, middle-aged women, what she called "cows in tracksuits." My father wasn't so much a Casanova as a disorganized and distracted man—impulsive too. Maybe his problem was simply ADD or some other chemical malady that would now be treated with two or three drugs that he could chew each morning like a Flintstones vitamin. Whatever the cause of his behavior, he never changed it, and my mother stuck with him through thirty years of this unchangeability.

Because the bee spraying and the skunk removal were sched-uled for the same day, we considered it something of an event. My sister took off from work and arranged for some other parent to collect her kids from softball or T-ball or whatever sport it was kids played in kindergarten before beginning a long personal his-tory of sitting on their ass. It was a hot and humid late-August afternoon, and I had made it through five days at my mother's gnome cottage without getting stung. We were having a rather swell time considering the circumstances, but I was nonetheless ready to go home, even though "home" for me consisted of an expensive apartment devoid of a working closet.

The bee man worked for a company called The Bee Man. He whistled while he worked, just like they used to do in Disney movies. For months my mother had been feeling him out as a potential boyfriend for me, mainly because of the whistling but also because he was single, tanned, and handsome and shared her views on the nature of happiness—which is that there is no such thing, only the well-chosen habit of being perceived as optimistic. He was also a few inches shorter than me and believed that the reason behind divorce rates being so high was "women with wacko ideas." Plus, he lived a good six-hour drive away. If you overlooked these minor complications, dating the bee man did not seem like such a stretch.

Unfortunately, I had little opportunity to chat with the bee man, because after we learned that he used to date my sister's sister-in-law who now lived in North Carolina, he and my sister yapped incessantly about her many faults as well as those of his ex-wife who, coincidentally, now lived in South Carolina. "The Carolinas," he said, shaking his head, "overrun by women with wacko ideas."

When the bee man was finished spraying he told my mother she was "all set for a while" and smiled at her affectionately. My mother told me that on one of his earlier missions she ended up singing "I Got Stung" with him. She always loved Elvis but could never play his records because my father thought him a "big fat hillbilly." My mother had her share of clandestine loves—Elvis and Gerry and the Pacemakers spring most readily to mind, but during my lifetime she'd add to her repertoire every five years or so. I remember the Dwight Yokum period like it was yesterday; then there was the strange dalliance with Evan Dando on account of the democratic miracle of VH1. My mother was at least twenty-five years older than the bee man, true, but why couldn't she go out with him? Our warped cultural norms, that's why. I like to think she'd be a hot ticket among her age peers on a Royal Viking cruise even though she has officially sworn off men—all men on account of one man. Widowhood did not stop my mother from being faithful in the same way that marriage did not stop my father from having girlfriends.

The skunk man, Vern, was happily married with four kids, so a fix-up with this pest-control professional was not an option for me or my mother. Vern had been referred to my mother by the guy who carted away his heaviest-ever groundhogs last year. Vern's was a skunks-only operation that he ran out of Binghamton. He trapped animals all over the region but always released them in the same place—a glade in Apalachin that he referred to as Skunk Hollow. He was expensive, but he was "the best," and in widowhood and retirement my mother was dead set on having "the best" of everything for this gnome cottage under siege—like her absurdly expensive new Swedish washing machine that rinsed your clothes five times and bled them of all life and color.

Everything with Vern was black and white—literally. His truck, his overalls, his cowhide-print canvas tote bag in which he carried the bait, although he referred to the rotting fruit as "smackerels." "You're feeding them SnackWells?" my mother asked at this part of the orientation. "No, Mom, *smackerels*," I said. "It's what Winnie the Pooh always wants to have."

"Oh, don't go putting cutesy pictures in my head!" she yelled. "This is hard for me as it is!"

"The trick is not to scare them," Vern told us. That's why he talked to them ("Why, hello there, skunky skunkies") and sang to them while transporting them from "confiscation site" to his truck. Always during the "drive to liberation" he played on the stereo the song "Muskrat Love" by the Captain and Tennille and sang along as he drove. There even speakers in the truck bed so that the skunks, a captive audience, could enjoy the song with Vern.

Vern placed a big cage containing a smorgasbord of rotting

smackerels near the small hole dug at the base of my mother's front porch. The cage's door slid open and was held above the entry with a ripcord device. "Now we kick back and wait," he said as we gathered on the other side of his truck in the driveway.

"What are the little ones officially called?" my mother, ever the conversationalist, wanted to know.

"The poets call them kittens," I ventured.

"The poets drink too much!" my mother exclaimed.

"The poets need to get some Time-Life books out of the library," Laura said.

"Skunklets," Vern replied, confirming my notion that he was a man who stuck to the script. "Least that's what I call them."

As if on cue, the mother skunk emerged from the hole, tentatively waddled toward the cage, sniffing and displacing the grass with her wide, bushy form. With most skunks I've seen, the white stripe invariably has yellowed from so much skunk activity—you'd think we'd call it a yellow stripe. But we're a nation that loves to see everything in terms of Vern's truck—no shades of gray—and in this respect the skunk seems very American. I had a boyfriend from Berlin who abandoned his postdoc position at MIT and the States altogether not long after encountering skunk smell on a camping trip to New Hampshire: "We don't have such animals in Germany" were his parting words to me.

As the mom entered the cage, out came the skunklets—one, two, three, four, single file.

"I just love these little critters," Vern said, sounding like he was going to get misty. Of course my mother picked right up on the sentimentality, putting her hand to her mouth to suppress some kind of emotive hiccup. Fortunately for me, the Hallmark moment tanked when Laura's cell phone rang with an obnoxious sound her family must have selected. The skunks looked apprehensive for a minute but then turned their attention back to the smorgasbord; still, I felt like such a voyeuristic creep crouching behind the truck. How could you help but feel that what we were doing was sinister? Luring the innocents to a nonexistent land of milk and honey so as to render them "displaced" like the Oakies, like the Joad family. And then I thought about the political economy of my mother's yard, and it seemed so typical of any current administration that the single mother with the dependents gets evicted while the testosterone-happy slacker under the shed gets to stay.

With the entire family feasting on rotting smackerels, Vern pulled a cord and the cage door shut. You'd think there'd have been more panic—or spraying God forbid—but the skunks continued eating their dinner in a clump of black and yellow. As he approached the cage, Vern started to whistle just like the bee man. He called the animals "my furry friends" and "old pals o' mine." I was feeling hopeful for their new life in the wilds of Apalachin, but suddenly, after Vern had set the cage in the truck bed, something popped out of the abandoned hole. A fifth skunklet emerged and darted out to where the cage had been. He sniffed the grass with his tiny sniffer and then hopped off over the daunting height of my mother's unmowed grass in the direction of the woodchuck's peach tree. Separated from his family, out there all alone. My mother and sister started to cry at the exact same instant, as if part of a genome study. I, too, was moved, but not to tears. "C'mon, you guys," I said, trying to maintain a stiff upper lip on Vern's behalf, to prevent him from feeling bad. "You wouldn't understand," Laura protested. "You're not a mother." Vern put his arms around the two distraught women, creating the ideal photo-op triumvirate.

"Just go, Vern, please," my mother said, gently elbowing him away.

Vern hung his head as he walked back to the truck. He turned on the music in the truck bed when he started the engine: *Muskrat, muskrat, candlelight / Doing the town and doing it right in the evening.*

"How can you bear to look at them?" Laura asked me as I waved off the clan with the ardor of a Von Trapp. Maybe it was because I wasn't a mother (if you didn't count Augie), or because they seemed so happy chowing down in the cage. "It's like in *Home Alone*," I replied with a shrug, "your favorite movie. She's not even going to notice until they're in Florida."

Like the Hallmark moment before it, the Oprah moment was shot to high heaven when Laura listened to the message on her cell phone. "Uh-oh," she said, sniffling, handing me the phone. "Get a load of this." I put the phone to my ear to hear Larry's voice: "Laura, you gotta run over to Pudgie's and pick up the pizza for Bob and me. We can't get out. There's a police barricade around the building. Jeoff's holding someone hostage in his apartment." Apparently Larry and his friend had been working in the garage when the hostage situation materialized.

"And he was the one normal guy!" Laura exclaimed, grabbing the phone and smacking it against her head.

"I knew there was only one," I said.

"And now, alas, there are none," my mother said, looking at where the skunk family had lived so happily.

Because of the hostage aspect, the three of us were pretty somber driving first to Pudgie's for the pizza and then to the crime scene. "I just hope it's not a child," my mother kept saying. "But he's not that type at all," Laura protested, looking genuinely perplexed. "Jeoff's a really nice guy."

The police barricade at the apartment complex consisted of yellow tape that looked like it had been applied to anything that wasn't moving. There were two cruisers, an ambulance, four cops, lots of bystanders, and one longhaired ENT who I think also works mornings at the Dunkin Donuts. The strange thing about this hostage situation was that the person Jeoffry was holding hostage was himself. It seems that he'd called the police and told them he was in his apartment holding a gun to his head. We learned from Judy, the rather hefty woman who ran Beauty Matters, that Jeoffry's girlfriend had recently broken up with him. The girlfriend was a client at the salon, and when she was there yesterday for her single-process color and foil-wrap frost he had listened through the wall to her talking about her new boyfriend.

Then he barged into the salon and there was a big scene, but according to Judy it ended on a pitiful note, with Jeoffry sobbing.

A woman standing next to Judy said that a few hours earlier Jeoffry had run out of Red Lobster, acting crazy.

"Were you there at Red Lobster to see him do that?" my mother asked.

"Nah," she said, "but these stories travel fast." This woman had had an appointment with Judy and was clearly dismayed about the barricade that prevented them from being in the salon next to Jeoffry's apartment. This woman was even heftier than Judy, what my mother used to call "a big girl"; her hips spread out like an oxen yoke. She wore Lycra leggings that coddled and amplified each and every cellulite dimple, and her hair was an issue unto itself—an elaborate product-based architecture, like a theme park for mice. I noticed that my mother and I were both slightly transfixed by this woman, and I had to wonder whether we were thinking the same thing: *Daddy'd be having an affair with her in no time!* The thought of my father in shenanigans with this large woman threatened to make me relive all of the broken-home Sturm und Drang of my high school years. To clear my mind of such dysfunctionality, I wondered what the liberated skunks were doing—whether the Joad family stuck together in the wilds of Apalachin and if the little guy alone had found another clan to pal around with. Uncannily, my mother picked up the psychic baton to declare, "I hope that little skunk finds an adoptive family." I nodded with sympathy. Busting up a family—who'd want that on her conscience? My mother certainly didn't need that in addition to the bees.

Because all of the cops knew Bob from poker and other recreational forms of gambling, he was allowed to step over (nay, onto) the barricade to collect the pizza. Bob was always dressed in the fashion of NFL players when they have to look presentable for TV cameras in the locker room—shower slides and really weird kinds of shorts. Every time I saw him he had a grease-covered ace bandage wound around a different part of his body, and this occasion was no exception. "Old football injury?" I asked, looking at his left knee. "The new stools at the Old Pioneer," he said, seizing the pizza. "They're so high ya get a nosebleed, go all lightheaded."

As Bob headed for the garage, one of the cops was talking to Jeoffry through a bullhorn. "Jeoff, man, ya gotta come out so we can all clear outta here—hang up our holsters, hit the OP." And Jeoffry shouted back, "I'm gonna do it! I'm gonna pull the trigger!" His projection was flawless; he didn't even need a bullhorn, and I doubt he took all the voice and articulation classes that I did.

With this Larry came breezing out from the garage, stepping over the yellow tape while eating a slice of pizza. He stood next to Laura and shook his head. "Ain't there something missing in this equation?"

"It takes two to tango," my mother said, raising her eyebrows.

Now Bob was back, too, with two slices of pizza and his barstool injury. "Where the heck did he get the gun anyway?" he wanted to know.

"I think they give them out at Red Lobster," Laura said.

"At Red Lobster?" my mother asked with a quizzical frown that quickly turned upside down, into a smile of enlightenment. "Oh, I get it," she said. "You go to the lobster tank and pick your own lobster, and then you go over to the fish barrel where they give you a gun so that you can shoot your own fish."

"And the gun's yours to take," my sister said, nodding.

"With your lobster bib," I added.

"He must be really crazy about that girl," Larry said.

"Or just really crazy," Bob said.

"Like Augie Doggie," my mother offered in a chirpy voice. That's what she and Laura called my ex-boyfriend, and from this Larry came up with "the Dogster." When I told Augie about this nickname he thought I said "the Dog Star," so he decided to name his projected record label Sirius. "You can't be Sirius" all of his friends told him—everybody has a record label or a useless software package or some big fat wireless enterprise out there under a permutation of "Sirius." But you couldn't tell that to the First Man.

"Here," Laura said, handing me her phone, "maybe you should call the Dogster and make sure he's not holding anyone hostage in your closet."

"Speaking of hostage," Larry whispered, motioning toward the woman with the leggings, "how many pounds d'ya suppose she's got trapped inside those pants?"

My mother shook her head as if recoiling from the sight of a grisly automobile accident. "Why is it that the most unathletic people in our country go around in tracksuits?" She completely ignored our shushing, and I longed to reply, "For the same reason that the most narcissistic people want to write and record love songs."

"Is she really going to do the decathlon?" my mother continued, not even feigning a whisper. "Is that what we're to make of that tracksuit?"

"Mom," Laura said, exasperated, "what is it with you and 'tracksuits'? You gotta stop watching *The Golden Girls*."

My mother's expression indicated that a thought transition was in progress. "You should give Augie Doggie another chance," she said, turning to look at me. "He's loyal—that counts for so much these days. At least he isn't having affairs with cows in tracksuits who sew draperies."

"Cows in tracksuits who sew draperies," Laura repeated.

"Sounds like *The Jerry Springer Show*," Larry said.

"Or Animal Planet," Bob said.

"He's sad about losing you," my mother continued, still looking at me.

I just stared back at her—startled, I suppose, to hear my own mother campaigning on Augie's behalf. My family didn't particularly like Augie, but then they didn't think he was any worse than my other boyfriends—"sprung from the very same mold" is how my mother saw it. "A Jell-O mold" in my sister's estimation. I didn't know whether my mother's uncharacteristic behavior was due to the heat, the stress of the skunk removal, or the stress of Jeoffry Thresher holding himself hostage.

"If he's sad, Mom," I finally said, "it's not about me. It's about his brother's million dollars."

She nodded in the "Ah, so" way of Charlie Chan. "The Wendy's money."

"The Wendy's money," everyone repeated.

It is suggested—by Bob I guess—that I use the phone in my hand to call Larry's mother and ask her to come over and talk to Jeoffry. They needed someone to "talk him out," and because no member of the law-enforcement team at hand wanted to hunt down a minister in this heat, they thought that someone from Jeoffry's church would do just as well.

"Don't call Lorraine," Laura said sternly, looking at her husband.

"Why don't you talk to him, Helen?" Larry proposed to my mother. "You're somebody's mother."

"Your wife's somebody's mother!" my mother exclaimed.

"Barely," he said with a snigger.

Laura whacked her husband but agreed that my mother should try talking to Jeoffry.

With this there ensued a buzz of enthusiasm—you could feel it—so I guess my mother had no choice in the matter. Two cops, each of whom had been our paperboy at one time or another, ushered her to the front of the crime scene area, facing the Beauty Matters salon. One of them—Guido I think—handed her the bullhorn. Then all four cops shifted their weight on their feet as if the woman were some kind of expert at the FTA. Even the ENT who looked like Jimmy Page stood at respectful attention.

For some reason my mother felt compelled to straighten her hair before she spoke. "Jeoffry, this is your landlord's mother," she began.

"Oh, brother!" Bob said. "That's sure gonna make him come flyin' right outta there."

"I'm gonna do it!" Jeoffry shouted back. "I'm gonna pull the trigger!" This was obviously his refrain; there was definitely something musical about it—very much like that old Pete Wingfield song Augie was always singing: "*I'm eighteen with a bullet / Got my finger on the trigger, I'm gonna pull it.*"

"Don't do that, Jeoffry," my mother continued. "It's too hot tonight, that's for sure. What you need is a good blast of AC."

"Great!" Laura said, tilting her head back. "His apartment's the only one that wasn't rewired."

Larry shook his head. "Plug in an air conditioner and bye-bye refrigerator."

"When I need a good blast of AC," my mother began, proceeding happily along on her roll, "I go to the Starbucks at the Arnot Mall. It's always about thirty degrees in there, even in the winter. It's too cold to drink your coffee there. They say it's all climate-controlled for the beans—and I say that's all for the birds. What's more important—beans or people? I always thought 'beans' were the lowest of everything—'he doesn't know beans about fixing things' and 'it doesn't amount to a hill of beans'—but apparently I was wrong."

You had to wonder where on earth my mother was heading with this. But then given what seemed a psychic connection I had with her, I felt that I knew what she was really thinking: that whenever she went to the Starbucks at the Arnot Mall she'd see one of those cows in tracksuits who sew draperies (hence the chill).

"What I'd like to tell you about, Jeoffry," she continued, "is my own tenant, the one who lives under my shed. He's a woodchuck, not a person, but he still must have what they call 'interpersonal relationships' with other woodchucks. So far I haven't seen any other woodchucks around, but it's inevitable. Sometimes I think he came to live under my shed after some disastrous relationship—maybe he had his heart broken. It must happen in the animal world. But the reason I bring him up is that in the animal world there's no such thing as 'my one and only.' Animals know that, just like in the song that goes *don't forget that love's just a game, and it will always come again.* Of course there's those sea lions with the harems, but let's not think about them."

I often thought that my mother was the real poet in our family. She didn't go to college, professing to be illiterate, but she was a big talker, which I like to think indicative of her being a big thinker. It seemed very natural for her to be speaking through a bullhorn, and I wondered if there was a way for her to carry one around in the future, to be known hereabouts as "that nice lady who orders her coffee through a bullhorn." Perhaps she should've used this kind of device to speak to my father. "I don't want to yell at you," she was always saying to him while he dressed and groomed for work, ignoring her conversation as he selected the appropriate tie for the evening's trysting venue. A wife who's always yelling was, in my mother's book, the worst thing a woman could be. "Don't give in to stereotypes," she'd advise Laura and me whenever we encountered some woman publicly behaving like the wife in "The Lockhorns."

Somehow, with a series of tangents whose navigational sequence I doubt anyone in the crowd could retrace, my mother was talking about her own marriage. "I never made very many friends, Jeoffry, because my husband never liked having 'extra people around.'" I guess she was indicating that he shouldn't be a recluse, should go out and socialize lest he wind up like her. "And that's just the thing we all want in life, Jeoffry—extra people around."

I often thought that my father should've been a hermit, should've lived in a cave—then if he wanted to have affairs he could've hit on other cave dwellers. He shouldn't have lived the life he did—he should never have married, let alone had kids. My father's ideal life was probably that of my mother's bachelor woodchuck, and I had to wonder if my mother was allowing the woodchuck to stay precisely because she thought my father had been reincarnated as this animal. And that scenario angered me—my mother providing the marmot reincarnation of my father with a *Green Acres*–type spread and maybe even plaster of Paris lions around his main entrance.

"I'm not coming up with the right words here, Jeoffry," my mother continued, obviously frustrated. "I'm not the poetic one. You know what I'm going to do? I'm going to turn the microphone over to my other daughter, Gwendolyn, your landlord's sister."

"Ouch" I felt my head say, as if both temples got dented by her words.

"Gweny studied poetry for . . . how many years was it we paid for? Kept going and going with those degrees, like she was doing the decathlon. And after all this work she's got a nice office job that has nothing to do with poetry."

Larry flashed me a wide grin. "Sure you don't wanna put a gun to your head, too?"

"Nice little cubicle, et cetera, et cetera," my mother continued.

"Next she'll be announcing your bra size," Laura said.

"Shoulda put my hearing aid in!" Bob shouted, pounding his chest and belching.

"Oh, don't let me go off onto that old bugbear," my mother said in the self-pooh-poohing manner she thought made her sound like a colorful sitcom character. "Let's say we have Gweny recite some poetry to cool us all off."

As my mother made a daytime-television gesture of holding out the bullhorn toward me, everyone tepidly applauded with apprehension—or maybe dread. She smiled at me and shrugged, as if this were her only alternative—open mike night at the hostage standoff.

"Here's your fifteen minutes," my sister said. "Don't blow it."

"Or he'll sure blow it," Bob said.

Taking the bullhorn from my mother, I thought how I couldn't imagine what Jeoffry's ex-girlfriend was like beyond the foil-wrap frost and single-process color. From this debacle you'd think she'd be one of those knockout girls from the L'Oreal haircolor ads, but common sense told me that she was probably just like Jeoffry. Two people, both dumber than the same sack of hammers. We have such a passionate reaction to the most unremarkable people, the most unexceptional people, because in the large scheme of things everyday people just keep on loving everyday people.

Facing the Beauty Matters salon, I felt that the fickle universe had for me one word and one word only: Keats! But Keats was all about dogged love (*a foil-wrapped thing of beauty, however dumb, is a joy forever*), to-the-grave love. In the Keatsian universe you got shot by Cupid, stung by a big honey bee, then you keeled over and died. Caught off guard, I resorted to Donne, my default setting: "Send home my long strayed eyes to me, / Which (Oh) too long have dwelt on thee." I relished the rhyming kick of these two lines like I would a limerick about a young man from Kenosha, but it didn't seem natural—this reciting poetry through a bullhorn in my hometown—so I stopped. Stopping was my default setting when it came to life. "Quitting" was probably a better word. Every activity of my current existence seemed to lead to this confession: *I quit poetry*. Yes, it's true that I quit poetry, but that doesn't mean the love was never there. I loved poetry so much, in fact, that I didn't know what to do with it. The situation was very similar to my first encounter with that certain kind of white paste in kindergarten. I simultaneously longed to squish it between my fingers, eat it, and make love to it (though at that point I had no idea what "making love" meant). Poetry for me could never be a job; it was more like a unisex cologne that I'd want to smell on myself but also on some guy I loved—with the result that if I wore the stuff I could self-seduce. My problem, in a nutshell, is not that I didn't love poetry. My problem is that I'm not that good at things.

"My mother's right about the woodchuck, Jeoffry," I declared after an awkward pause. My impromptu plan was to regale him with animal-world analogies to the bachelor lifestyle, but I wasn't sure which strand of the bachelor lifestyle I should hype: Frank Sinatra or Ethan Frome. Which scenario did a person in Jeoffry's situation — desperation — really want (or need) to hear? "I know like I know the back of my hand," I began after even further hesitation, "that my mother's woodchuck will find someone soon and the two of them will be happy as clams, just like in that old Captain and Tennille song." That song, I thought — that seemed the kind of thing appropriate for this crowd. "You probably don't know that old song," I continued, "but it goes something like *Muskrat Suzie, Muskrat Sam, do the jitterbug out in Muskrat Land.*" I was speaking the words rather than singing them, and for this reason I reminded myself of an old stodge — William Shatner, say, or Charlton Heston. I forgot the lyrics from that point on but made do with "*and they shimmy . . . and do something with Jimmy.*"

"No!" Jeoffry yelled abruptly, giving us all a stir. "It's *And they shimmy . . . Sam is so skinny!*"

The crowd was now basking in collective amazement.

"You know that song?" I asked, sounding incredulous to show solidarity with the assemblage. There was silence, so I ventured even more bastardized lyrics: "*Whirling and twirling the tango, somebody playing the banjo . . .*"

"Stop!" he yelled. "It's *And they whirl and they twirl and they tango / Singing and jinging a jango!*"

This was indeed surreal to me — especially the concept of any life form "jinging a jango."

"That's my favorite song!" he shouted from his apartment.

Here the crowd gasped in unison, as if Jeoffry's revelation were on the echelon of "I'm really his father!" or "He's still alive!"

During this odd silence you could actually hear Jeoffry crying — he even sobbed with flawless projection. "OK, OK!" he finally shouted. "I'm comin' out!" There was a surge of applause, and presently Jeoffry emerged from the house, shaking his head.

179 | *Tenants*

"She's the only thing!" he said over and over. It was sad, because now he was wailing, had his arm up across his face, as if his tears were gluing the crook of his elbow to his eyes.

"Let's have the gun, Jeoff," one of the cops said.

"Don't have one," he replied, wiping his eyes with his arm as he unburied his face. "No gun."

He was holding his Game Boy in his right hand, and you had to figure that he was either playing it all the while or else holding it to his head, for verisimilitude.

I couldn't believe that I, too, was now crying at the spectacle. You'd think the skunk separation/deportation would've done it, not this.

"I can't believe that was his favorite song," Larry said, shaking his head.

"I remember that song," Bob said, rather tenderly. "The varmints were eating bacon and cheese."

"It was such a nice thing Gweny said about the groundhog and his bride," my mother mused.

"Muskrats, Mom," Laura clarified.

"What if Daddy'd been like that?" my mother continued. "So loyal to one person. A lunatic maybe, but what fidelity."

Of course no one could think of a reply. It was disturbing to think that this person holding himself hostage with a Game Boy was suddenly a paragon of virtue to be held up against my dead father the womanizer, but the women in my family seem to have a habit of cutting a lot of slack for the male of the species. After all, my sister was a lot smarter than my brother-in-law, and my mother didn't divorce my philandering father; he had a circuit overload and died. How could anyone put up with my father all those years? My mother's reply to any and all inquirers: "I loved him." "Why did you love him?" "I just did." My mother's "I just did" didn't seem that distant in its absence of logic from Jeoffry Thresher's "She's the only thing!"

"I stand by what I said about giving Augie another chance," my mother said to me.

"Augie's a crapshoot, Mom," I said; then I blew my nose on something handed to me by the woman with the oxen-yoke hips.

"It's a risk, Gweny, but you can't go around being afraid of things."

"I'm not afraid of things," I said, looking at the Wendy's napkin in my hand.

"You're afraid of my washing machine."

She was right about that, and she was right about the wood-chuck's main entrance being wider than his rear entrance, so maybe she was right about other things as well—like that Augie was sad about losing me. Was he sad about "losing" me? Even more important, was there any logical reason for my mother to be pushing for us to get back together? I had to wonder if she wanted me to have an unhappy relationship like her own so as to bring us even closer together in commiseration and conspiracy and cynicism. But then Augie was nothing like my father, just like my brother-in-law was nothing like my father, and my mother really pushed for my sister to marry Larry. My brother-in-law was sociable—he liked having the extra people around and he loved Elvis. Ditto for Augie: loved the extra people, loved the King. But did he love me?

Perhaps my mother's dalliance with wizardry allowed her to see things—like maybe she perceived that Augie and I were perfectly suited to each other, united by our mediocrity, by our being not that good at things. Perhaps my mother saw that together we became a tad less mediocre. I certainly proved a beneficial liaison for Augie in extra-financial ways. For one thing, I got him to see the beauty of slant rhyme—consonance and dissonance, euphony and cacophony. His subsequent songs were nice though still easy to forget if you weren't sleeping with the songwriter. And I was a good companion to his adolescent behavior. In grocery stores he'd sing along with the Melissa Manchester and Lionel Richie soft-rock Muzak like he was a chicken, and I'd walk along beside him as if to say, "Yes, I am *with* this chicken." But was any reciprocation going on here? I can't really say how I benefited from grocery shopping with a musical chicken, so in this respect I was already like my mother—giving indiscriminately and getting nothing in return.

Aside from too much yellow police tape, the hostage incident had no detrimental effects on the local landscape. Laura and Larry allowed Jeoffry Thresher to stay in his apartment, Judy from Beauty Matters still wanted him to change lightbulbs, Red Lobster did not fire him for running off in the middle of his shift, and the police could find nothing to arrest him for. Laura and Larry even bit the bullet and agreed to rewire his unit as well, so he could always have AC and not turn into such a hothead on some other sweltering August afternoon. On the animal front, my mother's woodchuck did the unprecedented and took on a subletter—the little orphaned skunk moved in to claim the woodchuck's rear entrance. I don't know why my mother was certain from the start that both woodchuck and skunk were male, but this scenario certainly made for more of a head-scratcher. After all, what would a woodchuck and a skunk do together besides go into a bar in some joke Bob would tell Larry? My mother talks about her shed ménage in more innocent tones, like it was the kind of crowd-pleasing French movie that becomes popular in America—*La Cage aux Fauves.*

If the bachelor woodchuck can stay and the foundling skunk can stay and Jeoffry Thresher can stay, shouldn't Augie Doggie get to stay as well? And does letting Augie "stay" mean taking back as my boyfriend this guy believing in the counterculture and the Wendy's money and his Sirius label and slant-rhyming love songs? In many respects he was a lunatic, maybe even dangerous. After all, that song he was always singing went *"I got my finger right there on the trigger / I'm gonna pull it, pull it, pull it / You better start makin' plans, baby / This old house is too small now."* And if Augie's shallow and misguided brother ever did give him a sliver of the pie, would Augie share any of it with me, to somehow make amends for all of his schmoozing? The sharing in both instances

I find doubtful, especially in light of "the irreparable breach" that occurred during Augie's childhood—that time he and his brother were giving each other karate chops and one of them tried to use their mother as a shield while she was on the phone with a guy from the Spiegel catalog. A melee ensued, groundings were issued, and the relationship between the brothers was never the same during the intervening twenty-something years.

Despite my family legacy, I'm having a hard time with the idea of giving Augie "another chance," like he was a senior citizen at the keno table. What I can see myself doing is getting hold of some Captain and Tennille and playing "Muskrat Love" outside his closet—playing it over and over like the American military did to skunk out Noriega. Or maybe I should concede defeat to the breakaway republic and look for a new apartment—let him try to cough up the rent himself. After all, there were way too many guitar picks scattered around the place—down the sofa cushions, under rugs, in the sink trap. It seemed like they'd be there for decades—when I moved out, when he moved out, through guttings and floor sandings and repartitions. Then I thought of the woodchuck's peach pits also being there under my mother's shed forever, under earth and limestone and all that other stuff that comes with the ages. I thought of Augie's guitar picks and the woodchuck's peach pits like critical remnants of an archeological site—like the fossilized hickory shells they found while excavating in Shakespeare's Globe Theatre. An enduring layer of one generation's quotidian dreck—ossified, calcified, whatever. One giant continuum of the man part of mankind—don't pay rent, trash the place, behave like animals. And all of it—somehow—in the name of love.

The Rest of Esther

"Is this your first job in development?" I was asked by the senior major-gifts officer the day I started working at the School of Theology. I don't think I even answered the officer's question, taken aback as I was by the realization that I was now working in something that people consider a "field." I didn't know diddly-squat about development; I also didn't know that someone could be an "officer" of major gifts. "Do they wear badges?" my friends had wanted to know, because my friends, like myself, had been completely ignorant of the field of development. "What are 'major gifts'?" was something else they wanted to know. At the outset, this seemed obvious to me: gold, frankincense, and myrrh. Minor gifts, I guessed, were things like Bic lighters, a box of Fannie Farmer mint parfaits, free detailing with your Scrub-a-Dub car wash. Now that I know about this field, however, and now that I've come to think of these individuals who outrank me by a million and one grade levels as major *grift* officers, I think much differently about "job" and "development" being used in any sentence having to do with me.

Text had been my domain—data entry to be precise—but I decided it might be illuminating to make a foray into the world of numbers by being the one who enters financial contributions into the School of Theology's database. This, in addition to my chronic inability to buy into God in any format, was the impetus. Religion and fundraising seemed to me odd bedfellows (I can be intentionally naïve), and I thought that getting involved with these bedfellows might teach me something about the paradoxical nature of the universe. After all, I would be at the crux of the universal paradox because I would be typing in check amounts followed by any number of zeros. I started off in a more subordinate position, but I am now the sole "gifts processor" because my boss, Dennis, quit six months after I got here—had a nervous breakdown or else got a job in Swaziland. Who knows what happens to people who, after twelve years of processing major and minor gifts, go out for "a bite to eat" and never come back? Dennis went AWOL, and because they could never find anyone qualified to do do do what he did did did so well, I am doing it by default.

These days the School of Theology is known for its Former Deans, because its Former Deans are the cyber-age equivalent of Western Civ's Bad Popes. Although the Former Deans' offenses are more shameful than heinous, this is nonetheless what has earned the school so many entries in the *Times* database. Right before I started working here, the school finally hired a dean of some integrity—a rabbi theologian who was a big civil rights activist in the sixties and a friend of both Bill and Hillary when this still meant something. The recent initiative has been getting the dean out to lecture to alums around the country and rehabilitate the school's ailing reputation. Unfortunately for both him and the school, the man is on the verge of a nervous breakdown. His hands are full with diversity issues—the primary one being that there are no African Americans on the faculty even though one-third of the student body is black. He recently got into big trouble fielding questions at the open forum demanded by the newly formed Student Action Committee. I attended the forum because of some asinine idea about civic responsibility, and boy did I regret it. After just a few questions, the event devolved into a pale imitation of *Welcome Back, Kotter.* As the dean was leaving the podium, some wiseguy asked him, "So how come there are no Jewish spirituals?" "Sure there are," he replied. "Haven't you ever heard 'Moishe's in the Cold, Cold Ground'?" Everyone booed.

Minutes later, the dean was asked by a reporter for the university's student newspaper, "Is it clear to you what the Student Action Committee wants the school to do?" "Sure!" he shouted. "End the war in Vietnam and change our name to H. Rap Brown Junior High!" Needless to say, that evening did not bode well for diversity at the School of Theology.

Luckily for everyone involved, the faculty have tended to be more tame than the deans, but we do have our mavericks. For instance, there's the Catholic priest who used to moonlight as a wrestler in Chiapas, appearing under the stage name El Padre. Now that he's gainfully ensconced within academia, he goes by Father Carlos Anguiano, although most people still call him El Padre. He's known around campus for wearing his vinyl wrestling mask on the first day of classes each semester. Some flack has arisen about his plan to start a Web site for Catholics who want to make their confessions online, but not as much flack as that surrounding the talk-show-circuit professor who cites Dead Sea documents as evidence that Jesus was schizophrenic. He was just on *Oprah* talking about his "skeptical colleagues" and his "puritanical colleagues" and his "backwater colleagues"—that is, the various members of the School of Theology faculty who have been slashing his tires for months. There's also the Evangelical who's expressed his support for a proposal to corral all of the nation's homosexuals into a colony somewhere in the New Mexican desert, near Alamagordo, along the lines of Biospheres 1 and 2. And how could you gloss over Sister Edna from Iceland, who looks and dresses like the musician Patti Smith and wants to start an online magazine for nuns called *Modern Bride of Christ?*

Despite the fact that it's part of a major university with a nontaxable GNP equivalent to France on a bad day, the School of Theology doesn't get much money from its alumni—not in comparison to the School of Global Startups, the School of Baronial Robbery, the School of Making Itsy-Bitsy Plastic Things Cheaper in Malaysian Orphanages. The Theology campus is a pretty ramshackle place, and there is a campaign under way to

renovate a couple of buildings and add a massive courtyard between them so as to suggest a museum in Spain or maybe a hotel
lobby in Singapore. No one knows what religion is supposed to
look like anymore, but at this university regulations require that
religion be accessorized by winding brick sidewalks understat-
edly adorned with cedar mulch and red rhododendrons. Topping
the School of Theology's short list of courtyard options is a replica
of Richard Serra's *Tilted Arc,* constructed by the proportions of
Disneyland's Main Street (i.e., two-thirds the size of real life).
Also under consideration are replicas of all the Buddhist temples
destroyed by the Taliban in Afghanistan and a gigantic bronze
statue of Nietzsche shaking hands with Kierkegaard. I have no
idea how the *Tilted Arc* relates to religion—maybe it has something to do with Noah and the kinds of animals that might have
(sadly) fallen overboard during their incredible journey. In any
event, the goal for the courtyard is ecumenicalism without any
loss of Protestant good taste. Coincidentally or not, my under-
standing of ecumenicalism is that it involves plastic animals, because a few years ago legislators somewhere voted that crèches
had to be removed from city hall Christmas displays unless they
were accompanied by plastic animals—which, by my reckoning,
means that plastic animals are what make the baby Jesus palatable
to Jews, Muslims, and tree huggers.

Regardless of all these high-concept courtyard plans, the renovation campaign thus far is a nickel-and-dime affair. As the senior
grift officer put it at the first staff meeting I attended, "What we
really need is one good death." We have tons of files on all kinds
of rich and/or well-connected people for whom we have yet to hit
pay dirt. There are files for one or two dead presidents and way
too many files for the widows of statesmen and diplomats—doy-
ennes whose nicknames sound like the title of an animated Japanese feature film. The biggest fish that got away from the School
of Theology was known as Maundi Thursday, a prospect they'd
courted religiously for fifteen years. When she died she gave all
her money to the Ogden Nash Children's Hospital. The dean at

the time (a snippy Californian who was eventually driven out of town on a rail) was less upset at losing the estate than by the fact that the estate was given to something associated with such bad poetry.

Ever since I started working here, the major gift initiative has been landing the estate of Esther Janus, a nonagenarian known for having all of her faculties intact—also for having survived every variety of cancer with her carcass intact. "The Janus Fund" is how the grift officers refer to Esther, demonstrating that they do have faith in something. If Esther gave her money to the School of Theology, there'd have to be a ceremony to scatter her ashes somewhere on the grounds, because this is the stipulation for whatever bequest Esther Janus makes—the scattering of the ashes, the physical dispersal of her remains, at the actual site of her bequest. Although my colleagues are more concerned with getting their mitts on the money, I've been trying to envision how the dispersal of Esther's ashes could be integrated with the school's renovation plans. Perhaps they would use a leaf blower to project her ashes onto the *Tilted Arc* coated with still-wet polyurethane. Or maybe they would set designated portions of Esther's ashes in little dishes in front of all the Buddhist temples. Or maybe something could be rigged up so that ashes fell like snow on the bronze likenesses of Nietzsche the syphilitic madman as he shook the hand of Kierkegaard the hunchback.

The Janus Fund had been simmering on the back burner here in the development office for quite a while as Esther plodded along with the less-well-endowed multitudes, but all that changed one Tuesday last month. It was a quiet day, on my end at least. I had volunteered to help Elmer the temp make nametags for some event whose guest list featured a lot of retired faculty members and their wives—Ineke, Ingamor, Ursula, Dagmar, like a reunion of Lufthansa flight attendants. Elmer was telling me the details of that time his brother's lips were bitten off by the family cocker spaniel when one of the grift officers burst upon the scene. "OK, you guys, listen up," he shouted. "Esther wants blood."

"You mean like a *Sopranos* thing?" Elmer asked.

"No, like a Red Cross thing," the officer snapped. He then informed us that Esther was having some kind of big, risky surgery for pancreatic reasons and wanted to amass her own plasma supply. This news prompted Elmer to lift his shirt and show us the tattoo he got on his back some months earlier—a big Year of the Snake cobra. "That's great," the grift officer said sarcastically, "should I applaud?" I volunteered to translate: "You can't give blood if you've recently had a tattoo."

If I had to describe in sound-bite terms this particular officer and his colleagues to whom I refer in grift terminology, I'd say meritocracy-in-denial, because although most of them have doctoral degrees—I don't know from where or in what, but I suspect things like medieval fly-fishing or Umbrian basket-weaving—they would all much prefer to have come from money. Just last week the senior grift officer told me she had to leave work early to speak with her spiritual advisor. I had thought she was making a poignant euphemism for prayer. "You're going to church?" I asked. "No," she said in a tone I imagined her using on her Guatemalan cleaning women. "I have an appointment with Doohong Rinpoche. I need him to help me focus my meditation on how my husband and I can begin to buy art. Big art. And I can't be late this time—he's wicked expensive." She and her colleagues had recently attended a catered dinner at the Newton home of a major prospect—the ditched wife of a yuppie snack-food entrepreneur—and had a bad case of dollar-sign art on the brain. At the last staff meeting, when she was supposed to be regaling us with her fundraising accomplishments of the past week, the senior grift officer just sighed winsomely: "I want a Pollock," she said, "maybe a Rothko." The director of development graciously translated for the nonexempt personnel present: "I hardly have to say that everything at Swooni's was museum quality."

Being a self-styled prole, I am beginning to be really bugged by the meritocracy-in-denial in this department, this class of people who go around saying "excellent" to each other like it was their Skull and Bones password. My grade-level equivalents are two just-graduated bright young things who say "totally" and "exactly" to each other and primarily play around on the Internet all day. You can chat them up about music or what friends in New York they're planning on visiting this weekend, but that's about it. My only marginally classifiable sociodemographic compatriot is Elmer the temp, just sprung from the Coast Guard and hoping to land a job with the INS. The problem with Elmer, however, is that he has no discernible personality. Truth is, I sorely miss Dennis. When he was training me in the gift-processing aspects of development, he liked to quote from Scripture—for instance, Acts of the Apostles: "It is hard for thee to kick against the pricks." Often when he went out to buy his lunch, he'd eat it at the vacant guard station in the lobby, still wearing his winter overcoat. At the time I didn't fully appreciate Dennis's *Weltanschauung* because I was irritated by his Daffy Duck lisp. Now, however, I wish I had socialized more—I wish I'd gotten the chance to meet his wife, whom he said came from a long line of Belgian contortionists. He told me that in their bathroom they have photographs of his wife's grandmother's stage poses that greatly disturbed many houseguests.

As for the just-hatched Bleed for Esther initiative, the two bright young things got themselves off the hook by reason of body piercings—though it was left up to the imagination in what erogenous zones the piercings were made. Four grift officers and one director of development yielded five negligibly valid reasons why none of them could give blood. I never expected to stoop to this level of corporate kiss-ass-ness, but I struck a bargain—the day off plus two extra vacation days if I gave blood for Esther Janus.

The hospital at which Esther was having her surgery is by far *la crème de la crème* of hospitals in a hospital-happy city. I had my appendix out here when I was twenty-two and had no health insurance. I still owe them $12,000. At the time, I offered to give up my worldly possessions—a Lincoln Head Cent penny collection—but they stopped sending me invoices.

"I'm here to give all the blood I can to crack-addicted infants," I said after a half hour's worth of routing through the hospital's innards.

"Excuse me?" said a guy wearing a lab coat that I doubt he'd ever need to shield him from spurting blood.

"The rich old lady," I said.

With all the avidness of a parking booth attendant, he handed me a clipboard holding a form to fill out. "Have a seat with the others," he said, nodding at the minuscule waiting room crammed with people and their varying degrees of attitude. Approaching this assemblage was like boarding a Greyhound bus—no one would make eye contact, presumably to dissuade me from taking an adjacent seat. Ironically or not, I was surprised to find just one empty seat in the room, as if the whole thing were planned.

"I guess this really is blood money," I said to the woman on my left. She was flipping through a magazine—*Teen People*, I guess—and moving her whole right arm in the process. I was afraid her hand would slip and she'd slap me in the face.

"Yeah, whatever," she said, not bothering to look up.

It was apparent that "the others" in the waiting room had also come from the development world—lower-echelon, slag-heap recruits no doubt, but still classifiably development.

"So how many extra vacation days did you finagle?" I asked the guy on my right.

"I'm sorry," he said, "but I have no idea why you think I'd want to have a conversation with you." I realized from his pinky ring that he was a solid member of the grift establishment. "Don't be sorry," I said cheerfully. "You just looked to me like someone who might have been in the Coast Guard with Elmer." Fortunately for both of us, his number was called; then it was Miss *Teen People*, and then ten or so other numbers before they got to the "17" on my clipboard.

I've given blood so many times (though never for money) that I could do it in my sleep. With me, it's always slow at the start because I have small veins that have been further constricted by too many double lattes. The Red Cross workers have to do a lot of fancy handwork in the race to siphon enough blood before the seventeen-minute deadline elapses, and then they apologize profusely for the bruise on my arm, the hematoma. I usually walk away from the gurney thinking about poetry—Little Hematoma by the shores of Gitche Gumee—and actually look forward to the snack table where you recuperate with apple juice and Animal Crackers. At this hospital the crackers weren't the official Nabisco variety but a knockoff called Animal Snacks. With my hematoma and ice pack, I held up each Animal Snack that I planned on eating to see if the cookie looked like the animal illustration on the package. I was happily engrossed in this activity when someone in white came to fetch me from the table. "Mrs. Janus would like to see you, as a donor."

It was odd to think of myself as a "donor." At the School of Theology, we rate donors by "capacity" and "readiness," like they were cuts of beef or earthquakes. There are high-net-worth prospects and a group called "the heavy hitters," all of whom need to be "massaged" with "events" and not solicited for so much as a penny before the appropriate time, like a bottle of Ernest and Julio Gallo Pink Catawba. Hitting up a heavy hitter at the right moment was as delicate a maneuver as getting an in-captivity panda pregnant and into the birthing room—at least this is how the grift officers saw it when justifying exorbitant salaries (theirs) within the nonprofit sector.

The person in white who addressed me as "donor" gave me directions to get to the part of the hospital where Esther was holed up—up one elevator, down another; up a third elevator and down a fourth. The journey reminded me of those old Mickey Mouse cartoons in which Mickey drives his jalopy up and down hills, but only the bottom half of his body moves with the car so that he stretches and contracts like a rubber band. In those cartoons, however, Mickey was all zippity doo-dah because he was usually off to pick up Minnie for a date. Taking these elevators only stretched my patience; it wasn't at all like going on a date.

I found Esther in a room resembling a penthouse suite. No exaggeration—the place was huge and lavish, with white furniture like one of those Miami hotels frequented by Madonna and her retinue. I didn't know this kind of setup was allowed in a democracy—maybe in Argentina, I thought, but surely not here amid the Crisis in Health Care. But then I had to remember that this whole tableau was just the next logical installment of my unsentimental education in philanthropy. Since I started working at the School of Theology, I've been misreading those milk billboards as "Got money?" Word from the mountain seems to be that no matter how you choose to fuck up your life, just be sure you got money. That's all that matters, whoever you are, wherever you are. If you've got money, you can have milk mustaches up to your eyebrows and people will still want to be your friend.

Lying in a bed raised to the appropriate angle, surrounded by so much state-of-the-art gadgetry, Esther looked as diminutive and as shrink-wrapped in wrinkles as any ninety-five-year-old woman I've seen, though she didn't appear weak, faltering, feeble—any of those adjectives we reserve for age heaped upon age. "So who sent ya?" she yelled after I crossed the penthouse threshold.

"School of Theology," I replied promptly, like I was at boot camp.

"Too many Buddhists if you ask me. Idol lackeys. Still got that pedophile dean?" She was squinting at me, had even pulled her shoulders up from the bed to get a look at what form of human I was, so I moved closer to the gadgetry, out of common courtesy.

"I think he's working for Unicef," I said, trying to sound compliant. This was very difficult for me—compliancy—though I must have attempted it sometime in my past.

"I like that El Padre fella, though," she said. "Sort of."

"A lot of people do, sort of."

"Who else ya like there?"

I felt like a bookie— "who d'ya like in the fifth?" and all that. "I don't know," I said (and this was a genuine hedge— "like" was not a word I associate with the School of Theology). "There's a nun who wants to start a magazine, Sister Edna. I guess I like her. She's a good person."

"Did ya know that Mae West gave all her old Cadillacs to convents?" she asked. "It depressed her to see nuns riding the bus."

I said I didn't know that about Mae West.

She looked at me warily. "So whaddya know about Lot's wife?"

"Didn't she turn to stone?"

"Sure as hell she did!" she yelled. "And she's gonna fall off a cliff and into the Dead Sea if someone doesn't do something about it."

At this point the intelligent blood donor would surely pose any number of pointed questions, but I'd been distracted by Esther's exuberance, her sharpness, the strength of her voice, and was having a hard time acclimating myself to the dilemma of Lot's wife. "Is that bad?" I asked.

"Of course that's bad!" she hollered. "What's wrong with you, girl? Can't go around these days with your head stuck in the sand."

I wanted to tell her that sticking your head in the sand was now a national pastime, but you couldn't be impertinent to this kind of woman, especially when you'd already committed yourself to such a heroic stab at compliancy.

"Lot's wife," she continued, "think about that for a minute: she doesn't even have a name. But she doesn't care what the heck her husband tells her to do, doesn't care what the heck her husband's saying about God. And I say good for her. What happened to Lot? Who knows? Who talks about Lot without meaning his wife? Who cares about Lot! He's history. But Lot's wife is still standing."

From this synopsis, I could only envision Lot's wife looking like Elton John still standing in those big rhinestone glasses and hair implants—still standing up while playing the piano.

"And that's good?" I asked skeptically.

"What the heck is wrong with you!" she shouted. *"She's still standing."* Then she thought for a minute. "But she's breaking off, parts of her right and left, even as we speak."

At the "even as we speak" prompt, a nurse pushing a big cart of Pfizer wares came in to check Esther's blood and blood pressure and do a few other nasty little things I didn't care to know about.

"Stuart!" she shouted. "You need to put in the video!" Then she looked at me, feigning exasperation. "He's my assistant." Again she shouted, "Where the heck is he—out there molesting the orderlies?"

"You're the fifth screening today," said the young man who glided into the room from somewhere beyond and proceeded to put a videocassette into the hospital's TV-on-an-AV-stand. "Lot like a lottery, isn't it?" he said, lifting his eyebrows like Bugs Bunny.

The video wasn't old but had a score and narration that somehow reminded me of a junior high film loop about the Andes. From it I learned that in 1995, geologists claimed to have identified the probable site of the biblical cities of Sodom and Gomorrah and presented a theory as to why the edifice that people have long been calling Lot's wife was created. First we get the biblical background—the story that Sodom and Gomorrah were destroyed by fire and brimstone because of their residents' sinfulness and that, being considered a good man, Lot was warned of God's punishment, but his wife disobeyed God's sole condition that he not look back at the burning city and was transformed into a pillar of salt. The geologists analyzed local soil and rock to trace Sodom and Gomorrah to a specific Dead Sea peninsula and worked out the reason the cities vanished around 1900 B.C. The area was an earthquake zone, made up of saturated soil and highly flammable bitumen that, when subjected to a large earthquake, will liquefy. The geologists say that there was probably an earthquake that destroyed the cities, and the surging water of the Dead Sea might have thrown up salt floes to resemble a woman wearing a long dress with short sleeves and carrying an object on her head. The geologists dramatizing the scientific discovery were very tanned and sounded Australian. Whenever I watch these PBS-style archaeological documentaries I always think that it's the same groups of guys, whatever it is they're digging up. I picture them all driving 1979 Volvo station wagons with rock-climbing cords and dynamite in the back.

When the video was over, the three of us sat there. Now what? If anything in real life amounted to what Henry James called an embraceable impasse, this was it, because I had no idea what this situation wanted from the likes of me.

Finally, Esther broke the silence. "So I could give all my money to this outfit," she said, "this research crew, this university group, this . . ."

"Bunch of tan guys," I volunteered.

"I could give all my money to this bunch of tan guys," she continued, "so that they can do something to keep Lot's wife from falling."

"It's great they'd know how to do that," I said, as blithe as any idiot you'd pull off the street.

"So why do you want my money?" she hollered.

"It's the School of Theology," I said. "They want your money."

"And you'd be the SWAT team?" Stuart proposed.

"More like the wet nurse," I said, looking down at the bandage on my arm.

"You believe in God?" Esther asked me. It was more like a threat, maybe a dare.

"I don't know," I said, remembering that it would behoove any development professional to be on the alert for trick questions.

"Stuart here does," she said, waving her arm toward her assistant.

I looked at Stuart, who nodded. "Lutheran," he said.

"Though Lutherans don't really count," Esther said, coughing.

"I thought it was the Unitarians who didn't really count," I said, "you know, like in 'one, two, three . . .'"

"I was a Catholic since the cradle," Esther said, waving her hand at me, as if shooing off so many goofy Protestant excuses for bake sales and saints downgraded to walk-on roles. "Divorced four times, cardinal and venal sins left and right, all the way through. Don't think I ever once thought of talking to someone's God. Husbands when they died all went out singin' like canaries. Teenage mistress, bastard children, extortion, obstruction of justice . . . what else was there to confess?"

"Arson, indecent exposure, grand theft auto," Stuart said.

"Stuart here used to be a tap dancer in Arizona," she said, holding out her arm as if to grab something hanging on him. "Tell the girl about your tap dancing career."

"It was a thrilling period of my life."

"That's all you have to say?"

"I'm reformed now."

"He's dating a gay dentist!" she shouted at me.

"Yes," Stuart concurred. "And how lucky for me that he turned out to be a gay dentist and not the regular kind."

It was at the reiteration of "gay dentist" that I realized something important: this was fun, sitting here with the two of them. I felt like I was having a vacation day already.

"So where do *you* think my remains should be scattered?" Esther asked me.

"What are my options?" I asked, looking at Stuart.

"No particular options," Stuart said. "She means in the open field of life."

"He's got a way with words, doesn't he?" Esther said. "Though it goes to his head."

"I don't know," I said, still anticipating that trick question in regard to Esther's remains. "Probably the Dead Sea."

"You'd want to be dumped into the Dead Sea?" Esther shouted.

I tried to emulate the informed hesitation of the mental health professionals I've seen interviewed on *Good Morning America*. "It seems to me that the Dead Sea would be the logical place to wind up if you're dead."

"Good point," Stuart said, but I could tell that they expected more from the way they looked at me.

"That's why it doesn't seem like such a catastrophe to me if Lot's wife were to fall in there," I continued. "I mean, maybe that's what she wants after all these years of just standing there, holding that whatever on her head. What is that on her head anyway? Was it the family luggage or just something dumb she grabbed during the fire?"

"So you think Lot's wife should give in after all this time?" Esther asked.

"Would it be giving in or simply laying herself to rest?"

"What are you doing asking the questions?" she shouted.

"I always seem to have them," I said.

"Like what?" Stuart asked.

"OK, for one, why is it important for you to be scattered somewhere?"

"Take a lesson here, missy," Esther said, shaking a finger at me. "Ya can't scatter money these days; it just won't grow. Money!" she said, throwing up her hands. "What the heck do you do with it anyway? You toss some of it here, some of it there" — at this she limply flung her hands from one side to the other. "Say you're the one I give it to. You get hold of my money, and what do you do with it? You'd be just like those trailer-park types who sue Phillip Morris. Buy junk, drink it away. Money just turns to dirt. I've seen it my whole life. I oughta know, 'cause all I ever wanted was more money. All I did was spend my husbands' money."

Here she paused, as if reading my thoughts. After all, everyone in "the local development community" knew the sequence of Esther's husbands—one in New Zealand butter, another in fire-hydrant valves, another in plastic drinking cups, another in sealed-air packaging. As far as the romantic aspects of one's trade are concerned, it went from bad to worse for Esther, but in direct proportion to the increased size of the alimony and/or inherited estate.

"My ashes," she continued, "I gotta feeling about my ashes. I think my ashes are gonna do a lot more than my money, believe you me. I got this feeling that my ashes are what they used to call *kismet*."

"Like that Eartha Kitt musical," Stuart whispered to me.

"I believe in my ashes," Esther continued, reclining back on her pillow, turning her head to the side. "I can't think of anything else I believe in."

"Lot's wife, Esther's ashes," Stuart said, "same sort of carbon bonds."

"If your ashes are that powerful," I told Esther, "then I wouldn't choose the Dead Sea. They should go where they're really needed—where people are living."

"That's a very United Nations approach," Stuart said.

"So does Lois Lane here have any other questions for me?" Esther asked.

"Yeah," I said. "Why are you even having this surgery?"

"She's dying of cancer," Stuart said, "in case you haven't heard."

"Are you in pain?" I asked Esther.

"Are you?" she shouted.

"I don't think so," I said. "At least not yet."

"Well, avoid it if you can," she said, looking immensely irritated. "That's my advice to you." Then she thought for a minute. "What is it you do for a living?"

"I run numbers."

"You're a bookie?"

"I record the checks that people send in to the School of Theology."

"Filthy lucre," she said, shaking her head. "Didn't your mother ever tell you money was dirty?"

"My mother was always a big fan of money—still is."

"Well get yourself out of that business!" she shouted. "You hear me? Get out of that business, and while you're at it get your head out of the sand."

With this, I could tell I was officially dismissed.

"Is she in pain?" I asked Stuart after he ushered me into the hallway.

"Not too much," he said. Then he looked uncharacteristically pensive (it was amazing I could say "uncharacteristically" about this man I'd just met). "She's ninety-five; all of her friends have been dead for decades. She doesn't want to go out sucking on morphine."

"So she chose the surgery?"

"Not *chose*—more like demanded it. Finding a guy to do it—that was a pain in the neck. 'Ethics!'"

"You mean she's doing all this—getting everyone's blood—with the intention of dying?"

"If it walks like a duck."

"So this was all planned?"

"Everything's 'planned' these days," he said with a laugh. "You should know that better than most—'*planned* giving' and all, your biz."

My "biz" certainly felt like a contaminated one—a hazardous-waste receptacle of personnel—as I made my way out of the hospital. Like so many people, I don't really have a legitimate job title let alone a vocation let alone an avocation. Riding the elevators, I longed to be an archaeologist or a geologist or a dentist—even a contortionist—anything but a processor of major and minor gifts. Whatever I was, I wasn't even doing it for the money, and this realization put a damper on any conception of this excursion as being like a vacation day—day of reckoning was more like it. Plus, what a waste of blood! It was highly disconcerting to realize that "needless bloodshed" wasn't confined to the streets of Bogotá or the Red Cross's faulty refrigerators: even (or perhaps especially) country-club hospitals were getting into the act.

The School of Theology's Bleed for Esther initiative ultimately featured three installments: I gave blood on Wednesday, Esther had the operation on Thursday, and on Friday she died of complications. Needless to say, the grift officers were elated to hear the news. "Good work!" the senior officer said, slapping me on the back. "What did you put in your blood that day?"

"I drank a lot of Dr. Pepper beforehand," I said insolently, although I doubt that any of them would recognize insolence, even at close range.

Two weeks later, however, the officers weren't so happy, because it was announced that Esther Janus had bequeathed her estate to the Agape/Gnosis Foundation, an international consortium committed to nonviolent conflict resolution between Israel and Palestine; hence her ashes would be scattered around the West Bank. It was a scandal in all sectors of development. "Why?" I was asked imploringly by one despondent money-grubber after another, as if I had some divinatory sense in the matter. "I don't know," I said. "Maybe it was because Lot's wife is larger than life, whereas if we built the *Tilted Arc*, it would be two-thirds the size of life. Or maybe Esther just wanted world peace."

The grift officers weren't even mollified by the fact that Esther left a tidy little sum to our own Sister Edna—a bequest restricted to the establishment of a magazine called *Modern Bride of Christ*. "Nonendowment," the director scoffed. "Might as well be throwing peanuts to the organ grinder."

Although the Esther Janus Delegation—an assortment of Nobel laureates, high-ranking Carter administration officials, Quakers, and former tap dancers—has been appointed to make a pilgrimage to Jerusalem to scatter Esther's ashes at strategic points along the West Bank, every Janus near and far seems to be contesting the will, so who knows if world peace will be subsidized by Esther. I forgot that I had written down the information about Sister Edna for Stuart when I left Esther's room, and I was shocked to realize that I'd finally done something right in a professional capacity—and also to learn that Esther had selected me to be a member of the illustrious Esther Janus Delegation. I consider this quite an honor, though I'm not too happy about the part where I have to pay for the entire trip—including the bulletproof vest that every delegate is required to wear—out of pocket and then be reimbursed once Esther's assets are unfrozen. And after I return from visiting a war zone (if I do in fact return), I'm sure I'll be wanting a change on the work front. You don't have to be an international peace delegate to know when it's time to head back to text versus running the numbers. I have already applied for a data-entry job at the Medical School, the psychiatric department, where they are studying depression in the workplace. Apparently the director is a three-hundred-pound ogre who wears Bermuda shorts all winter. The downside is that you could very well get depressed in that kind of workplace; the upside is that that kind of workplace might very well be a cure for depression, just like this kind of workplace was a cure for religion—or at least a cure for living with my head in the sand.

The Flannery O'Connor Award for Short Fiction

David Walton, *Evening Out*
Leigh Allison Wilson, *From the Bottom Up*
Sandra Thompson, *Close-Ups*
Susan Neville, *The Invention of Flight*
Mary Hood, *How Far She Went*
François Camoin, *Why Men Are Afraid of Women*
Molly Giles, *Rough Translations*
Daniel Curley, *Living with Snakes*
Peter Meinke, *The Piano Tuner*
Tony Ardizzone, *The Evening News*
Salvatore La Puma, *The Boys of Bensonhurst*
Melissa Pritchard, *Spirit Seizures*
Philip F. Deaver, *Silent Retreats*
Gail Galloway Adams, *The Purchase of Order*
Carole L. Glickfeld, *Useful Gifts*
Antonya Nelson, *The Expendables*
Nancy Zafris, *The People I Know*
Debra Monroe, *The Source of Trouble*
Robert H. Abel, *Ghost Traps*
T. M. McNally, *Low Flying Aircraft*
Alfred DePew, *The Melancholy of Departure*
Dennis Hathaway, *The Consequences of Desire*
Rita Ciresi, *Mother Rocket*
Dianne Nelson, *A Brief History of Male Nudes in America*
Christopher McIlroy, *All My Relations*
Alyce Miller, *The Nature of Longing*
Carol Lee Lorenzo, *Nervous Dancer*
C. M. Mayo, *Sky over El Nido*